Arthur F Mathews '06

SNAKE CATCHER

SNAKE CATCHER

NAIYER MASUD

Translated from Urdu by
MUHAMMAD UMAR MEMON

Interlink Books

An imprint of Interlink Publishing Group, Inc.
Northampton, Massachusetts

First published in 2006 by

INTERLINK BOOKS
An imprint of Interlink Publishing Group, Inc.
46 Crosby Street, Northampton, Massachusetts 01060
www.interlinkbooks.com

Library of Congress Cataloging-in-Publication Data

Naiyer Masud.
  [Short stories. English. Selections]
  Snake catcher / by Naiyer Masud ; translated from Urdu by Muhammad Umar
Memon.
     p. cm.
  Short stories.
  ISBN 1-56656-629-0 (hardback)
  I. Memon, Muhammad Umar, 1939- II. Title.
  PK2200.N2199A265 2005

                                          2005013183

Stories "Obscure Domains of Fear and Desire" ("Oojhal"), "Woman in Black" ("Nusrat"), "Snake Catcher" ("Maar-Geer"), and "Resting Place" ("Maskan") are from the author's first collection *Seemiya* (Lucknow, India: Nusrat Publishers, 1984), pp. 5–40, 41–60, 61–116, and 209–232 respectively. "Ganjefa" ("Ganjifa") and "Weather Vane" ("Baad-Numa") first appeared in the *Annual of Urdu Studies* No. 12 (1997), 231–264 and No. 15 (2000), 650–664. "Lamentation" ("Nudba") and "Custody" ("Tahveel") appeared in the author's third collection *Taa'uus Chaman ki Mayna* (Karachi: Aaj ki Kitaaben, 1997), pp. 53–69 and 95–137. "Epistle" ("Muraasala") is from his second collection *'Itr-e Kaafuur* (Lucknow, India: Nusrat Publishers, 1990), pp. 11–30. "Allam and Son" (" 'Allaam aur Beta") and "The Big Garbage Dump" ("Bara Kuraa-Ghar") are taken from the quarterly *Aaj* No. 33 (2001) 61–73 and No. 29 (1991) 63–89.

    The story "Obscure Domains of Fear and Desire," co-translated with Javaid Qazi, was previously published, copyright © 1999 *Essence of Camphor* by Naiyer Masud. Reprinted by permission of The New Press, www.thenewpress.com.

    I would like to thank Elizabeth Bell and Jane Shum for their invaluable help in polishing the translations.

Printed and bound in the United States of America
10 9 8 7 6 5 4 3 2 1

Table of Contents

Introduction

Hai ghaib-e ghaib jis-ko samajhte hain ham shuhuud
Hain khvaab men hanoz jo jaage hain khvaab men
(The absent of the absent: what we see is merest seeming
It is the dream into which we awaken from dreaming.)
—Ghalib

Naiyer Masud, little known outside India and Pakistan, is both a scholar of Persian and Urdu and a short-story writer. Passionately involved with fiction, he began writing stories in his early boyhood but didn't start publishing until the 1970s. The five stories in his first collection, *Seemiya* (an Arabic word that can mean a number of things, among them "metamorphosis" or "the art of creating illusions"), initially appeared individually in an Indian literary magazine and went largely without critical comment. When they later appeared together they were greeted warmly but, as is often the case with first publications, dismissively. Some Urdu critics praised his work in casual newspaper columns or in coffeehouse banter, but none of them could tell the reader what was good or bad about it, or even where it led. The message, the meaning, the experience remained tenaciously elusive.

The world of *Seemiya* and *'Itr-e Kaafuur* (Essence of Camphor), his second collection, pulled reader and critic alike straight into the center of a vortex—at once seductive and inaccessible. Entirely original, unlike anything that preceded them in the history of Urdu fiction, these stories stood in a class by themselves. Here one encountered order, neatness, and decorum, qualities that dispelled any notion of "unreality." Masud's fictional world demanded respect, an admission of its unique ontological orientation, but gave no clue as to what its existentialist identity or purpose might be. While a mirror-image of the real world in its outer form, at a deeper, more emblematic level it sought to subvert that image. And even though each element in it appeared palpably real, oddly, the aggregate didn't add up to anything known.

The shimmering but elusive quality of the stories may derive from a number of factors, not the least of which is the terse and highly-clipped Urdu prose, which shuns even the slightest trace of hollow rhetoric, so stark in its suppression of qualifiers that it unsettles the mind. No or few idioms, no verbal pyrotechnics of any kind. It is Urdu all right, but it does not read like ordinary Urdu. It is attenuated yet overlain with invisible density and is evocative of absence. This economy, this avoidance of even an occasional exaggeration or embellishment, lends an element of unfamiliarity, if not of unreality. Words are selected with extreme care, not for their meanings but for their predisposition to evoke a silence and stillness in which the elusive becomes self-evident, but only in the form of a montage of inter-penetrating images hazily defined. Rarely has Urdu seen a writer more jealously protective of his verbal choices. There is absolutely nothing arbitrary or rushed about them. Those of us who have worked in consultation with him on translations of his stories know only too well his insistence on keeping the same word, often even the same word order of the different verbal elements as they appear in a sentence. And, above all, how he objects to the slightest emphasis, even when such emphasis might be creatively exploited in the translation.

Another factor may be Masud's use of certain elements identified with the architecture of spatial narratives. For instance, key words deployed at varying intervals horizontally across the fictional space. These words seek to carry the meaning—or whatever its equivalent may be in Masud's stories—incrementally forward, often even modifying the meaning in unexpected ways, keeping it always in a state of flux, always evolving. Often these words are woven so seamlessly into the narrative structure that one misses them altogether.

Another device used in his first collection, *Seemiya*, is the recurrence of certain images that are retrieved, in part, across several stories through a staggered time sequence. "*Seemiya*," writes Muhammad Salim-ur-Rahman, is

> a collection of five intertextured stories. Read individually, each story seems perfectly self-contained and autonomous. They share, however, a certain opaqueness. Read together they convey the impression of an organic whole, as if deep down there were a prolific intermingling of roots. At the same time their latent mystery, instead of moving toward a resolution, merely deepens.... Its components can be analyzed and meanings tagged to them, but seen as a whole they defy any consensus of interpretation.*

To give the reader some idea of the above formulation, I have included here four stories from *Seemiya*, retaining the order of their appearance in the original Urdu collection.

The tendency of the human mind is to subdue (fathom, sort out, catalogue, close) and move on. But Masud's narratives work against this tendency, against completion and closure. The reader experiences things in dynamic motion, not as objects with fixed perimeters in a state of repose or quiescence, so there is no way to be done with them and move on. Circularity has no terminus. Finishing one of his stories does not bring the reader to the expected tying up of threads and closure. What it does bring is a continuing engagement with the unspoken and the ineffable, lodged in the deepest recesses of memory.

*See his "Once Below a Time: A Short Essay on *Seemiya*," in the *Annual of Urdu Studies* No. 12 (1997), 290.

The tendency away from closure might itself stem from the denial, at the level of observation and experience, of the division of time into past, present, and future. It is as if all time is an eternity that is *necessarily* present. Experience, which can only be a single indivisible entity, is continuous; indeed it is coeval with consciousness. Ultimately, the two may be the same thing. The matter may be less abstruse from the point of view of Sufi metaphysics, where Reality = Being reduces temporality to pure nonexistence, except in relation to the created world—which is devoid of reality in and of itself.

But as stories, Masud's work falls squarely within the limits of the created world. And it is here that the suspension of the defining temporal conventions creates the dizzying sensation of disjuncture. At the same time, it jars the reader into the recognition that behind the apparent multiplicity of his work lies a single concern: the experience of being. Therefore no limits or order-producing perimeters or boundaries are possible. Each story is a variation on a single theme. Just as the present is an imaginary point along a continuum where consciousness may choose to place it, a story is a discrete embodiment only insofar as consciousness chooses to see it as such. In essence, it has no beginning and, therefore, no end.

In the process of working closely with Masud's fictional universe, I'm nowhere closer to its "meaning" today than I was some years ago when I first started. But, increasingly, I feel that to insist on some palpable meaning, or even a shard of meaning, in reflexive fiction such as Masud's is to put the wrong foot forward. "Meaning" inevitably has to do with the domain of logic, discursive reason, empiricism. It is inherently suggestive of a split, a dichotomy, a state of divorce and rupture. Whence its inability to deal with reality except piecemeal. Our generic expectations from the short story proceed from the basic premise that objects have meaning. These expectations are not likely to be met in a perusal of Masud's short stories. These stories are preoccupied instead with being. *To be*, and not *to mean*. The maze is entered for its own sake and not to subdue or to get somewhere.

Keeping in mind the prevailing culture where Masud has grown up, his predilection to preface his work with quotations from Persian mystical lore predisposes me to think that the subject matter of his stories (if one could be rash enough to use the phrase "subject matter") is most accessible experientially, in something like a visionary flash, in the realm of pure reflection. If the stories do not begin at a discrete logical point, if they don't close at the end of the day, if they fail to reach resolution and appear to be open-ended, it is precisely because they do not deal with reality as something divisible or linear. Perhaps their sole purpose is to induce silence, in which the calmed self might begin to experience Being.

Having said this it seems, nevertheless, that one particular aspect of the "experience of being" stands out in the stories collected here: the effect of Time. Time brings with it separation, loss, disintegration, and decay, at every level of experience—both within the individual and between individuals, within the community and between communities, and so on. Our experience of Time's effect is unconscious until one day, having grown old, we realize that we and the society around us have become its victims. The young, meanwhile, remain oblivious.

Naiyer Masud was born on 16 November 1936 in Lucknow, India. His parents both came from families of physicians (hakims), but in both families the practice of traditional medicine had effectively ended with his grandfathers. Coincidentally, Masud's wife also comes from a family of practitioners of traditional medicine, and in that family too the ancestral profession had terminated, in this instance with her father. Naiyer Masud's father, Syed Masud Hasan Rizvi Adeeb, was a professor of Persian at Lucknow University and a renowned scholar of Persian and Urdu. His library was well regarded for its sizable collection of rare books and manuscripts. "I owe the greater part of my literary training to him and to this collection," Masud admitted to me in a letter, dated 20 June 1997. "I was educated in ordinary schools and was an average student, more interested in reading all kinds of other books, novels and short story collections, than my course textbooks." Nevertheless, he holds two Ph.D. degrees, one in Urdu from Allahabad University, the other in Persian from Lucknow University, which he joined in 1965 as a professor of Persian and where he remained until his retirement a few years ago.

He married in 1971 and shares with his wife three daughters and a son. The family lives in the house that Masud's father had built and appropriately named "Adabistan" ("Abode of Literature" or "Abode of Cultured Living"). He finds social life tedious and travel bothersome. Any prospect of spending time away from his native Lucknow makes him nervous, but he did visit Tehran for a few days in 1977, at the invitation of Iran's Ministry of Culture, to participate in a conference of teachers of Persian. "But," he assures, "correspondence with friends, my job at the university, and visitors have saved me from becoming entirely cut off from the outside world."

In his boyhood Masud wrote some poetry, short stories, and plays that were published in children's magazines. Later, starting in 1965, he devoted his energies to writing research papers. His friendship with Shamsur Rahman Faruqi, Urdu literature's most astute critic, revived his desire to write fiction. He wrote his first short story, "Nusrat," here translated as "The Woman in Black," in 1971. This and the other four short stories included in the collection *Seemiya* initially appeared in Faruqi's magazine *Shab-Khoon*. "I'm very slow at writing," he remarks. "I've written only 22 short stories in the last 25 years." He is also very fond of translating, but regrets that he hasn't been able to undertake as much of it as he would have liked. "Some twenty pieces of Kafka, fifteen short stories and a few poems from Persian, that's as much as I have translated."

In the same letter he mentions his interest in calligraphy, painting, and music. "There was a time when I could play a few instruments," he writes. "I can also manage minor repair jobs around the house which have to do with plumbing, masonry, electrical work and carpentry. But I did learn the art of book-binding formally. My true occupation, at any rate, is reading and, occasionally, writing."

Masud has published some two dozen titles including fiction, children's books, translations, and research. His fiction includes: *Seemiya* (Lucknow: Kitaabnagar, Nusrat Publishers, 1984; reprint, Lahore: Qausain, 1987); *'Itr-e Kaafuur* (a collection of seven short stories; Lucknow: Nizami Press, 1990; reprint, Karachi: Aaj ki Kitaaben, 1999); and *Taa'uus Chaman ki Mayna* (The Myna from Peacock Garden, a collection of ten short stories; Karachi: Aaj ki Kitaaben, 1997). Notable among his translations is a volume of Franz Kafka's short stories and parables entitled *Kaafka ke Afsaane* (Lucknow: Kitaabnagar, 1978) and numerous contemporary Iranian short stories that have appeared in the quarterly *Aaj*.

—Muhammad Umar Memon

Obscure Domains of Fear and Desire

Ba kuja sar niham keh chun zanjiir
Har dare halqa-e dare digar-ast
(Hide—but where?
Each door I close opens another.)

—*Anonymous*
(found in a ghazal by Mir Taqi Mir)

Thou holdest mine eyes waking;
I am so troubled that I cannot speak.
I have considered the days of old,
the years of ancient times.

—*Psalm 77*

"We kept looking at each other, in silence, for the longest time ever. Our faces didn't betray any kind of curiosity. His eyes had an intensity, a brightness, but throughout this time, never for a moment did they seem to be devoid of feeling. I could not understand if his eyes were trying to say something or were merely observing me, but I felt we were coming to some silent understanding. All of a sudden a terrible feeling of despair came over me. It was the first time I'd felt like this since I'd come to this house. Just then his nurse placed her hand on my arm and led me out of the room.

"Outside, as I spoke with his nurse, I realized that my speech was a shortcoming and that the patient was traveling far ahead of me on a road I knew nothing about."

I have given up talking, not looking. It isn't easy to stop looking if one happens to possess a pair of eyes. Keeping quiet, even though one has a tongue, is relatively easy. At times I do get an urge to close my eyes. But so far they are still open. This may be due to the presence of the person who is looking after me. She is my last link with that old house where I opened my eyes for the first time and learned to talk. When I lived in that house, she was just a cute little doll, only a year-and-a-half old. And so affectionate toward me. I would call for her as soon as I entered the house and then she would cling to me the whole time I was there.

Now she has no memory of those days. All she's been told is that I am the last representative of her family. She does not know much else about me. In spite of this, she is very fond of me. She thinks this is the very first time she has seen me. She does not remember that I used to call her my "Little Bride." Actually, I started calling her that because she would refer to me as her bridegroom whenever someone in the family asked her who I was. This amused everyone. They would all laugh and then just to tease her, someone would claim me as a "bridegroom." When she heard this she would have a regular little tantrum. Among those who teased her were several older relatives, both male and female. In those days, her small world was crowded with rivals. But even then, the ranks of her rivals did not include the person for whom she had the warmest feelings, not counting her mother or myself. And in return, this woman cared more deeply for the little girl than anyone else.

1

She was at least two years older than me. Twelve years prior to the time I'm talking about, I had seen her at my older brother's wedding.

She was the younger sister of my brother's wife. But due to a complicated pattern of kinship, she also happened to be my aunt.

At the time of my brother's marriage, she was a mature young woman and I was a mere boy—a shy, awkward stripling. She adopted toward me the attitude of someone much older than myself. Of course, we often chatted, shared jokes, and teased each other. But despite all this informality, she maintained the air of an elder. However, I never detected any affectation in that attitude, which perhaps would have irritated me. She treated me not as though she were much older than I, but as though I were quite a bit younger than she. And I liked that.

There were times, however, when I got the distinct impression that I was, after all, just her young nephew. This happened when she compared her hometown with mine and insisted that hers was a much better place. I would immediately leap to the defense of my town and argue with her endlessly in a rather childish manner. During those years, she visited us once in a while and stayed with us for long periods of time. And during this particular visit she had been with us for three or four days.

I came into the house and, as usual, I called out to my "Little Bride" as soon as I'd stepped into the courtyard. But the house was silent. No one seemed to be home. However, Aunt was there. She had just emerged from the bathroom after her bath and had sat down in a sunlit spot to dry her hair. I asked her where all the others were and she said they had all gone to a wedding somewhere. Not knowing what else to say, I asked her about my "Little Bride" even though I had a hunch that she might have gone to the wedding with the others. I went and sat next to Aunt and we started talking about this and that. Most of the time we talked about my "Little Bride" and chuckled over her antics. After a while Aunt's hair was dry and she stood up to tie it in a bun. In an effort to arrange her hair, she raised both arms with her hands at the back of her head. Her bare waist arched slightly backward, her bust rose and then fell back a little, causing her locks to fall away from her. I saw this in a fraction of a second but it had no particular effect on me. She continued to put up her hair in a chignon and we went on talking. Suddenly one of her earrings fell off and landed near her foot. I quickly bent down to retrieve it for her. As I knelt at her feet, my eyes fell upon the pale curve of her instep and I was reminded once again that she had just taken a bath. I picked up the earring and tried to put it back in her ear while I kept up a rapid patter of conversation. I could smell the musky odor that rose from her moist body. She continued to fiddle with her hair and I kept on trying to put her earring back in. But for some reason I couldn't get it to stay and her earlobe began to turn red. I must have jabbed her with the post of the earring. A little cry came from her throat and she chided me mildly. She then took the earring from me with a smile and quickly put it in by herself. Soon afterwards, she went up to her room and I went to mine.

A little later, I went upstairs looking for a book. On the way back, I glanced over toward Aunt's room. She stood in front of the bamboo screen. Her hair hung loosely about her shoulders and her eyes looked as though she had just woken up. I went into her room and again we started talking about the same sort of trifles. She started to tie up her hair all over again and once again I saw what I had seen earlier. Seeing her waist bend backwards once again, I felt a bit uneasy. We talked about the wedding that my entire family had gone to attend and I told her that there was a great difference in height between the bride and bridegroom. Exaggerating rather wildly, I insisted that the bride barely came up to the waist of the bridegroom.

Aunt laughed at this and said, "Anyway, at least she's a little taller than your bride."

We started talking once again about my "Little Bride," whose absence made the house seem quite empty. I was about to introduce some other topic when Aunt stood up from the bed and came toward me.

"Let's see if you're taller than I am," she said with a smile.

Grinning we came and stood facing each other. She moved closer to me. Once again I became aware of the fragrance that rose from her body, a warm, moist odor that reminded me that she had just bathed. We drew still closer and her forehead almost touched my lips.

"You're much shorter than me," I told her.

"I am not," she retorted and stood up on her toes. Then she giggled: "How about now?"

I grabbed her waist with both hands and tried to push her downwards.

"You're cheating," I told her. And bending down, I grabbed both her ankles and tried to plant them back on the floor. When I stood up again, she wasn't laughing anymore. I clasped her waist firmly with both hands once again.

"You're being unfair," I said to her as the grip of my hands tightened on her waist.

Her arms rose, moved toward my neck, but then stopped. I felt as though I were standing in a vast pool of silence that stretched all around us. My hold on her waist tightened still more.

"The door," she said in a faint whisper.

I pulled her close to the door without letting go of her waist. Then I released her slowly, bolted the door and turned toward her again. I remembered how she had always behaved like an older relative toward me and I felt angry at her for the first time, but just as suddenly the anger melted into an awareness of her tremendous physical appeal. I bent over and held her legs. I was still bent over with my grip around her legs progressively tightening when I felt her fingers twist in my hair. She pulled me up with a violent intensity and my head bumped her chest. Then, with her fingers still locked in my hair, she moved back toward the bed. When we got to its edge, I eased her onto it, helping her feet up with my hands. But she suddenly broke free and stood up. I looked at her.

She murmured: "The door that leads up the stairs . . . it's open."

"But there's no one in the house."

"Someone will come."

Silently we went down the stairs and bolted the door at the bottom. Then we came back up together, went into her room and bolted the door from the inside. Apart from the tremors running through our bodies, we seemed fairly calm, exactly the way we were when we talked to each other under normal circumstances. She paused near the bed, adjusted her hair once again, and taking off her earrings she put them next to the pillow. In a flash of recollection, I remembered all those stories I'd heard about love affairs that started after the lovers stood together and compared their heights. But I decided at once that these stories were all imaginary, wishful tales and the only true Reality was this experience I was having with this woman, who was a distant aunt—but an aunt who also happened to be the younger sister of my brother's wife. I picked her up gently and made her lie down on the bed, reflecting that just a short time earlier I had entered the house calling for my "Little Bride." It's possible that the same thought may have crossed her mind. A light tremor ran through our bodies. I had just begun to lean toward her when she suddenly sat up straight. Fear flickered in her eyes.

"Someone is watching," she said softly and pointed at the door. I turned my head to look and also got the impression that someone was peeking through the crack between the double doors. The person appeared to move away and then return to look again. This went on for a few minutes. Both of us continued to stare in silence. Finally, I got up and opened the door. The bamboo screen which hung in front was swaying back and forth gently. I pushed at it with my hands and then closed the door once again. The sunlight streaming in through the door crack created a pattern of shifting light and shade as the bamboo screen moved in the breeze. I turned back toward Aunt. A weak smile flickered around her lips but I could hear her heart throbbing loudly in her chest, and her hands and feet were cold as ice. I sat down in a chair next to her bed and began telling her tall tales of strange optical illusions. She told me a few similar stories and pretty soon we were chatting away as we always did. Not one word was exchanged about anything that had transpired only a few minutes earlier. At length she said to me, "The others should be coming home soon."

At that moment it occurred to me that the door leading up the stairs had been bolted from the inside. Just then we began to hear the voices of family members. I got up, opened wide the door of the room and went out. Aunt was right behind me. I unbolted the door that led up the stairs and then we came back to her room and continued to make small talk. After a while, I heard a noise and saw that my "Little Bride" stood at the door. She really did look like a bride. Aunt uttered a joyful shout, grabbed the little girl, pulled her into her lap and started to kiss her over and over again with a passionate intensity. The little girl shrieked with laughter and struggled to escape from her embrace. Apparently, in the house where the wedding had taken place some overly enthusiastic girls had painted her up like a bride and decked her out with garlands. A few minutes later her mother came up to the room along with some other children. By this time the little girl was sitting in my lap and I was asking her about the fancy food she'd eaten at the house where the wedding had been. She could only pronounce the names of a few dishes and kept repeating them over and over. Her mother tried to pick her up but she refused to budge from my lap.

"Oh, she is such a shameless bride," Aunt said and everyone burst out laughing.

At some point we all came down onto the verandah where the other members of the family had gathered. Aunt kept showing my "Little Bride" how to act shy, and every now and then bursts of laughter rose up from the assembled throng.

2

By the time the sun had gone down, I'd made many attempts to catch Aunt alone. But she sat imprisoned in a circle of women, listening to anecdotes about the wedding. During the night, I tried three times to open the door that led up the stairs but it appeared to be bolted from the other side. I knew that a couple of women—themselves never married and perpetual hangers-on in the household—also slept in her room, but even so I wanted to go upstairs. Next day, from morning till noon, I saw her sitting with the other ladies of the family. I never did like spending much time with women so I uttered some casual remarks to her and did my best to stay away. By the late afternoon all my family members had retired to their rooms and most of the doors that opened onto the courtyard were now bolted from within. I went up the stairs and lifted the bamboo screen from Aunt's door. She lay on the bed fast asleep. I looked at her for the longest time. I had a hunch that she was merely pretending to be asleep. She lay with her head tilted backwards on the pillow and her hands clenched tightly into fists. She had removed her earrings and placed them next to her pillow. The scenes that had taken place in this very room just the day before flashed through my mind, but I drew a complete blank when I tried to remember what had happened during the moments that followed. It seemed to me that I had just picked her up in my arms and placed her on the bed. I stepped inside the room and turned to close the door but noticed one of those extraneous women sitting with her back against the balcony, winding some woolen yarn into a ball. She gave me an enthusiastic greeting and the utterly superfluous bit of information that Aunt was sleeping. I pretended to be looking for a book and then, complaining about not being able to find it, I left the room. But while I was searching, I looked over at Aunt several times. She seemed to be fast asleep after all.

Late in the afternoon, I saw the extraneous woman come downstairs and once again I went up and peered into Aunt's room. She was standing in front of a mirror combing her hair with her back toward me, while another extraneous woman recited a tale of woe about the first time she was beaten by her husband. I'd heard this story many times before; in fact, it had been a source of entertainment in our house for quite some time. Aunt laughed and then, noticing me in the mirror, asked me to sit down. But I questioned her about the imaginary book I had been searching for and went back downstairs.

I was away from the house for most of the evening. I had been sent to take care of some family matter, but I botched the whole business and returned home late at night. The doors of all the rooms were closed from within, including the one that led up the stairs. I went into my room and closed the door. For a while I tried to summon the image of Aunt, but I failed. I did manage to evoke her scent very briefly. As I slipped into sleep, I felt sure I would see her in my dreams. But the first phase of my sleep remained blank. Then toward midnight I dreamt that the extraneous women were dressed up as brides and were making obscene gestures at each other. Soon after that I woke up and only managed to get back to sleep toward dawn. At daybreak I woke up again from a dreamless sleep. My head felt foggy and confused. I decided to go and take a shower. In the bathroom I got the feeling that Aunt had just been there and I shook my head again and again to clear my senses. When I emerged from the bathroom I saw Aunt sitting in the sun drying her hair. One of my elders went up to her and began a lengthy discourse on the various ancient branches of our family. On the verandah the same two extraneous women I had seen yesterday were quarreling over something, but the presence of the old gentleman forced them to keep their voices low. Three other women in the same category soon joined the fray and contributed their half-witted views to reconcile the two or perhaps add fuel to the fire. Aunt listened to the elderly relative very attentively and covered her head as a sign of respect. I left her talking to this gentleman and went upstairs. But I came to a dead stop outside Aunt's room. Another extraneous woman was standing outside the bamboo screen. She asked me if Aunt had taken her bath. I told the old hag that I wasn't responsible for bathing Aunt and went downstairs again. Up to now I'd had no idea we had so many extraneous women crawling about our house. Their only practical use seemed to be to help with domestic chores, whether exacting or easy. Downstairs, the elderly gentleman was still pacing in front of Aunt. He had dealt with the past history of the family and was starting on the present.

Late in the afternoon I was sent out once again. But the situation that I'd been trying to deal with since yesterday deteriorated even more and I returned without accomplishing anything. That night I woke up many times. It occurred to me that the customary visit of Aunt as our house guest was almost at an end and the hour of her departure was drawing near. In the morning I felt as though my head was full of fog once again, and in spite of a cold shower I couldn't get rid of this heavy-headedness. I felt sure that if I found Aunt alone somewhere I would surely kill her. I didn't much care how I would do this either. I decided that I'd better stay away from her that day.

Much later, just as I emerged from my room, I saw her. She sat talking with some other women of the family and motioned with her hand for me to come over. The verandah was unusually quiet. The little girl slept in her mother's lap. Clearly she was ill. I took her into my lap and questioned her mother about her condition. Then the old gentleman, one of my elders, came onto the verandah and the atmosphere became even more somber. He made an effort to moderate his loud voice and asked about the child. But the little girl woke up. She looked as though she had almost recovered. The old gentleman began to tease her about her bridegroom. From the way the child responded, it became clear to us that she had not realized she was in my lap. The old gentleman then queried her regarding my whereabouts. Her response made everyone laugh. Finally, I tickled her lightly. She realized who I was and she began to giggle in embarrassment. The elderly relative picked her up and took her away. She was quite fond of him also and had woken up several times during the night calling for him.

As soon as the old gentleman left, the atmosphere of the room changed and peals of laughter rang out again and again. While they were all talking Aunt and I began to argue about what the date was that day. As we debated back and forth the others looked on with keen interest. Aunt simply couldn't be convinced. From where we sat I could see the corner of a calendar that hung in a room next to the verandah. Long ago a relative had drawn it up for us. With it you could tell the date of any day in any year. But this took a long time and you had to do several lengthy calculations. Eager to prove our cases, we got up to examine this calendar. Both of us entered the room together. But as soon as we were behind the door we clung to each other convulsively and almost sank to the floor. Then just as abruptly we got up and went out. The little girl's mother asked us if we had decided who was right, but just then there was some laughter, and then some more. Aunt was looking pale. Anyone coming in on us at that moment would undoubtedly have assumed that we had just come out of the room after spending quite a long time together.

That day I successfully finished the task I had mishandled twice before and returned home even later than the previous night. Everybody was in bed so I also went in and lay down. From the moment that Aunt had gotten up from the bed and come toward me to compare heights, to the time we had entered the room with the millennium calendar, I hadn't given much thought to how she might be feeling. I hadn't even considered that she might be totally unaffected by it all. Even so, I thought about killing her. All night long I was assaulted in turn by remorse, the allure of her physical charms, and the longing to meet her alone again.

In the morning when I came out of my room after a sleepless night, I was in the throes of remorse. So when an extraneous woman, the first one to rise, told me that Aunt's brother had arrived late at night with some bad news and that they had both gone away together, the only thought that came to my fogged brain was that I wished I'd been able to apologize to her.

None of the elders in my family could believe it when I told them that I had grown tired of my sheltered life and that I wanted to be on my own. And when they expressed reluctance, I was quite unable to assuage their doubts and concerns. Nevertheless, I succeeded in making them give in to my demands, mainly because they cared for me a great deal. Upon seeing all the elaborate arrangements they made for my journey, I realized how comfortable and secure I had been in that house and felt rather fed up with myself. A few days before my departure they gave me a small stone amulet inscribed with sacred names to wear around my neck. It was an heirloom that had been in our family for many generations. This increased my annoyance. Quietly I took the amulet off and put it back in the chest full of old clothes where it had always been kept.

My elders said good-bye to me in a subdued manner, and as I walked away from my home the voices I heard the longest were those of all the extraneous women. They were praying for my safe return.

3

I faced great hardships as I struggled to make myself independent. And in the end it was the good name of the family elders that helped me along. Thus, without moving a finger, indeed without even being aware of it, they helped me to stand on my own two feet. The work that I had undertaken involved inspecting houses. Initially, I had the feeling that I would fail in this profession because back then, apart from my own house, all other houses looked to me like piles of inorganic matter or half-dead vegetation. Sometimes I felt a vague hostility toward them, sometimes they looked like cheerless toys to me, and sometimes I stared at them for a long time as though they were foolish children, trying to hide something from me. Perhaps this is why, though I cannot seem to recall exactly when, houses began to assume a life of their own right before my eyes.

In the beginning I had no interest in the humanity that existed in these houses, though by merely looking at one I could make an estimate of how old it was, how and when certain improvements had been made over the years, as well as the speed with which Time passed inside these structures. I was sure that the speed of Time within these houses was not the same as it was on the outside. I also believed that the speed of Time could vary from one part of a house to the next. Therefore, when I calculated the rate of a home's deterioration and the years still left in the structure, the estimate usually bore no relationship to the outward appearance of the place. Still, none of my calculations were ever proved to be right or wrong, because even the smallest estimate of the years left in the life of a house was always larger than the years remaining in mine.

One day, as I was standing in front of a house, something about its closed front door gave me the impression that it had covered its face, either out of fear or to shield itself from something, or perhaps out of a sense of shame. I was unable to assess this house. Therefore, when I went in I examined every nook and cranny, every ceiling, wall, and floor very carefully. I wasted the entire day there without coming to any conclusion and at length came home only to spend most of the night thinking about this place. I reconsidered my assessment strategy and tried to remember all the details. At some point, it finally occurred to me that there was one part of this house that aroused fear and another part where one felt that some unknown desire was about to be fulfilled.

The next day I found myself standing in front of another house. The front door was closed, but it seemed to me that the house was staring at me with fearless, wide-open eyes. A short while later I was wandering inside it. When I entered a certain part of this house I became very apprehensive. Now I awaited the second sensation, and sure enough, in another part of the house, I got the feeling that some significant but unexpressed wish of mine was about to come true.

I was surprised at myself for having overlooked this fact until now. I returned to the houses I had seen many times and located these domains of fear and desire. No house, whether old or new, nor one among many of the same basic design, was without these domains. Looking for these domains of fear and desire became a vocation with me and, ultimately, this vocation proved harmful to my business. Because I was becoming convinced, asking the least bit of proof, that it was impossible to assess the life span of homes when they contained these domains of fear and desire. After suffering tremendous losses, I felt I had turned into an idiot, or was losing my mind altogether, and I decided to give up this vocation. But inspecting houses was my work and even if I did not look for these domains of fear and desire consciously, I would instinctively come to know where they were. All the same, I made an effort to cut down my interest in them.

Then one day I discovered a house where fear and desire existed in the same domain.

I stood there for a while, trying to decide whether I was experiencing fear or desire but I could not separate the two feelings. In this house fear was desire and desire, fear. I stood there for the longest time. The lady who owned the house wondered if I was having some kind of fit. She was a young woman and at the time there was no one else in the house except the two of us. She came close to me to examine me carefully and I realized that this domain of fear and desire was affecting her as well. She grabbed both my hands and then with a strange, cautious boldness she advised me to rest for a short while in the front room. I told her that I was quite well and, after a few minutes of conversation with her about business matters, I left the house. Perhaps it was after this day that I started taking an interest in the humanity that lived in these houses.

Eventually I could not imagine one without the other. In fact, at times I felt as though both were one and the same, because both intrigued me equally.

This interest increased my involvement with houses. Now I could look at a house in the most cursory manner and yet discover passageways that were secret or wide open, in use or abandoned. I could tell whether voices rising from one part of the house could reach other parts of the house. I'd examine each room very carefully to ascertain which parts of the room were visible from the crack between the door panels, or from the windows, or the skylights, and which parts could not be seen. In every room, I found a part that was not visible from the crack between the door panels nor from any window, nor from any skylight. In order to isolate this part, I would stand in the middle of the room and paint the whole place black in my imagination. Then, using only my eyes, I would spread white paint on all those parts that could be seen from the cracks or windows. In this manner, the parts that remained black were found to be the truly invisible parts of the room. Apart from certain rooms that were meant for children, I never did find a room in which the invisible part could not provide a hiding place for at least one man and one woman. Around this time, I began to concentrate on the shapes of these invisible parts. They made up the outlines of different images and at times had a truly amazing resemblance to certain objects. But I never did find a complete picture of anything. Everything appeared to be incomplete or broken, even though I examined countless such "invisible" parts. Some of these images had familiar shapes—of a lion, for instance, or a crab, or a pair of scales—but they all seemed like fragments. Other images resembled unknown objects and they looked incomplete although unfamiliar. They left a strange effect on the mind that was impossible to articulate.

One day I was in the outer room of a new house, looking at the image of the invisible part of the room. The image had an unfamiliar shape. As I examined this shape it occurred to me that long, long ago I had seen a decrepit old house in which the domain of desire had had exactly the same shape.

Until now I had only ascertained the boundaries of the domains of fear and desire in these houses. I had not thought about the shapes that could be formed from these outlines. But now I began to recall many—or, perhaps, all—shapes, and it occurred to me once again that either I was turning into an idiot or I was losing my mind altogether. Anyway, I became convinced that no one else could look at houses the way I did. I was also quite overwhelmed by the thought that no one else had the kind of rights that I had over the humanity that lived in these houses.

4

I didn't stay in any one place. I wandered through many cities and moved in and out of many homes. To me, at least, it began to look as though the cities were crowded with houses and the houses were filled with women. And every woman seemed to be within easy reach. Many women made advances toward me, and I made advances toward many. In this I also committed many blunders. For instance, some women whom I thought to be empty of, or unfamiliar with, or even full of hate for desires, turned out to be saturated with them and more than willing to do the utmost to fulfill them. In fact, at times they made advances so boldly that they frightened me. Other women who seemed to me to be oozing with desire, and just waiting for the slightest sign from me, turned out to be so naïve that when I made a pass at them they were unable to understand my intentions altogether. Some were overcome by depression, others were terrified. In fact, one got so worked up that she abandoned her calm and tranquil domestic life and actually left her home. She had a habit of arranging and rearranging her lustrous black tresses. I thought she wanted to draw my attention to her hair. She went away. That was totally unexpected. So I set out looking for her. I just wanted to tell her that her black hair had misled me, but she kept running away from me. Perhaps she thought that I was pursuing her like some sex-crazed animal. I never found her and I suspect that the fear I induced in her may have been the cause of her death. But I often console myself with the thought that she might have accidentally fallen into the river and resurfaced somewhere and been rescued.

5

After this, I gave up making passes at women. Instead, I took to waiting, wanting them to come after me. At times these waiting periods became rather protracted. During one such lengthy interval, I went to a new city where no one knew me. One morning, as I was wandering around the main bazaar of this city, a woman standing in front of some shops smiled at me and made a sign with her hand. She wanted me to come near. At first, I thought she might be a professional and I kept on walking. But then she called out my name. I stopped and turned toward her and she hurried over to me.

"Don't you know who I am?" she said with a smile.

I finally recognized her. Many years before she and I had been very close. She hadn't changed much except for the fact that she looked a little older. I was surprised that I had not been able to recognize her. But I was also pleased to run into someone in a strange town who actually knew me.

"What are you doing here?" I asked her.

"I live here," she said.

In a few minutes we were chatting away with the greatest informality. Again and again I got the feeling that she had become a prostitute. I had no experience with professionals. I couldn't even tell them apart from ordinary women. Then why did I suspect she was a professional? As I stood there staring at her, I became more and more suspicious. She noticed that I was examining her and a smug sort of look came over her face, revealing the source of my suspicions. For quite some time she had been making a play for me with words, eyes, and even body language. In the past, I had been the one who made advances. Several years earlier, during the period when I'd known her, she was already a woman of some maturity. And now she stood there acting coquettish and coy like a teenage girl. This saddened me. I examined her closely once again. Even now she was quite attractive. But she had also changed a great deal. As I stood there talking to this woman, I felt as though Time were speeding up, there, in that bazaar.

"Where do you live?" I asked her.

She pointed toward a neighborhood behind the shops.

"Come, I'll show you my house," she said. "If you have the time."

I had time. In the past, our relationship had begun pretty much in the same manner. She had shown me her house where she lived by herself in those days. Now we started walking side by side through the busy street. At a shop she stopped and bought a big padlock. She placed the lock and one key that went with it in her bag, and dangled the other key casually between her thumb and forefinger as she discussed the merits of a certain type of lock with the locksmith. Then, in an absent-minded way she handed me the key she had in her hand and we walked on.

She wants everything the way it used to be, I thought to myself, and once again it seemed to me that Time was speeding up in that bazaar.

"How much farther?" I asked her.

"We're almost there," she said, and turned into a broad side street.

Presently we found ourselves standing in front of an ancient wooden door that had just been given a fresh coat of paint. She removed the padlock that hung on this door, put it in her bag, and went inside. I stayed where I was. Then a smaller side door adjacent to the main door opened and she stepped out. She now had the new lock in her hand.

"You haven't forgotten, have you?" she asked and flashed a bold smile at me.

"I remember," I said.

I took the lock from her and she went back into the house through the small side door. I bolted the main door and locked it with my key and went into the house through the small side door, bolting it behind me. Now I found myself in a large room that contained many niches and alcoves but nothing in the way of furniture. I stepped out of the room into a spacious courtyard that had been enclosed by a wall. I noticed that a tall window made of weathered wood had been built into this wall. I started walking toward it when I heard a voice to my right:

"No, not there. Over here."

I turned and saw that adjacent to one corner of the wall and behind several small trees there was a verandah. The woman stood there under an arch. I went and sat down on a divan that had been placed there. Behind me there was a door. She opened the door and we went into a room. The room contained a bed and other domestic odds and ends that had been arranged neatly. She fell on the bed heavily, as though she were very tired, and I took a chair.

"So do you live here alone?" I asked her.

"Alone ... well, you could think of it as living alone. Actually, I live here with an old acquaintance—an elderly woman."

"Where is she now?"

"I really don't know. A few days ago she burst into tears abruptly and cried quietly all night long. In the morning she said, with the greatest reluctance, that she missed a certain home. All of a sudden she longed to be in the house where she'd spent her childhood. Soon afterwards she packed up all her things and went away. I'll introduce you to her when she returns."

"Why should I want to meet a melancholy old crone?"

"No, no. You don't understand. She can be very amusing. One minute she'll be telling you what a marvelous man her husband was. And the very next, she launches into a story about how he used to beat her up. She can be murderously funny."

"I have no desire to be murdered by the anecdotes of some old hag," I said, and left the room.

She came after me.

"What's the matter?" she asked.

"I'd like to see the house," I responded and went down into the courtyard.

"There isn't much to see," she said. "There's this verandah and this room, and that outer chamber. The rest of the structure has collapsed."

We were standing some distance away from the window, which had been built into the courtyard wall. I examined the wall carefully. It was apparent that the house had been one large structure and the wall had been put up to divide it into two halves.

"Who lives on the other side?" I asked her.

"I don't know," she said. "Perhaps no one."

Now we were standing near the window. The window had been poorly constructed out of rough planks. A board had been nailed diagonally across the two panels in order to seal it permanently. I was drumming softly on this board when I felt the ground under my feet shift. I placed my hands around the woman's waist and pulled her close to me. She looked a little surprised. I was also amazed at myself. I took a few steps back and then let her go. So the domain of desire is right here, I said to myself and then, stepping close to the window, I turned toward the woman again. She looked up at me and smiled.

"You've become rather aggressive," she said.

Once more the ground shifted under my feet and I shuddered.

And the domain of fear also, I thought with a causeless melancholy.

The woman stood in front of me, smiling. Somehow, she had succeeded in simulating a look of arousal. I lingered near the window for quite a while. It was a strip of ground barely two feet wide adjoining the window. The rest of the domain lay on the other side of that window.

"Who lives on the other side?" I asked.

"I told you, Mr. Impatient, no one."

"Come on, let's go," I said, moving close to her. We proceeded toward the verandah. Now she had really begun to feel aroused and she put her arms around my shoulders.

"It's very close and oppressive in there," she said in a whisper, and we stopped where we were. I recollected our old encounters when passion used to sweep her off her feet like a wind storm, and now, here in this house, she was either being overwhelmed by a storm of desire once again or leading me to believe that she was. In this house, or at least in this particular part of the house, Time moved more quickly than it did in the bazaar. A kind of affection began to stir in me for this woman who happened to be the only person I knew in this strange city.

"You haven't changed at all," she said softly.

"Well, along with Time …" I began and then suddenly, glancing upwards at the window, I saw something shiny in the crack between the frame and the upper edge of the panels. At exactly this time, the woman started to slip away from my grasp. She had closed her eyes, the way she used to. I took her in my arms and looked at the window once again. A pair of dark eyes was looking at us through the crack at the top. As I bent over the woman in my arms, I caught a fleeting glimpse of a red dress through the chinks between the boards. Slyly I looked up once again. The bright black eyes were locked on us. They were not looking into my eyes. They were focusing on our bodies. The idea that we were being watched by an unknown woman who was under the impression that I was unaware of her presence excited me, and I averted my face.

At this point we were standing very near the window. Slowly, very slowly I bent over this strip of ground until my head reached the bottom of the window. I had only the vaguest sensation that there was a woman with me and that I was holding on to her with both of my hands. I fixed my eyes on the lowest chink in the window. Looking down through the aperture, I saw a bare foot. Had the toe of this bare foot not twitched again and again, I would have thought that it had been molded in pure white wax. Behind the foot, at a distance that I could not determine, I saw an ancient arch of dark wood and the lower portion of a column. The foot took on a red glow from the shade of the dress, and I sensed the fragrance of a body in which another, more ancient odor was also implicated.

The toe rose from the ground and I saw that a long black string had been tied around it. I couldn't tell where the string led. If I'd wanted to, I could have reached in and grabbed the string, and perhaps I had decided to do just that. But the woman with me gripped my hands. Then she opened her eyes briefly and closed them tight again. She may have suspected that I wasn't focusing on her. So I became attentive to her. After a while, she rearranged her hair and said, "You haven't changed at all."

I looked at the window once again. There was no one on the other side. It was then that a question welled up inside me. Had this woman wanted to stage a show for a girlfriend? I kept on staring at the window for the longest time and then suddenly I turned toward the woman again and examined her face intently.

But a vacant look of satiation had settled over her expressionless face.

"You haven't changed either," I said to her, and went onto the verandah.

6

I went to see this woman nearly every day.

"Until the old lady returns," she told me the very first day, "this house is yours."

And, frankly, I did begin to think of it as my own house, and went there whenever I felt the urge. If the main door happened to be closed from the inside, I would knock and she would come and open it. I would sit and talk with her for a little while and then I'd go away. If the main door had a lock on it, I would produce my key, open the lock, and enter the house. Then I'd come back out through the side door, put the lock on the main door, re-enter the house through the side door, and bolt it behind me. She would meet me either on the verandah or in the room and I would end up returning late that day. But lately it seemed that almost every time I went to see her, I found the main door locked from the inside. I'd have to knock to be let in. She'd open the door and we would spend some time laughing and joking and then I would leave her.

One day I knocked on the door for a long time before realizing that it was locked from outside. It dawned on me that I had become used to knocking. I unlocked the door and went in. Then I came back out from the side door, put the lock on the main door, re-entered the house through the side door, bolted it behind me, and walked toward the verandah. The woman was not on the verandah and the door to her room was closed from outside. A couple of times in the past, she'd come home some time after my arrival. I opened the door to her room and lay down on her bed. I must have stayed there for a long time, in between sleeping and waking. Eventually, I left the room and went out onto the verandah. The afternoon was fading into evening. I was somewhat surprised at myself for having waited so long for her. Anyway, I waited a little longer and then went out through the side door, unlocked the main door, and went into the house again. I bolted the side door from the inside and was about to go out the main door when I stopped suddenly and turned back toward the verandah. I walked across the verandah into her room and changed the position of the bed.

She should know, I thought, and came back out onto the courtyard. I was going toward the main door when something made me stop in my tracks. I turned around slowly and looked at the window in the wall. A pair of dark eyes was looking straight into mine through the chink between the top of the window and the frame. I turned back toward the main door.

I should have known, I thought with groundless melancholy, and slowly turned and walked back toward the verandah. I went into the woman's room once again and pushed the bed back to its original position. Then I came out into the courtyard and crept along the wall that ran at an angle to the verandah. Staying close to the wall, I slowly inched forward in the direction of the window. When I got close to it, I bent down so far that my head almost touched the ground. Through the aperture at the bottom I could see the waxen foot with the black string still attached to the big toe. At first it remained perfectly still, but then it looked as though it had started to pull back. I reached under the crack suddenly, grabbed the black string and gave it several quick turns around two of my fingers. The foot struggled to retreat, but I pulled it back with equal force. Now, between my eyes and this foot, there was my intervening hand with the black string wrapped around the fingers. The string, apparently of silk, was very strong and clearly my fingers were about to be sliced off. I gave it several more turns around my fingers and then suddenly my hand came into contact with the toe.

The pull of the string was making it impossible for me to think clearly. When I had moved from the verandah toward the window, I had decided to make a play for her, but now I couldn't figure out what to do and my fingers were just about ready to drop off. The evening gloom fell over my eyes like a heavy blanket of darkness. I felt a cutting pain but at the same time it became possible for me to think. The very first thing that occurred to me was that I was not the only one in pain. In contrast to my tough and masculine hand, the delicate feminine foot was very soft and the thread that was cutting into my fingers was also tied to that foot. I pressed the toe gently and caressed the foot with two fingers that were free. It felt even softer than I had imagined it to be, but it was also cold as ice. Yet I could feel the warm current of blood surging under the delicate skin.

By now the blackness of night had spread everywhere and I could barely see the silhouettes of the small trees. I'm hurting her, I thought. Suddenly it occurred to me that up until now I had only pulled the string toward me once. I loosened the string around my fingers by a few turns and groped about the window with the other hand. I grasped the board that had been nailed obliquely across the window and tried to get up. But the board came loose and, precisely at that moment, the string unwound from my fingers. I placed both hands on the window to keep my balance but the window fell open since there was nothing to keep it closed now. Suddenly, I found myself on the other side of the window. In the darkness, I could barely see the dim outline of the dark wooden arch and a shadow moving slowly toward it.

I followed the shadow into a region of dense gloom beneath the arch and soon lost sight of myself.

This was my first experience with total darkness. I passed through the arch and went forward for a short distance. But then I found myself stopping. I tried to move north, east, south, west—in all four directions—but the darkness made it impossible for me to advance. I lost all sense of my whereabouts. Nor could I determine the position of the arch anymore. All I knew was that I was with an unknown woman in an unknown house and that—I was sure of this—we were alone. My long association with women and houses had given me the keen instincts of an animal. And now as I stood in the darkness, I peered about keenly just as an animal does. I took a deep breath. I was certain that the characteristic perfume emitted by ancient houses, which I'd begun to smell outside the door, would soon assail my nostrils. But this did not happen. And even though I knew it to be futile, I squinted into the darkness with such intensity that my features must have surely looked frightening. In spite of this, I could not cut through the darkness. As far as the sounds of voices were concerned, I had ceased to be conscious of them the moment I gave the very first turn of the black string around my fingers. Still, I made an unsuccessful effort to listen. It felt as though I had been standing there straining my senses for a very long time. Then it seemed as though I had just passed under the arch. Soon afterwards I felt two soft hands brush up against mine. I grasped them firmly and pulled them toward me.

After a long interval, I relaxed my grip, and my hands, exploring the elbows, arms, and shoulders, began to move toward the face. I tried to get a sense of individual features. But apart from a hint of long, thick eyelashes, I could not get an idea of how anything else looked. My hands wandered across her body, along her legs and down to her feet until my head touched the ground. I tugged at the string gently and then stood up. Now, once again, I felt soft hands clutching my own. Her palms pressed against my palms. And then in the darkness my hands became aware of color for the first time. Two white palms, upon which a pattern had been traced with red henna, moved from my palms to my wrists, then to my elbows, and from there to my shoulders and then further up until they cupped my face. Her fingers, which had red rings around them, passed over my cheeks and came to a stop at my neck. She tapped my neck three times and then her palms came to rest on my shoulders and stayed there for a long time. Groping slowly across my clothes, they reached down to my feet; they then vanished from that darkened scene for a few seconds and came to rest on my shoulders again. I remembered that ancient scent that had wafted toward me once, mingled with the odor of femininity. This odor is among those smells that are as old as the earth and were around long before flowers came into existence. It was an odor that brought to mind half-forgotten memories. However, at this moment it did not remind me of anything. In fact, I was fast forgetting what little I did remember.

The pressure of hands on my shoulders increased and then relaxed. And now, all at once, I became aware of the fulsome, palpable presence of a female body. It occurred to me that I was with a woman who had seen me with another woman—at least once—in broad daylight. I also realized that it was useless to try and see in the dark. I closed my eyes. I knew that closing them would not make any difference. And, truthfully, there was no difference, not for a while at least. But just when I'd forgotten the physical limitations of my eyes, I saw that I was slowly sinking into a lake of clear water. At the bottom of this lake I could see the ruins of ancient temples. I opened my eyes and was relieved to see only darkness all around. I recalled that there was a woman with me in this gloom. My breath felt the heat that was rising from her body. She is being swept along by a storm, I thought. Once more my eyes began to close and I could not keep them open no matter how hard I tried. Once again I saw the same clear-water lake. The ruins of ancient temples drifted up toward me until they hit my feet. But I couldn't feel them. Then, even as I was watching, the clear water of the lake became very dark and the ruins disappeared.

I don't know how long it was before I woke up. It was still pitch dark all around me. But on one side I saw the outline of the arch and beyond it the beginnings of dawn. I turned to the body lying motionless in the dark and let my hands wander all over it, touching everything. I placed my palms on hers, waiting for a long while for them to become moist with warmth. But they remained cold and dry. However, my hands did feel once again the bright red pattern on one of the palms. The shape of this pattern represented something unfamiliar. I stared hard at this shape and it became clear to me that the same shape resembled at once the domain of fear in a certain house, the domain of desire in a certain house, and the invisible part of yet another certain room. I tried to remember all the places where I had seen this shape and then it occurred to me that even though the shape was unfamiliar, it was, nevertheless, quite complete. For this reason, I had to struggle to convince myself that I had never seen this shape anywhere before. I made a futile attempt to pick up this shape from the palm of her hand. Then I touched it with my forehead, walked through the wooden arch, and went outside. The window resembled a dark stain. I went through it and emerged on the other side.

When I crossed the courtyard and made my way toward the main door, the morning birds were chirping in the small trees directly across from the verandah and some old woman there was coughing away.

7

I did not suddenly stop speaking. First of all, it never even dawned on me that I had given up speech. This because I never have been very talkative in the first place. The fact is, I just started devoting more time to thinking. After I came away from that house I slept for two days straight. I caught myself thinking even in my dreams and I continued to think after I woke up. The first thing that occurred to me was that I had gotten through that night with only the sense of touch to guide me. I had experienced everything by touch alone; rather, all that I had experienced was merely a transformed reflection of my sense of touch. Even so, I had missed nothing and, except for the first few minutes, I imagined that all five of my senses were being fully satisfied.

I never felt any curiosity about that woman. This reaction surprised me and I tried to force myself to think about her. But my mind rejected every image of her that I conjured up. I struggled with myself for many days but I was eventually forced to accept defeat. In the entire fierce encounter with my mind, I came to a realization: I wouldn't be able to recognize her even if I saw her from very close by. But she would recognize me instantly, whenever and wherever she saw me. This thought didn't disturb me that much, but then it didn't make me feel greatly at ease either. I accepted it like some worn-out and exhausted truth and gave up thinking about it. At about this time I realized that I had, more or less, also given up talking.

I have not sworn an oath of silence. It's just that I do not need to speak. This has been made possible for me by the kind people who live in this house. They spotted me somewhere, recognized me, and told me that for many generations our families had been very close. They brought me to this spacious house and graciously urged me to pick out whatever place I liked for my living quarters. I looked over the whole house and chose for myself— who knows, this might have pleased them—a section that had been unoccupied for a long time.

My bed is positioned exactly on top of the domain of fear. I have not been able to discover the domain of desire in this house. But that cannot be. So I have now become convinced that fear and desire converge here in exactly the same spot and that I have dominion over it.

Once I was walking about my room in the middle of the night when I happened to see this spot. It had assumed a black shape. This shape had an unfamiliar but complete outline. I kept on staring at this image for a long time. Then I examined the entire room carefully, peeking into each and every crevice, every window, every skylight. I stained the room white with my eyes, but the black shape remained untouched by this whiteness.

The shape of the invisible part—I thought ... At exactly this moment, I began to hear the chirping of the morning birds outside. I felt very strongly that if I tried even a little I would remember where I had seen this shape before. But I made something of a pact with myself never to make this effort. From that moment on I gave up talking.

The same day that I was introduced to my nurse, I moved a part of my bed a little distance away from the domain of fear and desire. She sits on this part of my bed and I just look at her. I believe that in this way I'm protecting her and also protecting myself.

—Co-translated with Javaid Qazi

The Woman in Black

My dreame thou brok'st not, but continued'st it
Thou art so truth, that thoughts of thee suffice,
To make dreames truth; and fables histories.

—*John Donne*

Savaar-e daulat-e javeed bar guzaar aamad
'Inaan-e ou na giriftand, az guzaar bi-raft
(The rider bearing the eternal treasure appeared on the path.
No one bade him halt. He traveled on.)

—*Anonymous*
(found in the papers of Fazl Allah Hurufi)

I do not remember the story of the bad woman now, but back in those days I took a keen interest in it. I remember I was overjoyed at learning that her case would be heard at our house, and that she would herself come to see it settled. Prior to this, the case of another notoriously bad woman had also been heard at our house, and my elders had brought it to a neat conclusion. But that happened when I was still in my nonage. I had only heard others speak of her, and they continued discussing her case amongst themselves until the case of this second bad woman came along and absorbed their attention.

On the day she was due to arrive, the outer room of our house was given a thorough cleanup and then furnished with additional seats. Several curios, some of them centuries old, were added to enhance the room's decor. The elders also called on me to help tidy up the place, and I did what was required of me with considerable enthusiasm. As I was moving a chair, I guessed from the conversation of my elders that this was the chair the bad woman would sit in. My heart began to pound. I could almost see her sitting right there. In fact, what aroused my interest in the matter was the opportunity it offered of looking squarely at a bad woman.

The elders alone were not going to try her; a number of outsiders were also expected to take part in the proceedings. These were honorable men to whom we had played host in the past as well. All the sumptuous reception arrangements were, as a matter of fact, intended primarily for their sake. My instructions, trickling in from the elders now and then, focused chiefly on ensuring that the honorable guests were properly looked after. But that wasn't where my interest lay.

A flurry of nervous activity swept over the elders as the time when everybody was set to arrive drew near. This obliged me to scurry back and forth several times from the side door of the house to the far outer room that formed a part of the house's façade. In the space between the side door and the outer room was a courtyard, the better part of which was overshadowed by a sprawling ancient tree bearing unusually tiny leaves. As the barrage of commands showed no sign of letting up, I too was infected by the same nervous tension and became breathless from my repeated rushed trips to the outer room. And yet I never failed, each time I passed under the tree, to raise my hand and give its branches a shake—it was an urge I could never resist, even now, when I was beside myself in all the excitement—and lift my eyes to look at the portico with the run-down roof that stood in a corner of the courtyard. The old surgeon lived in that portico. Every time I laid my hand on the branches he would call out, "Why do you meddle with that tree for no reason at all?"

But today he did not utter those words even once. He just sat there amid God knows what kind of medicines and ointments. He was so preoccupied with the paraphernalia before him that he forgot to defend the tree against my assaults. That day I saw him, for the first time ever, with the full array of his armamentarium; the fact is that he had given up the practice of surgery when I was still very young. He was an accomplished surgeon in his time, but I had only heard about his great expertise. To me he was merely an old man who pestered us with question after annoying question about everything and anything that transpired in the house. Old age had enhanced his nosiness. But most of his inquiries brought him no satisfaction: the elders rebuffed him, and I, for my part, gave him only incomplete and wrong answers that confused and befuddled him even more. As soon as the case of the bad woman surfaced, the old man was stung with curiosity. Every day he dragged himself out of the portico several times, only to walk back in, mumbling angrily. Today, however, when he should have been more excited than ever before, he was just quietly engrossed in his work, as if nothing else mattered.

For this I would certainly have teased him a bit. But by now I was feeling worked up—mainly because it was well past the time the invitees should have arrived, and in fact none had done so. The elders began to feel increasingly jittery; once more I found myself scrambling out the side door on my way to the outer room, giving the branches of the tree a tug as I made my way along. The tree, just as it had each time before, showered me with tiny yellow leaves. Brushing them off my hair and shoulders as I reached the outer room ... I saw there was nobody there.

I remained in the outer room for quite some time. Eventually the hushed stillness of the extravagantly decorated room began to bother me. Bored with the delay of the guests, I felt I no longer wanted to think about the bad woman, or the honorable guests either. It was then that I remembered Nusrat.

Hurrying by on my errands I had seen her, indeed every single time, sitting under the tree, leaning against it, staring straight ahead at the old surgeon or looking sideways at the ground, as her fingers traced lines in the dirt. And now I even seemed to recall that the first time I passed under the tree—or was it the second time?—she had turned to look at me. Perhaps she had also greeted me. But at the time I was too flustered to have returned her greeting, or even to have realized that she had actually raised her hand to me.

She had a sweet voice and she moved about nimbly. From time to time she came to our house to look after some sick relative of hers. Often I would notice how upon being called by someone she would pick her way from one part of the house to another with extreme caution, as if afraid she might step on something fragile and crush it. When she was present in the house, her name was heard quite often. But I rarely spoke to her: for one thing she talked in an exceedingly low voice, and for another, she kept her eyes lowered when she spoke. Yet she never failed to greet me.

At any rate, I started from the outer room, came to the tree, stopped and stood near it. I tugged at the branches lightly. The tree was in the throes of autumn and most of the leaves had turned pale and fallen. Here and there the branches were covered with spider webs, which caught many of the leaves as they came spiraling down. I looked at Nusrat. She sat leaning forward now, her head resting on her knees, her fingers still busily tracing lines. But then I saw her hand slacken and become motionless. Tiny yellow leaves covered her hair and shoulders, and she was dressed in white. It was bright and sunny under the tree, but too warm to sit outside.

"It isn't chilly out," I said.

She raised her head to look at me, and I asked, "Are you feeling cold, Nusrat?"

She sat up, her eyes still glued to the old surgeon.

"Are you feeling cold, Nusrat?"

"Not really," she said with a faint smile.

"Then why are you sitting here, in the sun?"

She didn't answer.

"Why don't you go in?" I said, pointing to the side door. "It's very hot here in the sun."

"Baba asked me to be here," she said looking at the old surgeon.

"Come on then. We'll go and sit with him," I said.

And although she seemed to be willing to follow my suggestion, she made no attempt to get up. I repeated my words and waited for a while for her to rise.

"I am not able to walk," she said softly, and with a slight nod of her head pointed at her feet.

Only then did I notice: Her feet were badly crushed, blackish-green and so swollen it was difficult to attribute them to a human body. The skin had been split open in several places, and a light red showed between the cracks. The right foot had been totally twisted out of shape and the left toes, bloated and curling round, were buried to half their length in the right sole. It looked as though they were being sucked into the right foot with a tremendous force and before long would break off and completely vanish into it. All of this looked like a murderous struggle, the sheer tension of which had caused a mesh of protruding blue veins to erupt ominously all across her calves.

"What happened, Nusrat?" I asked her again and again.

"Everybody says both feet will just have to be amputated," she said. "But Baba wants me to let him ..." Here her voice became so faint I could not hear the words that followed. I looked at the old surgeon. He was busy picking up some iron instruments one by one and peering at them, drawing them close to his eyes. Something was coming to a boil in a clay pot nearby and the portico was filled with smoke.

"Baba said I'm not to let anyone know," I heard Nusrat say. "He said he would do it today, because everyone would be busy elsewhere."

"But, Nusrat, how did this happen?"

Thereupon she told me the whole story. I've forgotten some of the details by now, others I couldn't make out as her voice, every now and then, dropped to a whisper. Perhaps she was in too much pain. She mentioned some men who were in a vehicle and wanted to get to a certain place in a hurry. Perhaps there had been an accident. But something was blocking the vehicle and had to be removed. Nusrat promptly pushed whatever it was aside. But before she could get out of the way the vehicle lurched forward and crushed both her feet. It rolled on without bothering to stop and Nusrat lay there unattended for a long time.

"What kind of people were they?" I exclaimed after hearing her out. "Didn't they even notice they'd run you over?"

"As a matter of fact, they did," she said. "That's why only the front wheel passed over my feet. They quickly swerved the vehicle to one side, maneuvering the rear wheel away from my feet."

"But they didn't stop?"

"They were in a hurry."

"You didn't stop them either?"

"They were in a hurry. Still I managed to say ..." her voice faded out.

"What did you say, Nusrat?"

"But maybe they could not hear me."

"What did you say, Nusrat?"

"I said: you see how helpless I am."

I couldn't help laughing at this.

"What a pointless thing to say!" I said. "What good could it possibly do? It wouldn't have made a bit of difference even if they had heard it."

"But what else could I have said?"

I had no answer to that. All the same I said, "Men like them are not likely to be affected by such a remark. 'You see how helpless I am,'" I said, mimicking the way she'd said it. "Didn't you realize the sort of people they were?"

"That's what people are like," she said, and once again put her face back on her knees.

Sensing she was not going to cry, I continued. "So what happened then? How did you get out of there?"

Just as she started to tell me about it I heard a few sharp sounds. I turned around and looked at the old surgeon. He was getting up, clutching his waist with his hands. Obviously, he was not the source of the sounds. I looked back at Nusrat. Her lips were moving but the racket drowned out her soft voice. Finally I did manage to guess where the sounds were coming from. I moved a few steps back to get a better view. I saw vehicles pulling up in front of the outer room. The bad woman had arrived.

I sprinted off.

Most of the seats in the outer room had been taken. Nearly all the honorable guests had also arrived. Their faces looked unusually serious, almost grim. My elders, being the hosts as well, were in something of a fix as to whether to look more hospitable or more grim. A number of women were also present. The bad woman was there too, as part of the audience. Contrary to my expectations, she didn't look significantly different from the others. She had draped herself in several mantles, one on top of the other, and the only thing her face betrayed was exhaustion. Although she was practically buried under her clothing, a part of her belly with prominent blue veins could still be seen clearly. Her lips parted a little as she breathed, fully exposing two of her front teeth, which remained visible as she kept breathing fast. I was disappointed when I saw her. A girl was sitting right next to her, and every now and then the bad woman leaned toward her to say something. Following one of her remarks the girl began to look around and her eyes fell on me. She got up and walked over to me. Then she said, "Would it be possible to get a drink of water?"

I hurried off at once. As I passed under the tree on my way to the side door I saw the old surgeon sitting in front of Nusrat and examining her feet very closely. Hearing my footsteps he raised his head and squinted at me in an effort to make out who I might be. Had I tugged at the branches, he would have recognized me at once. As I hastened to the outer room after fetching the glass of water from the house, I saw the old man still studying Nusrat's feet.

The bad woman drained the glass in a single draught and then handed it back to the girl, who then returned it to me. I had to bring her water three times over. There was time for all this only because some honorable guests still hadn't turned up. Time and again a sudden silence would descend on the room, prompting one or another of the elders to dispel it by clearing his throat and uttering some stuffy pleasantry to the guests seated near him.

The fourth time I brought the water it was the girl who took the glass from my hand and began to drink from it in small, unhurried sips. Two of her teeth, refracted and distorted by the glass and the water, appeared enormous. When she handed the glass back to me I casually put it down on the floor near the door, and the girl returned to the bad woman.

By now the atmosphere in the room had become so intolerably thick that I thought I might as well withdraw for a little while.

As I was passing under the tree I heard the voice of the old surgeon.

"Come here," he called to me. I turned to walk over to him.

"Come closer."

I drew nearer. He put his hand on my shoulder, pulling me down toward him.

"Her feet are stuck together," he whispered. "The first thing is to separate them. That is usually extremely painful. She may writhe and thrash about. Perhaps I won't be able to hold her still by myself. I may no longer have the strength."

I looked at Nusrat. There was panic in her eyes; still, she was trying to smile.

"Maybe if you talked to her and somehow kept her occupied ..." the old man whispered again. "Said things that would take her mind off me, completely off me. For if she suddenly jerked her feet, things would go badly for her. I mean her left toes would snap off. Don't let that happen. When I gesture to you, keep her mind off what I'm doing. Make sure she remains absolutely still, and I mean absolutely still."

Next he said something funny but couldn't make her laugh, so I began telling her some anecdotes from earlier in the old man's life. I spoke of achievements in the field of surgery about which I'd heard. In the meantime the old man went on examining her feet from various angles and placing them on the ground in different ways.

I talked for a long time. I told her interesting tidbits about our family. Then I began to talk about her. But it could not have amounted to much, or been very coherent. What did I really know about her? All the same, I tried not to let her sense that thought. I now had the distinct impression that she no longer was thinking about the old surgeon. Throughout, I would glance at him intermittently. I saw him indicate that I should be ready.

"And do you know, Nusrat, what came to my mind the very first time I saw you?" I couldn't even remember when that had been. Nonetheless I continued: "Do you know what crossed my mind that day? It seemed to me that you were walking on flowers." I realized at once what an awful mistake this was and hastily proceeded to say, "Should I tell you something about your hands, Nusrat—something I believe nobody else could ever tell you?"

Right then I saw the old man make that unmistakable sign. I quickly took hold of both her hands and pressed them hard.

"Should I tell you?" I whispered. Almost at once I heard harsh voices rise from the direction of the outer room and then melt away. Precisely then her hands trembled in my grasp. I saw her face turn blue, then red, and then ashen white. She bit her lips and her eyes expressed terrible agony.

"It's all right," I heard the old man say. "It's absolutely fine.

Well done! I will be able to heal her now. Just wait and see."

I turned toward the old man. He had spread his hands over Nusrat's feet, hiding them completely. I wanted to see what exactly he had done, but he sharply refused.

"Don't look at her feet," he said, "and don't let her look at them either."

I turned my face away and looked up at the spider webs stuck to the branches of the tree. It was absolutely quiet all around, except for the occasional soft clink of the surgical instruments. In anxious anticipation I waited for the old man to say something. And he did, finally, "You may go now, if you like, and attend to your own business. I can handle the rest myself."

Only then did I realize I was still holding her hands. She had put her face back down on her knees and her hands were damp with sweat. I let go of them, got up, and, even though aware that I was already too late, began to walk toward the outer room.

A deathly hush had now swept over the room. The chairs were in total disarray, and hastily scribbled scraps of paper lay near some of them. I collected the scraps. The scrawled writing marked the consultations that had taken place among the elders and honorable guests. I put the chairs back in order. I had a hard time deciphering the writing on the scraps, but once I had mastered it I tried to ascertain the events that had taken place during my absence. I arranged and rearranged the scraps in many different ways but failed completely to make any sense of them; as soon as I changed their order the events they were supposed to represent also underwent a complete change. I wasted a considerable amount of time juggling those scraps and was none the wiser for my effort. My interest, tremendously aroused by the sight of them, began to dampen and then vanish altogether. The room, lined with curios, began to suffocate me. I felt I couldn't stay there any longer. As I was leaving the room I noticed that the glass lay undisturbed near the door where I had set it. I didn't bother to pick it up; instead I headed straight for the tree.

But there was only the carpet of yellow leaves beneath it. I furtively looked at the portico of the old surgeon. It was empty, although still filled with smoke.

Soon afterwards my house began to empty out. My people, all of them, began to expire, one by one in quick succession; the elders died off even more swiftly: as though they were a heap of rice pressed by a damp hand against a surface, lifting them clear off. I looked on at all this, thinking that I must be in a dream and hoping I'd wake up from it. Occasionally I felt frightened. Anyway, in the end I found myself all alone in a rambling mansion, trying to get used to my loneliness somehow. I would visit each part of the house, anxious, always anxious, not to let even the smallest space remain unoccupied by me for too long. Anyone watching me in those days would surely have thought I was looking for something I had lost.

But one day it occurred to me that I had somehow completely neglected the outer room. So I went there. The main door stood open as usual and the heavy curtain across it stirred slowly. The light inside the room was dim, which made the farthest chairs appear hazy. In spite of the poor light I could still see the heavy layer of dust that had settled on the precious curios. The walls too had become coated with dust, and the portraits of the elders looked faded and dull. I touched the curios one at a time, leaving my fingerprints on them. I wiped the dust off the portraits of my elders with my hand. They became so vivid that I felt like talking to them. And when I spoke I could hear my voice resonate inside the room. I talked for a long time. Coming to one portrait, I broke my stride and stopped. The kind face peered at me with apprehension. A sense of loss overwhelmed me and I gently touched the portrait with my forehead.

"I remember everything," I said. "Everything."

Those anxious eyes just kept gazing at me.

"But nothing can be done now. I had no idea until this moment how the same house could look so completely deserted and yet so full of people. This very room ...," I swept the room with my glance, "this very room, once upon a time ...," my eyes caught the glass on the floor near the door, "why, even the bad woman...." Just then I heard the rustle of a dress, forcing me to turn around and look.

Someone had just gotten up from a chair in the distant gloom and was walking toward me. It was a woman. Is she the bad woman?—I wondered. But then I heard her voice.

"You wouldn't have recognized me," she said softly. She had drawn nearer now. I bent down and touched her feet to see if they were completely healed.

"This is wonderful!" I said. "I am so happy, Nusrat, that your feet are better now."

A long silence ensued during which neither of us said a word. Then I said, "I hope there are no scars."

One after the other she put her feet forward in the light filtering through the bottom of the heavy curtain.

"Even the scars have disappeared," she said.

Another long silence followed that I felt compelled to break. "After a few days," I began, "you won't even remember the terrible pain you had to endure. The scars would have been a reminder."

"But I *shall.*"

"That's what everyone imagines in the beginning. Without scars, though, one couldn't remember—neither the pain, nor even the old surgeon."

That seemed to disturb her and when she spoke again she did so hesitantly, as if trying to explain a mistake of hers.

"The scars would certainly have been there, but Baba himself ... He said there should be no scars." Then after a while she added, repeating her words two or three times, "I didn't say anything to him."

"You don't have to explain anything," I said, raising my hand. "I'm not blaming you at all. But the fact is that there are no scars now."

The stiffness in my speech was all too obvious to me. It was not right of me, I conceded to myself. But I couldn't help it. The loss of so many had left me saddened.

"You must be wondering, Nusrat, why I'm talking this way," I said. "You must be thinking it isn't the way I spoke to you that day under the tree."

"That was another day," Nusrat said, looking intently at her feet. Her voice grew softer as she added, "I was in a pitiable state that day."

She lifted her head to look at me. After a brief silence she said in a voice that was softer still, "That was a day of commiseration."

"And today?" I asked, my voice growing louder. "Is it not a day of commiseration also? Weren't you really looking forward to it?" I took a few quick steps forward and moved close to her. "But, Nusrat, let me tell you, my state is not pitiable."

"When did I ever say that?" There was sheer torment in her eyes and her voice was tremulous. "I couldn't even imagine it would turn out like this."

Suddenly her voice choked. She seemed ready to collapse. I quickly caught her arm to support her. After I had steadied her, I released her and moved back. Her face lost all its color and she stood there so perfectly still, so lost, for such a long time that she herself looked like one of the curios in the room. My dusty fingers had left marks on her arm.

I now began to feel contrite. "I am sorry, Nusrat," I said. "The room is full of dust and you are so fond of white clothes. And white does look lovely on you. I've heard many people admire you in white. As for me, I like black more. Do you know why?"

She raised her head to look at me. I repeated a line I had read somewhere—one I had never forgotten: "Because black is the color of nothingness."

A sense of loss overwhelmed me once again. I have no idea how much longer Nusrat stood there, waiting for me to say something more. But finally I saw her turn around slowly and walk toward the door. I heard the muted sound of the glass breaking and saw Nusrat hesitate for a moment near the door. Then she lifted the heavy curtain. Outside light invaded the room and, just as suddenly, vanished.

She was a soft-footed girl. I couldn't hear the sound of her receding footsteps.

I remembered that my prolonged stay in the room had caused me to neglect other parts of the house, and this prompted me to leave at once. Coming to the door my eyes caught the glass. It was broken now. I swept the pieces aside with my foot. The edges of some of the jagged pieces, I noticed, were stained with something—fresh blood, I recognized at once, even in the faint light.

Afterwards I had opportunity to pass under the tree many times. It had again filled out with dense foliage. The branches, unable to cope with the heavy burden of the leaves, had drooped so low over the ground that I had to crawl under them to get across. And if on occasion I walked totally absorbed in my thoughts, the soft leaves invariably struck me across the face. Which prompted me to think: Why not prune these branches that always get in my way?

One day I was going toward the side door. As I approached the tree I automatically bent down a little. But the leaves struck me in the face all the same and I noticed that the branches had drooped lower still. I was irritated. I thrust out my hand and pushed them away right and left, only to have them bounce back and strike me more forcefully than before. I began to feel terribly itchy on my face and neck and snapped off several branches, yanking them vigorously. I had to bend low to free myself from the tangle. As I straightened up and brushed the twigs and leaves off my body, I noticed someone sitting huddled against the trunk. It was not possible to make out the face of the figure because of the gloom cast by the thick foliage, but I recognized her all the same.

"Nusrat!" I called out, picking my way toward her. As I drew near I saw that she was dressed in black.

"Nusrat!" I called her softly and my eyes fell on her. Her features were not visible. I couldn't understand why this was so. I leaned forward and took a closer look. Dry yellow leaves covered her face like a veil. I wanted to remove the leaves from her face but saw that they were held together by cobwebs and my hand stopped halfway.

"Nusrat!" I called again, my voice growing fainter. I saw that the black mantle covered her from her shoulders to her feet. One of her hands was free of the cape and seemed to be resting on the ground. Her fingers were coated with dust and there was a maze of lines drawn in the dirt.

"Nusrat!" I said, but as a man talking only to himself. I shook her in an effort to wake her up. I tried to move her feet slowly. It was then that I saw: her feet under the black mantle formed an odd protuberance. I didn't touch her. Somehow I knew that beneath the mantle her feet were again misshapen.

I looked around. My sweeping eyes came to rest on the portico of the old surgeon. The floor was covered with the debris of the caved-in roof. There was no voice to be heard anywhere. Not a thing seemed to move. The chill under the tree increased suddenly and a severe trembling seized my body.

I stood up and ran in through the side door. I had taken only a few steps inside when I turned back to close it. I grabbed both panels of the door firmly and brought them together. As the door was about to close I peered through the slit that remained to see whether Nusrat was still sitting there as before. She was.

I shut the door and was never able to open it again.

Snake Catcher

Turn away no more;
Why wilt thou turn away?

—*William Blake*

Lang-o-luuk-o-chuftah-shakl-o-be-adab
Su'e ou miighez-o-ou-ra miitalab
(Though hobbling, bent over, and uncouth
Creep ever toward Him, seeking Him forevermore)

—*Rumi,* Masnavi

1

"Maar-Geer! Maar-Geer!"*

The cry would echo in the stillness of the night. The caller was sometimes an old man, sometimes a youth, sometimes a woman, and sometimes a child, so one might assume these cries would be quite different, but to me they always sounded the same.

"Maar-Geer! Maar-Geer!"

Whenever the cry rang out in the still night I was unable to figure out who the caller was. The call had the same quivering fear of death that spread across age and gender. I would be awakened from a deep sleep and know that a snake had bitten someone. A slight shudder would sweep through my body and I would want to go back to sleep and think of it as something I'd only heard in my dream. Just then I would feel the cold touch of two fingers on my neck and hear a faint "The cry's up" very close to my ear.

*I have retained the original phrase "Maar-Geer" ("Snake Catcher") where he is addressed by the people. —*Translator*

This obliged me to get out of my bed. By then the cry would have moved closer, now mixed with other voices.

"Maar-Geer! Maar-Geer!"

The sound of countless shuffling feet accompanied the cry; I would approach the door and open it, allowing in a small crowd of people. Some of them would be supporting a dying man. Sometimes one of them held a stick in his hand with a dead snake dangling from it. The sight made me shudder again. At that time, I had to deal with the crowd all by myself. I would make a space on the ground, and the dying man was laid out there. I would unroll a long—about the length of two men—narrow mat right beside him on which the uncoiled dead snake was then placed. I would grope around the dying man's body looking for the wound and, after I had found it, I would make him lie in such a way that the wound was accessible. I never asked how the snake had bitten him; still, some people went to great lengths relating the entire incident. They all spoke at once so I was never entirely able to hear about the actual incident. And besides, only a handful could describe it anyway. The one who had been through it all lay on the ground unconscious or simply mute with terror, so people spent more energy enlarging upon how they got the news and what they were doing at the time. As they continued talking they watched my usual routines, with their eyes roaming around searching for someone else the whole time.

Shortly afterward the Snake Catcher would appear before them and everyone would immediately become attentive to him, a whisper sweeping through the crowd from one end to the other.

"Maar-Geer! Maar-Geer!"

For a while he would remain absolutely silent, paying attention to no one. The people would also remain quiet, allowing their gaze to rest on him. Then he always asked the same question, "What happened?"

In response, the people didn't speak all at once, as though they had silently struck a deal among themselves and now only one of them would start slowly and, using a minimum of words, tell him what had happened. But it seemed as though the Snake Catcher didn't hear a single thing the man said. His eyes were fixed on the snake lying stretched out on the mat with its hood often terribly crushed. He always looked at the snake wistfully, sometimes even giving the impression that he considered the snake his patient. These moments felt inordinately long. Only then did he take notice of the victim, and I also looked closely at the victim's face for the first time along with him.

The face would be covered with beads of sweat. Sometimes the victim would be completely unconscious, but, even so, something like colors seemed to flow quickly just underneath the skin. Sometimes he was conscious, but appeared terribly frightened. Sometimes he seemed to be struck simultaneously by drowsiness and fear; I don't recall ever seeing fear and drowsiness together on anyone's face except that of a snakebite victim.

The victims could be of any age or gender, but the face of just about every victim invariably reflected a strange sense of his or her importance, as if being bitten by a snake was a personal achievement that no one else was capable of matching. I never saw despair on any victim's face, perhaps because once a victim had made it to the Snake Catcher alive he never died, and usually walked back on his own feet.

Now and then though, a victim went back as a corpse, but this happened only when he had already died en route to the Snake Catcher. The victim of a snakebite looks utterly dead when he dies; there's no need to even look at his face to confirm his death. Nevertheless the people who carry a victim can only be convinced of his death after they have brought him over to the Snake Catcher. Usually on such occasions I would know before the Snake Catcher's arrival that the victim was already dead. The skin of some victims had burst open. The people accompanying such victims didn't show much enthusiasm for talking about the incident before the Snake Catcher's arrival. They would just look at me intently, trying to gauge the condition of the patient, but I tried not to let anything show on my face. The Snake Catcher would arrive. First he would look for the mat but it wouldn't be in its place because I never saw a dead victim brought in along with the snake that had killed him. Only after that would the Snake Catcher look closely at the victim and then at me, and I would know what he wanted. I would unroll another mat that stood in a corner and throw it over the victim. After a few moments of total silence the Snake Catcher would leave the scene. The people would then pick up the dead body. I would remove the mat from on top of the body, roll it up and return it to the corner, and they would walk out carrying the corpse with them. They would start out in perfect silence but the minute they stepped out the door the sound of someone wailing would surely be heard.

This happened rarely, however. Usually a victim was rushed to the Snake Catcher before he had turned cold. In that event, the Snake Catcher wouldn't let him die, regardless of what kind of snake had bitten him. Whether the culprit accompanied its victim or not, the Snake Catcher would know with just one glance what kind of snake it had been.

In the first place, most victims had not been bitten by a poisonous snake, but their own fear pretty much did them in. Any plain, colored water would have sufficed to put them back on their feet. But the Snake Catcher would put them through a truly painful ordeal, sometimes scorching the spot that had been bitten and sometimes using sharp, pointed instruments to make incisions in the wound, which he then filled with certain kinds of medicinal powders that made the victims start to scream and thrash about. However, on a sign from him, several people would grab the victim tightly and muffle his cries. Something resembling a riot continued for a while and during this time the Snake Catcher turned his attention back to the dead snake. Eventually a daze would sweep over the victim and the people would carry him away.

But for those actually bitten by a poisonous snake, the Snake Catcher had any number of treatments. These changed according to the type and kind of offending snake. He smeared the wounds of some victims with a certain kind of clay, which he also diluted with water and made the person drink. On other wounds he applied the frothy juice from the freshly crushed green bark of some tree. On still others, he would suck out a fair amount of blood and then dribble a few drops of some medication, which I'm certain contained venom collected from some other kind of snake.

If, however, a victim had been bitten by a snake that was so venomous, or the venom from a snake had spread through his bloodstream to such an extent that no antidote would work, the Snake Catcher didn't even attempt to treat him with medicine. Instead, he took out his bezoar. The bezoar always performed uniformly and never failed.

I first observed the workings of the bezoar on myself—at least now it seems that I did.

2

I was running away from a dead girl. I didn't even know for certain whether she was really dead, still I was running away from her. I left my house far behind, then even my hometown. New settlements appeared; these, too, I left behind and now I was facing the jungle.

For some time already I had given up thinking altogether, but I stood there facing the jungle and spent a long time thinking. Right across from me was a corridor of trees and bushes that became darker up ahead, and I knew nothing about it. I was on a slight elevation and this jungle corridor was sloping downward. I had to make up my mind whether to enter it or not. But before that, I had to make up my mind about the dead girl—whether she was actually dead or had merely appeared to be dead. And I had to decide this not on the basis of the events but strictly on the basis of my own inclination. I was caught in the worst dilemma. In fact, I was even having difficulty deciding what it was I wanted to decide in the first place. I spent an entire night thinking, but when it was morning I was still unsure whether I was running away from her because I thought she was alive or because I thought she was dead. I wished that what happened hadn't happened. While I was wishing for this, I fell asleep and dreamt that what had actually happened hadn't really happened at all. Because of this I started to fall asleep in my dream, and I woke up.

I stepped into the jungle immediately.

This was my first encounter with the jungle. Here, the atmosphere felt damp, and continued to get damper and damper as I moved forward. I was wading through old trees and withered vines. Small pathways had been opened between the crooked lines of trees, but they were covered with a meshwork of countless roots, thick and thin, that jutted out from the earth and made it difficult to relate the roots to their corresponding trees. Now and then, though, I came upon a dead tree and some root in the meshwork snapped under my feet, letting me know that it, in fact, belonged to that tree.

The jungle didn't frighten me. I only encountered a few animals. When they sensed my footsteps, the small ones darted into the bushes where they would stand staring at me with wide-eyed wonder, reminding me of shy children. I saw innocence and bewilderment in the eyes of all the jungle animals. I didn't encounter any that were ferocious.

For some distance I looked around at the jungle with interest. Then I was reminded of the curios neatly arranged in the outer reception room of my house. I couldn't remember exactly what those curios were so I tried hard to recall each and every one of them.

One was a lion made of some kind of metal. It stood on its hind legs with its mouth wide open as though it were roaring. Its eyes were crafted from some precious stone and they had disappeared several generations before me. Yet the lion's only importance lay in its missing eyes. Close to the lion, but larger than it, was a horse molded from some reddish-brown material with a rider of the same material mounted on it. One of the rider's hands was poised in the manner of someone wielding a sword, but the hand was empty. The sword of that empty hand was sorely missed, but an elder of the family used to say that the rider had, in fact, held a scale, not a sword, in that hand. In my own time, mostly due to my own carelessness, the upper half of the rider's body had also broken off and a clever artisan had been commissioned to put it back together. I remember that when the upper half came off, it revealed that the inside material was of a rather dark red color and it gave off a strange scent, which conjured up memories of old things when it was inhaled. On the wall across from the lion and the rider hung a crab fashioned from numerous tiny chips of animal horn. The pieces had been put together in such a way that the slightest touch made the entire crab wobble and appear as if it were crawling along the wall. I hated this crab; sometimes I even feared it. It was a specimen of a craft practiced by some lost tribe whose name I could never remember.

The curios in the reception room also included a miniature palace built from tiny stone bricks of different colors. It was a complete palace with arches, columns, turrets, etc. The turrets, especially, were exceedingly beautiful and guests often marveled at the delicate workmanship of their ornamental serratures. It used to be said about this palace that at some point in time there really was a full-scale likeness of it, the ruins of which could still be seen, and that the miniature had been made to serve as a model for the actual palace. But some elders said that it was when the actual palace was destroyed that its builder made this miniature to keep the memory of the other palace alive. Now and then this miniature even came up for discussion among the elders. They would speculate in increasingly novel ways about the possible reasons for the palace's destruction and about the age of its architect, without ever resolving whether the miniature was the model for or the memorial of its life-size likeness. But at least this much was certain: there used to be a full-scale palace, in every respect exactly like its miniature counterpart, which had crumbled and, for that reason, the miniature was now considered only a memorial.

I often stood in front of the miniature palace and stared at it for so long that it began to look like the real, life-size palace. Not only that, I even heard sounds of life filtering out of it. Then, abruptly, I would regain control of myself and the palace would shrink back down with a jolt. Later on, I resolved to build myself a real palace patterned after it. I even informed the elders and guests in the reception room about my resolve and solicited their opinion about the changes I was considering making.

However, the most prominent among the reception room's curios was a palanquin sitting on top of an octagonal table in the center of the room. The table had been built especially for it. Made from a variety of metals and woods, the palanquin had layer upon layer of curtains, fashioned out of extremely fine, colorful fabric, over its doors. These were drawn back by cords with large tassels, revealing a space strewn with assorted cushions of various shapes. Tiny silver and gold vessels lay beside those cushions. I never could figure out the purpose for even one of them. Miniscule bells made of an exceptionally delicate metal hung from the palanquin's ceiling. These could often be heard tinkling softly, but only when the conversation in the reception room suddenly stopped. Then the tinkling of bells seemed to fill the entire room. The softness of the sound was another matter. It seemed as if the bells weren't tinkling softly somewhere nearby, but rather that they were echoes from bells ringing loudly somewhere quite far off.

The palanquin was the last curio to be added to the collection in the reception room—the only addition made after

I'd reached the age of discernment and understanding, and from that point of view, it was also the first addition. Somebody who looked a bit wild had brought it and had also stayed on with us for a while to oversee its suitable placement in the reception room, including the construction of the octagonal table. He revealed nothing about the palanquin's antiquity. A few of the guests believed that it was several hundred years old; however, some merchants asserted that it was, in fact, a specimen of the workmanship of the wild fellow himself and that it only appeared to be ancient. Still, no one doubted that if any one man had crafted this palanquin, he must have spent more or less his entire life doing it. At first the wild one was shown great hospitality, but later he was thrown out of our house in terrible disgrace, the reason for which I never discovered. In any case, the palanquin remained in its place on the octagonal table in the center of the reception room. Its greatest virtue—so it was claimed, though I had difficulty fathoming it—was that it drew all the other curios to itself, curios that before had seemed to scurry every which way. In the beginning, whenever the palanquin was mentioned in our house, the wild fellow was also invariably mentioned, but slowly all reference to him was dropped. The last time I heard him mentioned was when news arrived that a snake had bitten him.

At this point the thought that there could be snakes in the jungle occurred to me for the first time.

I was in a part of the jungle where green vines were spread out over the tree trunks and the ground. These vines had large, dark green leaves with light green, protruding veins and they were so succulent that when they were bent they snapped in the middle, releasing jets of water. And, in fact, the atmosphere there was suffused with exceedingly fine sprays of water. In short, that area of the jungle was completely different from the places where the presence of snakes might be suspected. But it was precisely here that the thought of snakes occurred to me and I began to imagine their presence near every moving leaf, so much so that it became difficult for me to press ahead. I stood there surrounded by a sea of green vines. The movement of their leaves resembled the rise and fall of waves, and the objects below them, which seemed to be crawling toward me, made it difficult even to stand. I scanned the area for a clearing, but there were green vines around me and it was impossible to tell where the terrain rose and fell beneath their large succulent leaves. That the terrain was uneven was beyond a doubt. I remembered how several times, as I trudged forward, I had been plunged up to my waist in leaves and, wading through these leaves with my hands, I had to climb up a slope. That is to say, the sensation of wading through the leaves was still fresh on my hands. At that moment I stood rooted to the ground, finding it difficult even to budge. Suddenly something stirred close to my feet and, without determining its direction, I moved. I stepped on something that was alive and that became even more alive. I felt a sort of prick on my foot. There was a movement in the leaves and a hood rose from beneath them. For a brief second I saw tiny eyes staring at me and then I heard what sounded like someone sighing nearby. Meanwhile, the hood dived under the leaves. The leaves swayed and I saw a long, slithering body retreat. The leaves churned violently and continued being churned up for some ways into the distance.

I felt that something warm had filled my ears. I started to wonder what it might be. Finally I shook my head; I realized a snake had bitten me. For a long time this thought attempted to become fixed in my mind in some way or other. I was feeling somewhat irritated. I already thought that there were snakes in that area and that I was within their striking range. This, perhaps, also gave me the strange belief that I was safe from them. My irritation arose precisely because this belief proved to be wrong. How did it happen that there actually was a snake where I had only suspected there might be one? But by then that warm thing in my ears had increased and I was once again overwhelmed by the thought that a snake had bitten me. A strong desire to be at home took hold of me and I started to run.

I was running in the direction I had walked in earlier, quite oblivious to the fact that I was, in this way, heading farther away from my home. I had definitely concluded that the faster I ran the sooner I would reach home, and several times I in fact imagined that the twists and turns of the jungle were familiar pathways around my house. Soon enough I was exhausted. I felt that something was slowly tightening around my body. I stopped. I was feeling sleepy, but I didn't want to sleep. The absence of another human in this jungle began to weigh heavily on me. My body had begun to sway from drowsiness. At one point I saw something resembling a black wall rising up in front of me. When I tried to look at it closely, it disappeared. At the same time, I felt that black walls were rising up on either side of me. Within seconds the first wall in front also reappeared, and then all of them fused together. Black walls surrounded me on all sides. They were not only shrinking gradually, they were also becoming taller as a mysterious silence and darkness wafted out from them and spread everywhere.

In that spreading silence I heard a voice: "Where did it go?"

I don't know how but I understood that the question was about the snake and was directed at me.

Meanwhile, the voice asked again: "What kind was it?"

I had no desire to respond to the question. It didn't even seem odd to me that I was trapped, as I was, within those black walls. Now, someone was feeling all over on my body. I heard another question: "Where did it bite you?"

I lay motionless, aware of someone's presence near me. Someone slowly lifted my eyelids and then let go. Someone tried, unsuccessfully, to hoist me up and carry me somewhere. A final wave of drowsiness swept over me, but, before sinking into the darkness, I heard a piercing scream right next to my ear: "Maar-Geer! Maar-Geer!"

That was the first and also the last time that the residents of the hamlet heard the Snake Catcher call out his own name. What transpired next has been related to me so many times that I can describe it as an eyewitness. Why, there are times when I imagine that I did actually witness everything myself.

The Snake Catcher's scream shot out of the jungle and carried all the way to the hamlet where the residents immediately rushed out. Although none of them was sure who had raised the cry, they all at least knew that a snake had bitten someone and that they had to carry the victim to the Snake Catcher. When they entered the mouth of the jungle, they found the Snake Catcher, his body scraped in several places, struggling to carry me on his back. The people from the hamlet quickly picked me up and ran back, just as they had come. The Snake Catcher kept abreast of them about half the way and then collapsed, so the people had to lug him too. They were terrified. When this procession entered the hamlet, a commotion swept across its entire length and, without anyone breathing a word, the news spread that a snake had bitten the Snake Catcher and that he had probably also died. However, when he came near his home the Snake Catcher started to walk on his feet. He opened the door himself, and by the time the people had stretched me out on the ground, he had already returned from the inner part of the house with the bezoar and the milk pot and was standing near my head. He searched for the wound over my entire body and pinched the two tiny holes located just above my left heel. He then took out the bezoar, which looked like a piece of some dark-colored stone. He touched the wound with it lightly. The wound pulled the stone toward it like a magnet and stuck to it—a clear signal that the snake's victim could still be saved. He started to pour milk from a small vessel over the wound, a drop at a time. A whisper swept through the crowd that still stood there dazed: "The bezoar is sucking the poison!"

The bezoar remained fastened to the wound for a short time and then came unstuck and fell down. Somebody informed someone else: "The poison has permeated the bezoar; it's fallen unconscious."

The Snake Catcher tossed the bezoar into the large milk pot. Another whisper went around: "Now it'll release the poison in the milk and refresh itself."

The Snake Catcher removed the bezoar from the pot and touched it against the wound once more. Again it became stuck there. Shortly afterward it came loose and fell unconscious, was again placed in the pot of milk, again removed and applied to the wound, and again it stuck to it. This routine was repeated several times, and each time the whisper, "Until it has sucked the poison out of every vein, it will go on sticking to the wound," was passed around. Finally, one time when the bezoar was removed from the milk and brought in contact with the wound, it didn't stick to it and rolled off. At that moment my body moved.

Only then did the hamlet's residents turn their attention to me: Who was I? What should be done with me? Before they started discussing the matter, the Snake Catcher, without raising his head, said, "Leave him with me."

3

For several days I remained suspended in a state somewhere between sleep and wakefulness. The Snake Catcher visited me two or three times every day. He would stand beside my head looking at me intently. He also made me drink a certain extract several times. Finally one day he stood me on my feet and signaled me to follow him. I was thinking that I would have difficulty walking, but after taking a step I realized that I was my usual self. I didn't talk to the Snake Catcher, however.

He made me go once around the entire hamlet. It was a small settlement and it looked more or less deserted to me at the time. When we came to the pathway leading out of the hamlet, he seized hold of my hand and started taking such giant strides that I almost had to run to keep up with him. Before long I began to breathe unevenly and started to sweat all over. He stopped after a while and stared at my face for the longest time. We started moving again and soon found ourselves at the mouth of the jungle. Here the Snake Catcher again looked at me intently for a long time and then grabbed my hand and led me into the jungle.

The same sea of green vines was surging before me as I wondered how on earth I had managed to get right into the middle of it and, if I actually had, how had I then managed to get out of it at all. At the moment, plunging into the vines seemed an impossibility. Although it was a bit sparse right at that spot, the jungle became progressively denser in some of the patches up ahead. No matter which direction we turned in, I always saw someone or other there. It seemed that humans, rather than animals, inhabited this jungle.

All of these men were busy with some kind of work. I saw one old man digging whitish roots out of the crumbly soil. Two men stood under a very tall tree holding a sheet of cloth tautly between them and giving instructions to a third man at the top of the tree. Elsewhere, some men were gathering different kinds of leaves into big piles, and I saw still others collecting resins and saps from tree trunks. Now and then someone could be seen coming from the jungle's more distant areas holding cages with small wild animals and birds inside. With all these people fearlessly engrossed in their respective tasks, the jungle now appeared absolutely fascinating to me. Their concentration was also fascinating: it seemed as if outside of their work they were oblivious to the presence of anyone else around them. But whenever the Snake Catcher passed one of them, the man would interrupt his work and resume it only after the Snake Catcher had moved on. They didn't look toward him, but when I passed by they smiled and shook their heads as if inquiring after me. They made signs to inform one another that I was there, then they looked at me and smiled. Several times I thought that I should smile back at them, but I continued to pass among them with the face and eyes of a dead man. This seemed to be quite appropriate and I rationalized that it was a consequence of my accompanying the Snake Catcher. Before long we had moved past these people.

We were now in the semi-dark areas of the jungle. Here, the Snake Catcher sat down on a thick root that jutted out of the ground and he signaled to me to sit down too. I did. He asked me, "Where were you coming from?"

I told him. With his thumbnail he kept scratching the bark of the tree whose root he was sitting on. I noticed that both of his thumbnails were unusually long and bluish. He kept gazing at the dark-green streaks that had begun to appear on the bark. He gazed at them for a long time. Then he rubbed his nail on his clothes to clean it off and asked me in a very soft voice, "Where did you say you were coming from?"

I told him once more. The dust-colored scrapings from the bark had accumulated on the protruding root. He gathered them up and rolled them into a loose ball between his palms and then put the ball inside his clothing to save it. After that he asked the question I was now expecting: "Where were you headed?"

I remained silent. He said, "If you didn't set out with a specific destination in mind, then this hamlet is just as good as any, although snakes abound here."

"In the jungle?" I asked.

"In the hamlet too," he said. "Because the two are close together, or rather the people have made them one."

I tried to think. Meanwhile he said, "Nobody's trying to stop you. If you really want to move on ..."

"Let me think it over. I'll tell you later."

"No need to tell," he said very gently. Then his tone changed and a touch of melancholy appeared. "The scar from the wound on your foot is now completely gone. Soon you won't even remember ever having been bitten by a snake."

"I *will* remember," I said and repeated the sentence silently in my heart.

"Familiar words," he said in an unsteady voice, "I've heard them before."

After that he didn't say anything further for a long time. I thought perhaps he was waiting for me to say something, but I found myself at a loss to say anything at all. Then he himself spoke up, "At first I was having difficulty determining what kind of snake bit you. I was already very tired and, besides, there wasn't much time—this is the reason I resorted to the bezoar. Later I had to come out here in the jungle to look for it."

I sensed the presence of a familiar odor somewhere near. Sometime, long ago, I was definitely familiar with it. A kind of haze began to spread through my brain, but it was cleared up by the voice of the Snake Catcher. He was pulling out a bag from the folds of his clothing.

"This is the one that bit you," he said, as he plunged his hand inside the bag and took out a writhing snake.

The snake had just started to coil itself around his hand when a cry was heard from somewhere in the distance, "Maar-Geer! Maar-Geer!" And several voices in our vicinity repeated that cry like an echo, "Maar-Geer! Maar-Geer!"

He stood up.

"They're calling," he said, swinging his hand and throwing the snake into the distance. The snake twisted its body a few times in midair and then fell into a bush with a slight thump, causing a couple of birds to take wing.

I watched him going back taking brisk long strides, and he soon disappeared from my view.

The familiar scent wafted by again in a gentle wave and suddenly I realized that it was coming from the green scratch marks on the trunk. As I was being drawn toward those green streaks, I heard the sound of approaching feet. The Snake Catcher was standing near me. He bent forward a little and put his hand on my shoulder.

"As I mentioned, snakes abound here," he said. "But I'm here too," and then, walking even more quickly than before, he went back.

I was still feeling the pressure of his hand on my shoulder. It came to mind that the same familiar odor was also present on his palms, and this reminded me that the very same smell also emanated from the broken torso of the rider about whom it could not be decided whether he had held a scale or a sword in his hand.

I don't remember well now how I started to help the Snake Catcher in his work. When I occasionally took a stroll through the hamlet, the residents treated me graciously, but much of their conversation focused on the Snake Catcher. They had no idea what he did in his spare time; they also didn't know, but were quite eager to find out, what he talked about with me, because outside of inquiring about the condition of victims of snakebites—and even that in the briefest of words—he never talked about anything more with them. So it didn't surprise me at all that these people displayed their curiosity about him to me, although they asked me less about him than they told me. The topic of these conversations invariably centered on when and how and whom he had saved from a snake's venom. They particularly pointed out to me the people—myself included— whom he had revived. In short, they told me about myself but they asked very little about me, not even my name. Rather, they themselves gave me a name in their local language that meant "Helper." Hearing this word repeated on several occasions, it finally occurred to me that I did, in fact, help the Snake Catcher and perhaps I had been living in this hamlet longer than I realized.

I would go to the jungle with him and gather the materials for his medicinal concoctions. These included minerals, vegetation, animals—in fact, everything. Sometimes we collected different types of clays and stones, sometimes different varieties of fruits and flowers, and sometimes the barks, roots, fibers, and resins of trees. Sometimes we went out for animals and birds, which he would round up easily, though I found it impossible myself, and I would then catch. On all these occasions he described to me the effects of each item in great detail. The effect always dealt exclusively with healing wounds, never with the treatment of snakebites. I was sure that he only used a few of these materials on the victims of snakebite, but which ones—that I could never figure out. He never revealed that to me either. The fact is, he never discussed the subject of snakes. But one day he suddenly started to talk about it.

That was on the hamlet's market day. Buyers from outlying areas had come. The merchandise consisted of whatever the people from the hamlet had been able to gather from the jungle. I had just returned after browsing through the market quickly. No matter where I went, I heard the Snake Catcher being talked about. These out-of-town buyers were especially interested in hearing about him, though he always stayed away from the market, and their desire to see the famous Snake Catcher of the hamlet, even if only for a fleeting moment, had remained unfulfilled until that market day. I had barely stepped inside when the cry rose from the direction of the market, "Maar-Geer! Maar-Geer!"

Before I knew it, the Snake Catcher was standing in front of me. He was agitated, and an excitement, a curiosity such as I'd never seen before was apparent on his face. His quick appearance following the cry was also something quite new to me. I started to clear a spot on the floor, but he stopped me. "No."

I looked at him. He said, "I have to go. A snake's been spotted somewhere."

I too then realized that this time the cry didn't have the quivering fear of death that always sent a shudder through my body. This situation was new to me and I was wondering whether he would ask me to accompany him. Just then the cry went up again, still about the same distance away as before, but more like a loud, collective cry, "Maar-Geer! Maar-Geer! Snake Catcher!"

I saw him dart off in the direction of the cry. I started out after him but he had soon outdistanced me and disappeared. The tumult was still increasing, but before I could reach the market it had subsided and eventually it faded away completely. As I walked further ahead I saw the dust in the market rising up so profusely that hardly anything could be seen there at all. I strained to hear the sounds, but silence, such as cannot be imagined on a market day, had spread everywhere. I stopped short. I kept staring at the swirls of dust twisting and turning in the air. I was thinking of going back when I heard a very loud, solitary voice rise from the market, "Who didn't know that I only catch snakes?"

It was the same voice that I had heard rising near my head the day I was bitten by the snake, but that day it didn't have this quality of molten stones. And now it rang out even louder than before, "Who didn't know?"

Perhaps something was said in response. The Snake Catcher's solitary voice was heard again, "If it's a python, it's a python; if it's a snake, it's a snake."

Beyond the clouds of dust I saw his trembling image. His hands were spread wide and he said in a voice that betrayed no emotion, "This is not the land of pythons. I've left that far behind."

His image froze for a second and then trembled again. Suddenly he came very close to me. The skin of his face was taut and his eyes had become very large. But he didn't see me. Perhaps I wasn't even visible to him. He was walking very fast. I moved out of his way and when he passed by me, I felt a chill flowing from his body. Even after thinking a long time, I wasn't any wiser, so I just stepped into the dust-enveloped market.

The market was in a state of turmoil. No customers could be seen. When I scanned the area I spotted them quite some distance

away, standing quietly in a group near their carts. The local people
had gathered into small groups of their own and they were talking
in whispers. The minute they saw me they darted toward me and
started talking all at the same time. For me, everything they said
at first added up to just this: the Snake Catcher was angry and
could I think of a way to appease him. "Python" or "snake" didn't
even once figure in what was said, although the foolishness of
someone was mentioned over and over. After a while they became
quiet waiting for a response from me. Perhaps my silence spoke
for itself and I was invited to listen to the whole story. A man,
famous throughout the hamlet for his cheerful disposition, was
chosen for the job. Drawing on totally unnecessary details, he
began telling, in a perfectly serious tone, how the market had
been set up and the order in which the customers had made their
appearance. In the middle of his narration someone suggested that
the incident should be recounted in the presence of the
customers. A couple of people rushed over to them and, after
talking with them, came back with the suggestion that everyone
should move to where they and their carts were stationed. And so,
avoiding the piles of merchandise, we went over to them. Now I
looked at the customers from up close.

Their faces reflected the usual weariness that comes from
an idle and uninteresting period waiting for something. These out-
of-towners—dissimilar in their clothing and temperaments, but
nonetheless similar in their circumstances—had perhaps adopted
this air of disinterest by mutual agreement. They looked at me
indifferently and paid absolutely no attention to the narrator,
which, however, didn't affect his engrossment in the least. Almost
as soon as he got there, he resumed: how a customer coming from
some distant place had encountered a python along the way that
had not quite swallowed its victim yet and was beginning to slow
down in its effort to do so while people stood all around it. The
customer somehow prevailed upon these people to load the reptile
onto his cart, taking every precaution so that it wouldn't escape.

When he arrived at the market and the subject of the Snake Catcher came up, he or one of his companions told the people there about the python. As a result, a veritable crowd immediately formed around his cart. Everyone was eager to see the python. The customer who had suddenly become the focus of everyone's attention opened, just slightly, the part of the cart that held the python. Everyone now saw the python slide out in one swift motion, fully alert and active. Soon it was slithering about in the market. Some people thought it even attacked them. Chaos erupted everywhere. The residents of the hamlet were hell-bent on destroying the python, while the customers who had come to shop at the market wanted to recapture it alive. This led to some unpleasantness, in the middle of which somebody mentioned the Snake Catcher and the cry went up. Meanwhile, the escaped python had wandered into that section of the market where small animals and birds were sold. By the time the Snake Catcher arrived it had already grabbed one of the animals in its mouth and people were surrounding it. For a while nobody even noticed that the Snake Catcher had arrived. Finally they looked at him, only to find him a different man, a completely different man. Never before had anyone seen him in such an angry state. He paid absolutely no attention to the python and went away still quite angry.

This account was rather long-winded, abounding in the names of commodities and individuals. Whenever the narrator mentioned a certain product, he found it necessary to also point to its mound in the market, indicating who it belonged to as well as who wanted to buy it. And whenever he mentioned the name of one of the hamlet's residents, he not only asked that individual to show himself to me, he also gave me a brief introduction to him. I recognized some of these individuals as snakebite victims. In any case, the narrative ended. Now several people started to talk at once again. All of them were afraid that the Snake Catcher would abandon the hamlet and they hoped I would talk him out of it. Each one feared that the Snake Catcher was particularly angry with him individually and took pains to point out that the suggestion to summon the Snake Catcher hadn't originated with him; some even claimed they had opposed the idea. The customers, however, were silent. But when I started to leave, a heavy hand grabbed on to my shoulder. I turned around to look. He was perhaps the oldest among the customers and he didn't see well. He drew me close to himself and said, "We've been duly informed that a python is a python. But do ask him this: those whom a snake has devoured alive, doesn't that snake count as a python for them?"

And then, straining his eyes, he stared at me for the longest time as though he expected me to answer.

"And don't forget to tell him that if he is indispensable for the hamlet, so are we," he was saying. "If it was ever necessary to decide which of us is more indispensable..." he hesitated, and it struck me that his voice wasn't consistent with his appearance at all.

"Should he so desire, you may also tell him my name," he said, letting go of my shoulder, but he didn't reveal his name to me.

As I trekked back, the residents of the hamlet accompanied me for some distance, but now they were talking among themselves, caught up in misgivings that eluded me. However, their conversation did reveal, but only vaguely, that the Snake Catcher didn't like the presence of the customers in the hamlet, nor they his. And yet they also definitely affirmed that neither the customers nor the Snake Catcher had actually expressed this displeasure openly.

I found the Snake Catcher sitting on the same mat that was used to cover the dead bodies of snake victims. When he saw me he moved over a bit to clear a place, and, after a slight hesitation, I also sat down on the same mat. He was rubbing his long, bluish thumbnails on his clothes, and he was silent. There was a faint rustling sound coming from the rubbing. After a while it seemed to me that the sound was coming from somewhere far away. Then it started to draw nearer, quickly gaining in intensity. Then it appeared to be coming from outside. It turned dark for a minute and I promptly got up. The sound grew progressively fainter and receded into the distance. I looked outside. The ground was wet and drops of water were falling from the leaves, but the sky was absolutely clear.

"Sit," he was saying. "This sort of rain does fall here occasionally."

I sat down.

"Where were you?"

I gave him a brief account of what had transpired at the market, but I skipped the conversation with the old customer and the thoughts expressed by the local residents afterward.

"They consider a python and a snake the same thing," he mumbled, as if complaining, "although they haven't seen either one. To them both are slithering creatures, one larger than the other. They know next to nothing about the difference in poisons." He looked at me and fell silent. My own silence didn't seem to be a proper response to his tone and I asked, "Doesn't the difference in poisons result from the difference in snakes?"

"A snake is one that has poison. The rest are merely colorful insects. Then again, a snake is a snake only as long as it can make use of its poison. That's why a dead snake is no longer a snake."

"But poisonous snakes come in different varieties ...?"

"It's poison that has varieties, not snakes."

"How about the snake ... the merely colorful insect, whose victim dies from fright ...?"

"For such a person it is a snake, though in reality ..." he stopped, resuming after a pause, "Why, you do have a way with words. I don't know why ... but this word 'variety' ... it applies to those who die from fright, not to those slithering creatures; and to those that slither this is the most poisonous variety of human. That's why you see me treat people of this variety the way I do."

I recalled the cries and the desperate ranting and raving of some victims brought to the Snake Catcher and I asked, "For the sake of those colorful insects?"

"For the sake of both ... but ..." he said quite amiably, "didn't you like what I said about the colorful insects? All right, just for your sake, I'll grant that there are two types of snakes: one from whose bite a man dies legitimately, and a second from whose bite a man dies illegitimately."

But this, in effect, amounted to two kinds of men, didn't it?—I thought, and perhaps he was also thinking the same thing, though neither of us said a word.

He remained silent for a long time. During this interval, he looked at his nails closely once, he ran his hand back and forth over the mat for a while, and then he said, "The place where I lived before I came here really had an overabundance of pythons. Because of my fascination with all things that kill, I would wander around observing pythons, always anxious to see one catch its prey. And I did see that sight many times, indeed, so many times that I began to understand the nature of the relationship a python has with its victim. I assume you know that every creature that hunts has a relationship with its prey."

I didn't know; all the same I nodded my head yes.

"Like any hunter ... like any hunting animal, a python seeks out prey only when it's hungry. It lies in wait, coiled around a tree. Sometimes it waits in a high place, sometimes very close to the ground, and sometimes, disappointed in one place, it moves on to another, waiting, waiting. Finally, a victim chances by and the python appears as though it isn't aware of the approaching prey.

"Suddenly, however, it springs, and it can be seen coiling around the victim. The victim writhes too, aware, almost immediately, that he's facing death, and he struggles harder to break free of the coils. But they increase and tighten around him. It's a fierce but quiet battle that sometimes goes on for a very long time. Eventually the intensity subsides. The thought of facing death, which before augmented the victim's will to survive, now weakens it. When this point is reached the python begins to devour its prey. But its eyes don't shine with victory."

He slowly closed his palms. "I've always looked closely into the eyes of both and have always found only a desolate stillness there, as if they're consciously avoiding each other. Behind that stillness their half-closed eyes sometimes show resignation, sometimes a peculiar embarrassment, and sometimes just weariness, as if they're merely fulfilling a responsibility, their hearts aren't in it. That's why sometimes—perhaps this is just a fancy on my part—I feel ..." He stopped. He reflected for a very long time, but he didn't finish.

"Why did you abandon the land of pythons?" I finally asked, but perhaps he didn't hear.

"Until his very last breath the victim struggles to break free from the python's coils, even though in the end the struggle is nothing more than merely carrying out the formality of living. It's a terribly revolting sight. But once caught by a python, the victim knows, from start to finish, that he's facing death, and why. He can feel the physical presence of the python until his last gasp, and the python can feel its victim's presence even long after that. For both of them it's a game played out in the open. And a game that's played out in the open ..." He stopped again and didn't finish. It seemed as if he had suddenly become aware of my presence, and he asked, "When the snake's poison was spreading through your body and you were nearing death, where was the snake itself at that time?"

"I don't know."

"It must have been somewhere quite far from you, and it's possible that it had meanwhile encountered something that took its mind off of you completely. You had perhaps seen it, so you were fleeing; but it's also possible that you hadn't seen it at all, and only thought that a small thorn had pricked your foot. At most you would have bent down and rubbed on the spot gently. Before long you would have forgotten that a thorn had ever pricked your foot. God knows how far you might have walked before the poison started spreading through your body, and you would have been at a loss to understand what was happening to you. It wouldn't even have occurred to you that the prick you had felt on your foot sometime somewhere was actually the thing that was killing you. You wouldn't have known whose prey you had become, and your hunter would have been no wiser than you. Why, for that matter, it's not even necessary that there should be a hunter. It's entirely possible that your hunter had already perished before you. But for you what difference would it have made whether it was alive or dead, near or far, because a snake doesn't play its game out in the open. Only a python does."

I mentioned the remark made by the old customer that, for a small animal, weren't a snake and a python alike.

"Yes," he said, "market customers think up such questions all too frequently, although they know that a snake is not like a python where humans are concerned, and a python is not a snake for anyone. They can't even begin to understand what a tremendous difference there is between the two."

I was reflecting on the difference when he asked, "Have you seen a python before today?"

When he found out that I hadn't before, or even today, he shifted a bit and I felt somewhat uneasy. Once again our conversation was heading toward a question. I was hoping the subject of our conversation would change somehow. For a moment I considered asking him about the cloud that had rained suddenly and then drifted away, but he himself threw a question at me, "What did they tell you about the python?"

I had to tell him that I hadn't asked them about it at all. I sensed that his gaze was fixed on me. There was silence for quite a while. Finally he said, "Well all right, if you don't want me to, I won't ask you anything about yourself."

Afterwards he talked for a long time about different snake poisons and their effects, but it seemed as if he was trying to refresh his own memory. Suddenly there was the sound of approaching feet and he gave a start.

Three strangers appeared.

One of them said, "We came here since you couldn't be found there."

The Snake Catcher stood up. "Oh, it's already so late in the evening!" he said with amazement.

The men kept looking over at me. Finally, one of them pointed at me and said, "In front of him?"

"No," he said. "Come." And making them go ahead of himself he ushered them into the inner area of the house.

They weren't residents of the hamlet, and they also definitely looked quite different from the customers I'd seen in the market. Still there was something about them, and it didn't take me long to conclude that they too were customers.

4

That very night, just before the crack of dawn, the cry went up and an unconscious man was brought in along with a dead snake. The people who accompanied him said that they had heard him scream but by the time they reached him he was already unconscious. They found the snake not far from him. They also said that the man had been bitten by a snake once before. They were discussing the details of the first episode when the Snake Catcher appeared in front of them.

"What happened?" he asked, bending over the unconscious man. He then examined the snake closely before leaning over the man one more time. He kept looking at the two by turns for quite some time. Finally, he withdrew to one side and said in a voice without any expression, "Take him away."

Perhaps this was an entirely unexpected situation for them. As they were consulting among themselves with their eyes, the Snake Catcher's somewhat loud voice was heard saying, "What did he tell you?"

I told him that the men had found him unconscious and that they had only heard him scream.

"He hasn't been bitten by a snake," he said, and left. The people who had brought the unconscious man had just started to say something when the man's condition took a turn for the worse and they rushed toward him.

Just then, off in the distance, the cry rose again: "Maar-Geer! Maar-Geer!"

The companions of the unconscious man picked him up and went out of the house. Shortly thereafter another group came in. It included a few people from the earlier group and it also brought an unconscious man, whose condition apparently didn't look good. I was given no details this time around. Instead, everyone remained silent, even when the Snake Catcher came and questioned them. Perhaps they were having difficulty deciding who should speak. But by now the Snake Catcher had already bent over the unconscious man. One of the group, who seemed very restless, came forward and stood close to the Snake Catcher. "Snakebite—wouldn't you say?" he asked, practically begging.

Looking at the dead snake stretched out on the mat the Snake Catcher shook his head affirmatively.

I noticed, for the first time, how a current of relief and joy washed over the entire group accompanying the snake's victim, even before the treatment had begun.

"Milk!" the Snake Catcher said, and some people dashed out. They had all guessed that the treatment would be done with the bezoar but their hope of watching the treatment was not satisfied because, after the milk had been brought in, the Snake Catcher had all of them step out.

The wound couldn't be found. The Snake Catcher himself made a wound on the victim's body. The bezoar even stuck to that. While I was dribbling milk over it, I heard him say, "I don't know what it is, perhaps no one does: is it something created by the ancients or by nature, like a stone or vegetation, or is it some kind of living thing?"

"Living thing?" I asked. At the same moment the bezoar tumbled down, unconscious.

"This unconsciousness," he said, "or perhaps temporary death—isn't it proof enough of its being a living thing? And then again, what proof is there that it isn't?"

He retrieved the bezoar from the milk pot and placed it on the wound.

"You'll be amazed to know," he said, "that I fear the snake more than anything."

I was amazed indeed. And I made it known that I was.

"But there are times when I fear the bezoar even more."

Just then the victim's body stirred and the Snake Catcher fixed his attention on him.

By the time the victim left, walking on his own feet, it had become sunny. Placing the bezoar between his palms and rubbing it slowly the Snake Catcher said, "It plays its game out in the open, but no one is able to understand it. Isn't that something to fear?"

"Perhaps," I said, "but if ..."

"And it's the killer of poison, which makes me absolutely sure that in some way or other it is itself lethal. But how? I have in my possession a thing that kills, but I don't know how it kills. That's why I fear it, and when fear is mixed with the thought that maybe this thing is alive ..."

I was feeling drowsy, but it was a strange kind of drowsiness. I had the feeling that I was becoming hollow and that if I fell asleep my body would simply disappear. I wanted him to go on talking so that I wouldn't fall asleep, but I was only able to hear one more sentence. "In exactly this same way, I also begin to fear myself sometimes."

Then I saw him dash toward me.

5

Up to now I haven't been able to figure out how much time I spent among those dim shadows. In the beginning I sensed nothing except the sounds of softly approaching feet. Later, along with those sounds, I could feel the sensation of hands touching me. Sometimes those hands fed me some liquid that immediately filled my nostrils with an odor resembling acrid smoke. I felt that there was a black curtain drawn in front of me all the time. Finally one day faint ripples began to appear on the curtain, gradually changing into murky shadows. At first these shadows were incomprehensible to me, but then they began to assume whatever form I wished, and it became something of a sport for me. Outside of these changing forms, which were entirely dependent on me for their existence, I nurtured absolutely no curiosity about anything else, and whatever came in contact with my senses seemed entirely natural to me, something that had been happening forever. Voices asked me questions, which didn't need to be understood to be answered. At times I even started answering when no question was asked and I supposed that I was, in this way, discharging myself of some major obligation. I was contented with my life in every way.

Once, though, I suddenly began feeling an aversion for my speech, and I fell silent in mid-sentence. Somebody asked me a question which I didn't understand. After that I mostly slept or dreamed. One of my dreams was that a snake had bitten me in a jungle in the midst of green vines. I was carried over to the Snake Catcher's and he was saying that I had not been bitten by a snake, but the people were imploring him, trying somehow to make him say that I had indeed been bitten by one. They moved forward toward him and drew back repeatedly, and their back and forth movements shook my body and interrupted my sleep.

The Snake Catcher was looking at me bent over. Finding me watching him, he retreated several steps, went to one side and stood there. I looked at him again and he came back over to me.

"It doesn't displease you to look at me—does it?" he asked.

I was lying on a pile of cushions. Some vessels, whose purpose I didn't understand, lay near me. There were large doors all around and each had several curtains of some exceedingly fine fabric hanging over it. The Snake Catcher pulled back the curtains of a door. The strong light that poured through the open door appeared very strange and unpleasant to me. But I didn't close my eyes. I was expecting to see something but didn't have a clue what it might be. Whatever was on the outside wasn't visible to me. The Snake Catcher drew the curtains together and I shut my eyes. I heard his voice. He was telling somebody, "Today I'll take him with me."

When my eyes opened next, the Snake Catcher was standing in front of me holding a light.

"Let's go," he said.

Several hands stood me up and I went out supported by those hands. Since the light was falling directly on my eyes, I was unable to see anyone. I was put on a seat in a carriage. When it moved, there was no one with me. Not even the light was with me. I drifted in and out of sleep the whole way. Finally the carriage stopped and I saw the Snake Catcher holding the light. He helped me get down. I could see his house up ahead.

"Try to walk on your own," he said. Taking slow steps I went through the door. Just then he said something and I turned around to look. The lights in the houses of the hamlet could be seen. The Snake Catcher had drawn near me. He no longer held the light in his hand and three murky shadows were getting on the carriage.

"Come in," I heard him say.

For several days I didn't step outside. Perhaps I didn't feel like it, or perhaps I imagined that the Snake Catcher didn't want me to. I had also dreamed up several vague explanations why he wanted it that way, but I don't remember what they were now. The fact is that, in the first place, during this time I saw very little of him. My memory was becoming keener now and I could recall everything in detail, though I had little success remembering things in the order they occurred. For instance, the incident of my being bitten by the snake seemed to me to have occurred after the Snake Catcher had grabbed the snake and tossed it away in the jungle. Inevitably I turned my attention to the medicinal ingredients the Snake Catcher collected from the jungle. I noticed there hadn't been any increase in their volume since his last trip when I accompanied him. I picked up each and every substance, and everything he had told me about it started to surface in my memory. I also found the substance he had scraped from the bark of the tree which emitted its familiar odor. The Snake Catcher had mentioned several of its effects, but here my memory faltered. Try as hard as I might, I couldn't remember a single one of those effects; why, when I strained my memory harder, I even forgot that it was a scraping of tree bark. This recurred several times. Then it began to happen that the minute I saw the scraping, or even so much as thought of it, its odor wafted into my nose, making it well-nigh impossible for me to stay inside the house.

On one such occasion I heard the noise of children, or a sound somewhat like rain coming down somewhere far off. I went out and started to walk in the direction of the sound. Noticing greenish clumps shifting this way and that up ahead in the distance, I went near them and saw that they were large-leafed vines being dragged around by small children who looked very excited by this game. Some children would jump into the vines and get dragged along with them for some distance, thrashing their arms and legs about as though they were playing in water and leaving behind them trails of broken bits of leaves. When they saw me their excitement increased and they started to shout, "Maar-Geer! Maar-Geer!"

For a while I didn't hear their voices. I saw people rushing down the roads on their way from the jungle. Within minutes a crowd formed around the children. Then suddenly everything became very quiet and I heard the Snake Catcher's voice behind me, "You shouldn't remain out-of-doors too long."

After he was gone, the children tried to resume playing with the vines but their elders stopped them and started to drag them away.

Then I noticed that, for the first time ever, they had returned from the jungle empty-handed.

6

I continued sleeping well into the next day. I was awakened by the sound of soft footsteps. Two men from the hamlet were standing beside my bed near my head. One of them who was well known for his cheerful disposition asked me, in a serious tone of voice how I was doing, and then he said, "You've changed a lot during this time, Helper. We all wanted to see you. We had the chance yesterday, but the cry ..." he suddenly became despondent. "But perhaps you had come out on account of the cry."

I told them that I had come out because of the noise of the children and it was they who had raised the cry when they saw me.

"If only you could tell him that ..." he became despondent once again. "How can it be, Helper, that children would not do what their elders do?"

His companion reminded him of something; hesitation began to show on his face. I said, "Yesterday when I saw you all returning empty-handed from the jungle ..."

"We knew it would sadden you," he said, his natural cheerfulness slowly returning. "Helper, we only want to see you."

He pointed outside. "They've all gathered out there. We know you shouldn't stay out-of-doors for long."

"And besides, you've just woken up," his companion added.

I got out of bed. It was the time when the local residents went out to the jungle. I found them assembled on the road. They gazed at me in wistful silence for the longest time, until I couldn't hold back any longer.

"It's all very hazy in my mind," I said. "All the same, ask what you have to …"

They drew close to me. Now they all started asking me questions. None of these questions indicated that they wanted me to answer it; the balance of their questions seemed not to even be directed toward me. Someone would ask a question, several others would reject it and ask questions of their own which were rejected in turn by still others. Pretty soon I guessed that their questions were actually directed toward one another and that they were having difficulty deciding what questions I could conceivably answer. Such weariness was etched on their faces and such despair oozed from their words that the thought that I was not one of them began to weigh heavily on me. Soon, though, I found myself inundated by questions that had somehow penetrated my hearing clearly. Was this the first time I was bitten by a snake? Had I been bitten two times or only the second time? Why did I choose to come to the hamlet via the jungle? Was I really sorry to see them return from the jungle empty-handed? Why then is the jungle being chopped down?

"Why then is the jungle being chopped down?" I repeated this last question.

"We had never thought about it," an old man said. "It has always provided sustenance for us, but now it is *we* who are chopping it down." He looked at his hands in despair.

"Are you chopping down the jungle?" I said.

"We have to do something, Helper. It may not be what we want, but others commission us to do it. And to tell you the truth, even now the jungle is sustaining our lives. But for how long?"

"This is a good hamlet, Helper," said another, even older, man. "Of course it has too many snakes. But then, it also has the Snake Catcher."

After that they turned toward the jungle. Only the old man remained, standing with his head bent low. I drew near him and put my hand on his shoulder. He lifted his head and looked at me with his gloomy eyes saying, "This hamlet used to be a good one, Helper."

Then he went to catch up with the rest of his companions.

"I would like to know," I said.

"I know you've been asked many questions," the Snake Catcher said. "But they themselves don't know whether or not you can answer those questions. Since you're a stranger they think you might know what they don't. It isn't a good thing to be a stranger, Helper." He used my name for the first time. "Or perhaps it is. And then again maybe not."

"I'd like to know," I repeated.

"You couldn't figure anything out from their questions?"

I only repeated to him the questions that I had heard clearly. He listened with his head bowed. After a while he lifted it. "Are you sure these questions were asked in that order?"

I was speechless. Actually, except for the last question about why the jungle was being chopped down, I didn't remember the order of the questions.

He looked at me intently. Several times his eyes were focused down on me and then raised up. Then he put his hand on mine and said in a very soft, low voice, "No? Don't try to remember; otherwise you'll be overwhelmed. What is first and what is last, forgetting that makes a huge difference, Helper. And this difference will correspond to the differences in the manner of forgetting."

"I'm having difficulty remembering the order of the questions."

"Try to forget it now. Be glad that you only encountered questions." He got up and began to pace. "Suppose the questions had also accompanied answers, some of which might have themselves been in the form of questions, and you had been unable to determine which answer went with which question, and which question came after which answer or question, and which question followed it, and every time ..." he choked on his words.

Is he crying? I wondered and looked at him, but his eyes were dry and his voice had cleared.

"...and every time, when you tried to remember but weren't sure, you would have regretted remembering even as much as you did," he said, and it was quite apparent that he was trying to remember something but was unsure about it.

"When I said that I'd like to know," I explained, "I meant ..."

"And what surprised me the most was that you wanted to know. You've changed quite a bit during this time, Helper."

"I was thinking of the people of the hamlet."

"They are a fine people," he said, and then his eyes also became gloomy and he said the same thing, "This used to be a good hamlet, Helper."

He got up to go. I came and stood in front of him.

"Why is the jungle being chopped down?" I asked.

"Really, you've changed a lot," he said with a tinge of regret. "Even so, you're a stranger, and here, in this matter, it isn't a bad thing to be a stranger. Anyway, Helper, I myself wanted to tell you something. It's not that I want to inform you about things; that's not my job." He made a low, grunting sound, and seeing him in this condition, at the time, I was reminded of trapped animals.

"When I said that I'd like to know ..."

"Look, Helper," he signaled me to sit down as he did so himself and said, "you know, everyone has to do something or other, and whoever does something must unavoidably deal with buyers. Even if he has nothing to sell, he still has to. A buyer looks for profit and only watches out for his own gain. Right? But what's even worse, if he sees only his gain but doesn't see the other's loss, he begins to have doubts about his own gain. And there are many buyers like this who only measure their gain by the loss of the other. No …" He stopped me even before I could open my mouth. "Don't say that it's not like that. It *is*. You perhaps doubt it. Sometimes I think about you. You don't have to deal with buyers nor are you a buyer yourself … Have you ever thought why you are like this?"

"I will now."

"Because you're a stranger. You were offended when I called you 'stranger'—but the fact is: you are a stranger, pure and simple. And as I said, this is not a bad thing, Helper. This is not something to take offense at."

"I wasn't offended," I said with perfect equanimity.

"Stranger," he mumbled. "This is why you felt the need to understand, even though you had been told that we have come into the midst of buyers."

"Didn't you have dealings with them before?"

"We did. But at that time the buyers used to come to us. Now that we've gone to them …" His words were drowned in a grunt, and once again I thought of trapped animals.

Suddenly it seemed as if he'd heard something. He got up, grabbed my hand and led me out of the house. He scanned the area, as if he was trying to determine the direction. I strained my ears. Just then a quivering animal sound was heard some distance away. Still holding on to my hand he walked in that direction but stopped after just a few steps. His eyes were riveted in the direction of the sound. It seemed as if he had become oblivious of my presence, but he said, "Actually, what I wanted to tell you, Helper, was that every buyer goes to great lengths to prevent people from understanding his operations. And he considers this necessary for his own gain as well as for the other's loss. So now don't ever say that you want to understand, because I myself don't understand." After that he started to move briskly in the direction of the sound.

We didn't have to go far. Coming to a mound of earth he halted. He let go of my hand and went halfway around it. He was now facing me from the other side. He gestured for me to back away and I had just barely done so when a snake quickly slithered out from behind. I hadn't yet noticed it when the Snake Catcher thrust himself between me and the snake. I had the feeling that he had gotten there by going right through the heap. The snake reared up but the Snake Catcher again stood in his way. The snake twisted to one side, the Snake Catcher again placed himself in its way. The snake's slithering track and the Catcher's footprints were both being formed on the soft, dry earth without a sound. Once again the snake turned around. But the Snake Catcher was again in front of him. There was a brief pause and then the snake lifted its head and spread out its hood. Turning to one side the Snake Catcher moved forward. The snake gyrated, pointing its hood toward him. The Snake Catcher spun lightly and advanced toward it. The snake's hood was again facing him. But now the Snake Catcher continued to move straight toward him. The snake's hood was swinging right and left and its tail was slowly flapping on the ground. The Snake Catcher had reached the snake. Suddenly one of his knees touched the ground, his hand moved forward, a bit of dust flew up, and the snake could be seen wrapped around his arm all the way up to his shoulder. Its deflated hood was held tightly in the Snake Catcher's fist.

Holding the snake this way he came over to me.

"How does it look?" he asked.

I discerned an awesome beauty in both of them; although, compared to the Snake Catcher, the snake looked like something brought into existence just recently.

"It hasn't bitten you—has it?" I asked, realizing myself how absurd my question was.

The Snake Catcher pressed against the snake's hood with his thumb and its mouth popped open. He lifted it up a bit higher to look. He was saying something to it under his breath that I couldn't hear clearly, but I did guess from it that the snake was a female.

"All the poison ever seen," he said, staring into the snake's eyes. Then he turned toward me. "Everyone has to do some work or other, Helper, and my work is with poisons."

Lately more snakes had started to appear in the hamlet. At least once a day a call went up. By now, I too had begun to understand the differences in this call so I didn't have to make any preparations when I heard it. The Snake Catcher would emerge from the inner part of the house and go out. He would return shortly and I would try not to look at him. He himself paid no attention to me. Sometimes he wasn't at home when the cry was raised and he could be seen rushing from the direction of the jungle or from some other direction. But after he had caught the snake he made straight for home. He usually stayed inside the house, or perhaps his house had another door that led to the outside. At any rate, other than catching an occasional glimpse of him, I hadn't had a conversation with him since the day he had caught the snake in my presence.

One day, though, I noticed that he came near me again and again. He would stare at me for some time and then go back in. Once, while this was going on, a cry was even raised, and when he returned from outside he lingered near me for a long time. Without looking at him, I just waited for him to speak, but he didn't say a word. A sound, like someone repeatedly opening and closing his palm, came from his hand periodically. One time I even thought that he was saying something, but it was barely audible. Finally, I looked toward him. As I had suspected, he was looking at me, but his face betrayed nothing. The snake wrapped around his arm was alternately tightening and loosening its coils. I started to say something, but checked myself. With his hand bent over, the Snake Catcher was now gazing at the snake. He turned around and came back, tripping slightly along the way.

By evening another cry went up. I had fallen asleep and was awakened by the cry. There was a silence everywhere. I stayed awake for some time and then, thinking that the cry had occurred in my dream, I was about to go back to sleep when I heard footsteps outside the house. Shortly afterward a small crowd of people came inside. I sat up startled. A dead snake was dangling from a stick that the man at the front of the crowd was holding in his hand. I tried hard but couldn't remember whether this time the cry had contained the quivering fear of death or not. I cleared a space on the ground and spread the thin mat over it. The crowd looked at me in silence. Then the man at the front moved forward. He tossed the snake, along with the stick, onto the mat and turned toward me saying, "We had to kill it."

After that they all went away in complete silence. The snake lay on the mat haphazardly.

I noticed a slight movement in it, despite the fact that its hood was badly crushed. The snake was exactly the same kind I had seen the Snake Catcher capture in my presence.

After lying awake for quite a while I went back to sleep.

Halfway through the night I woke up. I felt the sensation of two cold fingers on my neck. I sat up in bed. The Snake Catcher was standing in front of me. Then he sat down nearby. As before he remained silent.

"I didn't hear the cry," I said.

"There wasn't a cry," he said.

I looked around. The dead snake lay on the mat as haphazardly as before, though the direction of its hood had changed slightly. I looked toward the Snake Catcher.

"This time I am informing you, Helper," his cold hand clutched mine. "The bezoar has disappeared."

7

After a brief silence I asked, "When?"

"God knows," he said.

He remained absolutely speechless for quite a while. I got out of bed and stood up. "I'll look for it."

He motioned for me to sit down, and placing his hand on my shoulder he said to me very gently, "Such things don't disappear in order to be found again."

"Even so, perhaps …"

"It won't help to worry," he said. "It's a loss, surely; but worrying won't help."

He said it as though it was I, not he, who had sustained the loss and he was trying to console me. His manner was so genuine that for a while I really began to think of myself as deserving his sympathy. Soon, however, I regained my ability to consider the reality of it.

"The bezoar was only needed occasionally," I said.

"Yes, occasionally," he said. "It was the last resort, and it never failed."

"But you have many other remedies; you rarely made use of the bezoar."

"I understand, Helper," he said, "but you don't. It was the last remedy, and it never failed because it could take care of every poison. Of course there's no shortage of remedies, but it, and it alone, could neutralize certain poisons. I will have to fear those poisons from now on, in fact, I'll have to fear all poisons because it was the last alternative as an antidote for every poison."

But he didn't look frightened, rather, at the time, I thought his peaceful face appeared to be something one ought to fear.

"I'm not afraid, Helper," he said in a low voice. "But since its disappearance I'm seeing all this."

Afterwards a slight stupor came over him. Certainly he was seeing something at that moment. I extended my hand toward him. His half-opened eyes were riveted on me. My hand stopped midway and I began to see in his eyes everything that he, perhaps, was himself seeing: I see the Snake Catcher arrive at a place where a snake has been spotted. Many people are gathered together there. They make way for him the moment they see him, but the snake, instead of fleeing at his sight, coils up and spreads out its hood. The Snake Catcher moves toward it, slowly, cautiously. Suddenly the snake snaps, bites him, and flees. The people kill it and a crowd forms around the Snake Catcher. Next I see a crowd entering the house clamoring loudly. The condition of the unconscious man with them appears critical. Everyone looks terribly worried. The Snake Catcher comes forward. He looks at the victim and then stands there silently. The victim's condition grows progressively worse. The people continue looking at the Snake Catcher and then they start beseeching him; they only want him to say that it was, indeed, a snake that bit the man. But the Snake Catcher continues standing silently until the victim dies. The people pick the man up and go out, and the sound of weeping can be heard from outside. Just then another crowd files in. But as soon as they see the Snake Catcher they retreat quickly, move forward again, and then draw back again. Everyone's gaze is fixed on the Snake Catcher. There is only a raging silence in his half-open eyes and he is looking straight ahead. Then he began to slump over.

I tried to raise him up, but he did it himself and then he sat with his eyes opened fully.

"As it is, the hamlet was dying out on its own anyway, Helper," he said. "This is yet another factor in its demise. I came here from the land of pythons and started to work with poisons." He remained silent for quite a while with his eyes fixed on the dead snake.

Shortly before daybreak he stood up. I tried to give him some support but he shrank back a little. Twice he repeated the name of my city and looked at me. Then he drew near me and said, "Feel like going back home?"

I didn't reply. He turned around to leave, but after taking a few steps he came back. From the mat he picked up the stick that had held the dead snake and peered at it in silence for a long time. Then he said, "Don't tell anybody, Helper, but I'm certain that I've forgotten all the cures for treating snakebites."

When I looked up, he was already gone.

I stayed awake watching the sun rise and its rays grow stronger. I heard the sounds of the hamlet coming to life and of people setting out for the jungle. But all this time my ears were trained on the sounds that were coming from the inner part of the house. These were faint and of different kinds: of picking something up and putting it down, of patting, of dirt falling on dirt, of pushing something carefully from one place to another, and also a sound that was intermittent but persistent and incredibly soft but with a brutal force lurking behind it. I couldn't figure it out at all. But I didn't want to hear it now. I was wondering what I should do if it continued. Just then it stopped. So far I hadn't heard the Snake Catcher's voice and I was waiting for it. But it was absolutely quiet inside the house. I waited for a long time; the silence didn't let up. I felt as if the Snake Catcher's voice was some heady intoxication that I needed desperately, and I waited for this feeling to subside.

After waiting an appropriate amount of time I stepped into the inner part of the house.

Up until then I hadn't seen this part of the house. Here I found an assortment of bags, baskets, and objects resembling cages hanging from the walls or stored on high wooden shelves. There was also an assortment of small containers in different shapes, whose purpose escaped me, and, separate from them, lay a collection of small and large milk vessels. Several sticks, bent in a particular way, stood in a corner, and an empty bed lay near them. Some of the ingredients for medicines, most of which were stored in the section of the house where I lived, were lying in disorder under a shelf. I immediately returned to my living quarters and picked up, from the ingredients stored there, the ball of tree bark that emitted the familiar odor. As I was sniffing the ball, my gaze fell on the thin mat that was spread out on the ground. The dead snake was still lying there and had started to decompose. I didn't touch either the mat or the snake. Instead, I picked up the other mat that stood rolled up in the corner. Throughout this whole time the feeling that I was rendering great assistance to the Snake Catcher overwhelmed me.

I went into the interior of the house a second time and glanced again at the objects I had noticed on my first visit. I hadn't missed a single item. Now I began to look more closely at objects I had seen on earlier occasions.

On the floor snakes were scattered everywhere. They didn't move even though a few small animals frisked about in their midst. Whenever the animals brushed past a snake, it stirred slightly. The snakes were of different sizes, and some of them were really very beautiful. Here and there a snake had turned over and the neatly drawn lines on its white or yellowish belly were clearly visible. Each lay in its place in such a way that there could be no doubt that it was dead.

The hood on every one of the snakes was badly crushed, and none of them had any eyes left, though the mouths on some did seem to be open. The rest of their bodies were completely unscathed, except for a few whose tails also appeared to have been flattened. Had their eyes survived, I wondered, what kind of expression would they have shown? I immediately felt very bad about thinking such a thing and now I directed my attention to the place I had looked almost as soon as I had entered the inner part of the house. I moved toward it, stepping in the empty spaces between the snakes.

The Snake Catcher was lying on the floor near the bed. One of his hands was stretched out in front of him and the other was grabbing on to the bed's cushion in such a way that half of it had slid down. I gently restored it to its earlier condition and the Snake Catcher's hand came to rest on the floor.

His face was under his outstretched hand so I couldn't see it. I started to say something but stopped. I was still holding the rolled up mat in my hand. I unrolled it and threw it over his body. Then I returned to my part of the house.

Seeing the snake lying alone on the thin mat, it occurred to me how unusual it was that no cry had gone up that day. At the time, I couldn't even remember when I had heard the last cry, although I could remember each of the earlier ones complete with its particular details. I continued thinking until a thick darkness spread all around, and I stepped out into that darkness.

I came upon traces of human habitation for some distance. Finally, the hamlet was left far behind.

Resting Place

All my past life is mine no more;
The flying hours are gone,
Like transitory dreams given o'er,
Whose images are kept in store
By memory alone.
—*John Wilmot, Earl of Rochester*
from "Love and Life"

Zamaana gasht, to ham gard su'e khaana'-e kheesh
(Time has turned; you too turn back home)
—*Mirza Gada 'Ali Gada*
from the elegy "Imam-e tishna-jigar ne pas az namaaz-e 'isha"

I'm exhausted now, or rather, I now think that I had already
become tired a long time ago, perhaps after I had been
assured that I had no need to go elsewhere and that I was to
stay in this house from that day onward. I do recall vividly
though that I felt full of energy when I first set foot in this place.

1

The house's façade had caught my attention. When I stopped to
look at it, my glance fell on the garden in front and I walked in
through the gate. I proceeded toward the façade looking at the
garden over a hedge of brambles. A desire came over me to go

into the garden and examine each and every patch at length, but just then somebody asked me, "Who are you looking for?"

I was standing in front of a large room that formed part of the façade and the person sitting inside the room was looking at me intently. From his posture and expression it didn't take long for me to conclude that he was the owner, so when he asked me a second time, "Who are you looking for?" I replied, "You."

"Where are you coming from?"

"I've been wandering around."

"Come on in," he said, but then he himself came out.

"I was passing by," I said, "and saw this garden. I thought I might tell you, 'Let it be.'"

"Whatever for?"

"Everything in it is wild, some things are really very useful and not easily found. Please don't have it torn up."

"Yes," he said, looking at me with interest, "I thought so too: it has certain things that are useful and even rare. But I don't know anything about them."

"It's no easy job to lay out such a garden."

"It hasn't been laid out, just left to grow on its own," he said, then, hesitating a moment, he added, "Come, have a look from the inside."

We went down the two stone steps and came into the garden. I wandered around for a long time looking at the trees, vines and shrubs that grew haphazardly. The owner was walking behind me quietly. Whenever I began to explain something about a leaf, a tree trunk or a root by placing my hand on it, he quickly came up near to me and then fell back behind me again once I had moved on. If anyone saw us then, they would have perhaps taken me for the owner and him for the guest; actually I had started to think of myself as the owner, repeatedly deluded into thinking that I had a guest with me who was being shown around the garden for the first time.

Now we were in a dense arbor.

"You seem to know quite a lot about these things," he said.

"Not about all of them," I said, "but I do recognize them."

"You do?" he said, a little surprised. "So then ..."

"Each one has some kind of effect," I said. "I know the effect of certain ones, but not others; nonetheless I do recognize them all."

"Then tell me about this one," he said, lowering a branch that had long, thin leaves.

I told him the name of the tree and added, "But I can't tell you what its effect is."

Thereafter we started back toward the outer room. Going up the stone steps he turned around toward me and said, "You look quite tired."

"I've been wandering around," I replied.

We came to the door of the room in silence.

I saw that most of the seats in the room were occupied. I stopped at the door. The owner went in and took the same seat he had been sitting in earlier. In our encounter so far he had seemed like a rather serious and somewhat melancholy person, but among these people he appeared to be quite cheerful and carefree. Without paying much attention to the clothing or conversation of those present, I had surmised that most were guests but some were members of this household.

They were talking about the curios that decorated the room. The owner had apparently forgotten that I was there, but when I turned around to leave I heard his voice rise behind me: "Don't go yet," he said, standing near me. "Let me finish talking to the guests."

Turning towards the door he stopped short and said with a smile, "You, too, are a guest, in a manner of speaking, but it's possible ... All right, I'll send for you shortly." Then he went back inside.

I moved and stood a slight distance from the door. I could see a part of the garden from my vantage. The branches of the small trees that grew side by side in a row in this section seemed to be almost fused into one another, and a broad-leafed vine propped up against one of these trees had risen a bit higher, hanging over it and out past the hedge. I recognized all of them, one by one, but didn't know, or couldn't remember, what effect each had.

Finally I sensed that all the guests had left and only members of the household remained in the outer room. After a long conversation one of them got up. He came out and asked me to follow him.

There were four or five people, and each was looking at me with great interest. I remained silent as I stood before their eyes. Finally, the person who had come out for me asked, "Where all have you been?"

I told him a little.

"What all have you been doing?"

I told him a little about that too.

After that they talked among themselves secretively and I occupied myself by glancing at the curios. Then they broke into a loud laugh over something and the owner turned toward me. "We want to keep you with them," he pointed at the curios, "but the trouble is you're alive."

"These are all priceless objects," I said, "though each one has something missing."

"Even so, should you care to rest here for a few days," he said, ignoring my comment, "space could be found for you too."

I had not heard the exchange that took place among them; still it occurred to me that for some reason they wanted to populate an unoccupied portion of the house. And a desire to look at this unoccupied part came over me, so I blurted out that I was ready to rest there for a few days.

"Come back tomorrow about this time," the owner said, and I left.

I found the owner standing near the stone steps leading into the garden. Perhaps he was waiting for me.

"Come," he said, and led me toward the side door of the house. There was an enclosed area straight across from the door. It was scattered all over with tiny yellow leaves. I looked up: the leaves of the ancient tree that overshadowed the better part of the area were coming down steadily. I ran my hand over the tree's trunk, and the owner, brushing leaves off of his head and shoulders, pointed and said, "Over there."

I could see a portico up ahead. I entered it behind the owner. Most of its dilapidated roof had tilted slightly downward, the mortar having crumbled long ago. The walls, however, were sturdy. A small door could be seen in the wall on the left. The door looked as though it hadn't been opened for quite a long time. Its wood had lost its strength. I gently pushed on one of its panels, but it refused to budge.

"This was once an attached storeroom," the owner said, "but its roof has caved in. It's filled with rubble. So now there's just this portico."

"Its roof too ..."

"No," he said, "it's been like this from the beginning."

"But the door ..."

"The rubble has closed it off from inside," he said. "If you think you could live in this portico ..."

"I imagine I can," I said.

"You'll face three problems," he said. "A pack of dogs lives on the other side of the wall. Sometimes when they start barking they keep it up all night. This will disturb your sleep."

"I sleep little as it is," I said, "and when I do, I doubt that I can be woken up by the barking."

"And when it rains, water sprays come in here."

"But surely there must be some part or other where the spray doesn't reach."

"There is," he said, "but you'll have to get up repeatedly. Sometimes it starts to rain all of a sudden; then it'll bother you more."

"It won't bother me," I said.

"This isn't a good place," he said in a tone at once a little melancholy and a little apologetic. "I had wanted you to stay here and rest."

"I won't have any problem, really."

"And yes, the third problem," he remembered and pointed toward the floor. "Sometimes slither marks are seen here. I suspect the storeroom has ..." he stopped and shuddered slightly. I looked at the floor. It had obviously been swept clean just recently.

"A snake doesn't just bite someone on its own," I said. "Then again, not all snakes are poisonous."

"So you're sure you can rest here?"

"I imagine I can," I said, "but if that would inconvenience others ..."

"People only rarely come into this section," he said. "Nobody will be inconvenienced, in fact nobody will even notice that you're here."

2

People rarely came into this part of the house, just as the owner had said, although now and then some sulking child would wander into the compound, followed shortly afterward by an adult who would emerge from the side door and, after consoling the child, take him back inside the house. If a grown-up took longer in coming, I tried to amuse the child, but the children of this house weren't comfortable with me.

One day a child came out of the side door crying and sat down under the tree for a long time. Having failed in my attempt to amuse him, I waited for an adult to show up. But perhaps the house was going through some sort of commotion that day. The child had meanwhile stopped crying and started throwing clumps of dirt at the branches of the tree.

"Why do you bother the tree?" I asked him. But he had

already become oblivious to me. I also became oblivious to him. But when he suddenly started to scream, I looked at him. Blood was flowing down his forehead. I came out of the portico and picked him up in my lap. The wound was deep and the bleeding just wouldn't stop. Pressing down hard on the wound with my hand, I started off toward the garden with the child in my arms. Near the steps I heard a voice behind me, "What happened?" The owner had emerged from the outer room.

"What happened to him?" he asked, looking at the child with concern. I told him what had happened which only increased his concern.

"There's something wrong with his blood," he informed me. "His wounds become infected very quickly."

"This one won't," I said, descending into the garden.

The owner followed me. I put the boy down and sat him on the ground. He had calmed down now and was looking back and forth fearfully at me and the owner.

"He was injured at the very same spot once before," the owner said, "and nearly died."

Meanwhile I'd spotted the leaves I was looking for. I squeezed them, letting the juice drip onto the child's wound, and then covered the wound with the crushed pulp.

"Let this sit the whole night," I said. "I'll look at him again in the morning."

"Will this be enough?" the owner asked me skeptically.

"I'll look at him again in the morning," I repeated. The owner picked up the boy and went inside.

The child's wound had nearly healed by morning.

That's how I got started treating the wounds of the people who lived in this house. Before long they started sending even outsiders to me for treatment. Most of the wounds of the outsiders were very old, but all of them were treatable from the resources in the garden, although this sometimes required the use of fire and cooking vessels. On such occasions the owner had the vessels sent over to me from the house. Sometimes he also accompanied these things and watched me for a long time busy at my work.

One day as he was watching I put a brand new vessel on the fire and, when I tossed some roots into it, the inside of the vessel turned black. I told the owner, "Certain items ruin the vessels; this distracts me from my work."

"But whatever you prepare is far more valuable than the vessels."

"Even so," I said, "new vessels hamper my work. If you've got some old ones lying around …"

"I suppose that can be arranged," he said appearing to be thinking something, then got up and went back in.

Shortly thereafter the very boy who had injured his forehead came and left several odd-looking vessels near me. Some had their handles broken and some had their lids missing; still they were all quite sufficient for my purpose. As I was about to put one of them on the fire, my hand stopped and I pulled the vessel back up. I gathered up the whole lot and brought them over to the outer room.

The owner sat there in his usual chair, his head bent over. He lifted it when he heard my footsteps. I set the vessels on the floor near his feet and looked around at the curios. The gaping spaces between them gave the room a somewhat strange and unfinished appearance. Meanwhile the owner was looking intently at me.

"Why did you remove these?" I asked. He looked at me even more intently. I realized that my tone sounded demanding, but before I had had time to change it, he asked, "You're not pleased that I removed them?"

"They were here for a long time … perhaps even from the very beginning," I said. "Your room doesn't look right without them."

He remained quiet for a while, then a faint smile appeared

on his lips. "When you first came here," he began, "I mentioned that we wanted to keep you close beside them."

"I remember," I said, "but the problem was that I was alive."

"And still are," he said as his smile brightened. Then he suddenly turned very grave. "That's the reason you can't reside with them. But at least they can reside with you. Can they not?"

"They can," I said slowly, "because they are not alive."

"They are not alive," he repeated my last words like an echo.

"But without them this room …"

"I'll rearrange things," he said, "so the absence of those others isn't felt."

He stood up from the chair and quickly started to move the curios around. Then he stopped, turned toward me and said, "Although their absence makes your presence felt."

He turned back toward the curios. I picked up the vessels and returned to the portico.

Those vessels were made of old metal alloys. The effectiveness of whatever I prepared in them was increased many times over.

3

From then on one of these vessels was nearly always on the fire and I would feel compelled to make several trips to the garden every day. I went there even when it wasn't necessary to do so, just to stroll around among the vines and shrubs. Sometimes I even rested there, until I began to feel that my true place of rest was the garden, not the portico. Though I still spent most of my time in the portico. From here I could see clearly the changing conditions of the small-leafed tree.

Sometimes its branches became heavy with leaves, spreading a cool shade beneath it. Sometimes its leaves turned yellow and scattered all over the compound. Seeing sunshine under its bare branches one felt that the tree had withered away. But then new sprouts appeared on those branches, and sometimes the entire tree turned red with flowers even before the leaves had appeared. Slowly the flowers disappeared, replaced by green leaves that covered the tree.

One day I was looking at the naked branches of the tree imagining where new shoots might appear first. It seemed to me that light green dots had started to appear here and there on certain branches of the tree even as I was looking at it. When I came out of the portico and approached the tree to give those tiny green dots a closer look, I heard something like a noise coming from the house. Several people rushed out of the side door and ran toward the main entrance. Then some people came back and went in again through the same side door. That day, for the first time, I became curious about the goings-on inside the house, but I just stood quietly between the portico and the tree watching people as they filed in and out through the side door. At first everyone was silent, later they started to talk among themselves. Several times their eyes fell on me but nobody told me anything. The commotion inside the house was rising steadily. Finally I stopped someone who had just walked out of the side door. He hastily told me the reason for the commotion. The owner had died while he was still sitting in his chair in the outer room.

I sat down under the tree leaning against the trunk. I remembered that I had seen him just that morning. He had walked over to me from the outer room as I was going down the garden steps. Standing there, he had queried me for a long time about different kinds of wounds and their treatments. Then I had gone down into the garden. When I was returning with an assortment of barks and leaves, I again found him standing near the steps. He asked me about the effects of the leaves and barks I had, expressing, with feigned seriousness, his desire to be wounded sometime and to be treated by me. His last words rang out in my ears, "Provided," he had said, laughing, "the wound is one I would like."

God knows what sort of wound he had wished for himself? I wondered, and I felt a burning sensation in my nostrils. I looked up in front of me. The portico was filled with smoke, but I stayed under the tree. I knew that whatever was boiling in the old, uncovered cooking pot in the portico must have boiled over and put out the fire.

4

I didn't venture out of the portico for many days. Meanwhile calm had returned to the house and sulking children had again started to wander into the compound. Now they sometimes even talked to me a bit. It's through them that I guessed that the man who had come to usher me back into the outer room the very first day was now the owner.

One day the new owner sent a boy to get me and bring me to the outer room, but when I got there I found that the door was fastened from the inside. I left. A few days later he sent for me again, and again I found the door closed. This happened several times. Finally one day as I was going away I stopped and tapped gently on the door. It opened. The new owner was standing across from me.

"Come," he said, sitting down in the previous owner's chair.

"I came several times before," I said, stepping into the room, "but the door ..."

"Yes," he said, "I keep it closed."

I took a sweeping glance around the room. The former owner's portrait hung on the wall straight across from me and the gaps the vessels had left between the curios were still there. I went over near the portrait and started looking at it. "He always watched over us with great care," the present owner said. Then he talked about the deceased for quite some time while I looked at the portrait. Now and then my eyes came to rest on a space left vacant by a vessel.

Finally I said, "He watched over me with great care too."

"That's why I've called you here," he said. "He hoped that you wouldn't go anywhere else," he paused, and then added, "and I hope that too."

After a long silence I said, "I won't," and turned around to leave.

"But he wanted you to rest here," I heard him say. "You really must rest."

I sensed something in his voice, so I stopped at the door.

"I'm not in any difficulty here," I replied.

While I continued standing at the door he started to say something several times but hesitated. Finally he got out of his chair and came over to me.

"This disorderly garden doesn't go at all well with this house," he said, faltering. "Everyone had wanted it to be freshly laid out. He did too," he pointed at the portrait, "but …" he hesitated, and said after a pause, "the fact is, it doesn't look like a garden at all."

"The fact is, it's not a garden at all," I said softly.

After that I remained speechless for quite some time and so did he. Finally, he cleared his throat and said, "He cared for you a lot."

"If you would leave the door open for a bit …" I said, going out the door.

I went to the portico, gathered the vessels and hauled them back to the outer room. He was sitting in his chair.

"But he had given these to you," he said, looking at me intently.

"Empty spaces don't look pleasing," I said, returning the vessels to their places. He stared at me silently, then, when I'd finished my work and turned toward the door, he said, "You really must rest now and, as was his wish," he again pointed at the portrait. "You must stay on here."

5

I rest now. But I've allowed my curiosity to get the better of me. I want to know more and more about the things that transpire in this house. At first, the older people in the house answered my questions in great detail, then they may have begun to suspect that after asking a question I didn't really pay attention to their answer, or that I forgot the answer the minute I heard it. Later, they became convinced that I forgot my own question before they had even answered it. So now it doesn't surprise me that they don't like me asking them anything, and once one of them even blurted out, "You're afflicted with talking."

Children are no longer seen in the compound. Only one boy wanders in now and then. I know he's the one who will be the next owner of this house. He's very at ease with me, but whenever I ask him something he answers it in such a way that, were I to reflect on it, my mind would become completely muddled, but I don't reflect on it, although he thinks that I do. He's the one who told me about the plan for the new garden, which I couldn't understand. Nevertheless I kept asking him about each and every corner of it, always forgetting what I had just asked. Finally he got fed up and always said the same thing, "Why don't you come along and have a look at it yourself?" and he would go back inside the house without waiting for my answer.

People continue to come and go in this house and this boy keeps me informed about it. But he purposely only gives me incomplete information so that I will continue to ask him question after question, and he can continue to give me incomplete answers.

One day he ran over to me and said, "Your guest has arrived."

"My guest?"

"Now this portico will be taken away from you."

"Will the guest take it away?"

"No, the patient, not the guest."

"A patient? What illness does he have?"

The boy pressed his lips with his finger waving his hand back and forth as if saying no, and waited for my next question. But I didn't ask him anything. He looked at me for a while feigning fear, and then suddenly said in a tone filled with the same mock fear, "Run! He's coming," and took off, disappearing behind the side door.

I saw that a man had, in fact, entered the compound and had already walked up as far as the tree, with the owner and some other members of the household following behind. They stopped and stood under the tree. The owner was explaining something to the man. Then, taking slow steps, all of them came towards the portico. The guest's eyes were scanning the ground, as if he was searching for something. He was moving with deliberate slowness, but he didn't appear sick at all. He stopped a short distance away from me. Even now he was looking at the ground with half-closed eyes. The owner drew near him and said, "Just this portico." The man opened his eyes wide, lifted his head and twisted his neck giving just one glance at the compound, the tree, the side door, the portico and me, and then he turned around to leave. It seemed to me that everything he had glanced at disappeared into his eyes and then came back out within the space of a single second.

Now they were entering the side door. His eyes hadn't tarried on my face at all; still I was feeling as if I had just walked straight out of some maze.

6

I was bound to be curious about the patient. The boy visited me now and then and brought up the subject on his own, but since I knew he would never give a straight answer to any of my questions, I asked him about other things instead. Finally he stopped mentioning the patient altogether. But this only increased my dilemma further until one day I myself asked him, "How is your patient faring?"

"Why don't you ask the girl who comes to look after him," he said. "She comes here in this area too."

"Here?"

"She just sits for a long time under the tree," he said. "Perhaps you don't see well these days."

It occurred to me that on certain days I had, indeed, seen a girl under the tree, but I had thought of her as a guest.

"So she's his nurse?"

"No, she's *your* nurse," he said feeling bored, and he got up and went back into the house.

That same day, when the girl arrived and sat down under the tree, I came out of the portico. She saw me and greeted me. I approached her. She quickly stood up and I hurled one question after another at her about the sick man. However, I couldn't get much information out of her. She knew very little herself, but she did tell me as much as she knew.

What I found out from her was just this: for generations the relations between the families of the people who lived in this house and the family of the sick man had been very close. He had gone away somewhere. When the people of this house found him, none of his family except this girl remained alive. He didn't tell anyone where he had been, but he was willing to live in this house now.

"And what ailment does he have?" I inquired.

"He doesn't talk," the girl replied.

"Something wrong with his throat?"

"No, he's chosen on his own to give up talking."

"Why?"

"I don't know."

"Didn't you ask him?"

"What's the point? He's given up talking, hasn't he?"

I realized that my question was absurd.

After that, whenever she came into the compound, I would come out of the portico. She would greet me and I would spend a long time telling her all kinds of interesting stories. I had taken it upon myself to amuse her. Sometimes I also asked her about the sick man, invariably adding at the end, "I want to meet him at least once."

One day she told me that everybody in the house had gone out to some wedding and, if I wanted, I could meet with the sick man now.

The people here hadn't invited me inside the house up to now. Perhaps I really shouldn't go. I thought for a while and then followed the nurse through the side door. After passing through several sections of the house, we came into a section the greater part of which looked unoccupied. Coming to the open door of a room, she asked me to wait there and went in herself.

I saw the patient from the door. He was sitting on his bed and his eyes were apparently searching for something on the floor. After a while he lifted his head and looked at the girl, who beckoned for me to come in. After some hesitation I entered. The patient's eyes had again started to search for something on the floor but I somehow felt that he was, in reality, observing me. Finally, he lifted his head and turned his face toward me.

We kept looking at each other, in silence, for the longest time ever. Our faces didn't betray any kind of curiosity. His eyes had an intensity, a brightness, but throughout this time never for a moment did they seem to be devoid of feeling. I could not understand if his eyes were trying to say something or were merely observing me, but I felt we were coming to some silent understanding. All of a sudden a terrible feeling of despair came over me. It was the first time I'd felt like this since I'd come to this house. Just then his nurse placed her hand on my arm and led me out of the room.

Outside, as I spoke with his nurse, I realized that my speech was a shortcoming and that the patient was traveling far ahead of me on a road I knew nothing about.

7

Bouts of despair strike me; still, I let my curiosity grow as much as, or even more than, before. The people who live here still become flustered by my questions. I continue to tell the nurse all kinds of interesting stories and inquire after the patient's condition. But when I'm seized by an attack of despair, I feel as if tiny yellow leaves are coming down in a shower between the nurse and myself. The boy who must own this house one day begins to seem like a vanishing shadow. And the ceiling of my resting place feels as though it's right on top of my chest.

*Ganjefa** *

"... Ganjefa, as I've already mentioned, has eight suits, of which the higher ones are *taaj*, *zar-e safed*, *shamsheer*, and *ghulaam* and the lower ones are *chang*, *zar-e surkh*, *baraat*, and *qumaash*.

"The king of *zar-e surkh*, called *aaftaab* [sun], is the most important card in the game, followed by the king of *zar-e safed* which enjoys the title of *maahtaab* [moon]. *Maahtaab*, naturally, has a lower status than *aaftaab*, provided the latter is shining.

"... In the daytime he who holds the *aaftaab* card starts the game, with *maahtaab* carrying a lesser value, or rather no value at all, before it. At night, though, the power and value of the *aaftaab* is transferred over to *maahtaab* and *aaftaab* is reduced in status to that of an ordinary card."

Letters of the Famous

1

I began to feel bad about my life the night of the riots. On my way home from the cemetery that night, I was stopped several times and interrogated. Well, not quite interrogated—I was asked just three questions: "What's your name?" "Where do you live?" and "What do you do?" I answered the first two right away but invariably faltered at the third. While I would be thinking of an appropriate answer they would let me go with a stern order to return home immediately.

* *"Ganjefa"* or *"ganjifa"* is a game of cards (also means a pack of cards). For details, see Rudolf von Leyden, *Ganjifa, the Playing Cards of India* (London: Victoria and Albert Museum, 1982).

Then they would stop some other passerby and subject him to the same questions. During this exercise a couple of people even got beaten up. At first the thought that the third question might well result in my getting roughed up too scared me quite a bit, so I became nervous trying to answer it, but as I drew closer to my home I started to feel a bit testy about the question itself. When I was asked, "What do you do?" for the last time, I answered in my heart, "I live off the earnings of my mother."

Father had also lived off my mother's earnings. Asthma and addiction to playing the lottery had pretty much made him a good-for-nothing. I never saw him do anything other than cough away as he lay in bed, or tear up lottery tickets and toss them away. Mother managed to pay the expenses of the household from the money she earned doing chikan embroidery work. It was Mother again who had looked after my education, during which time she somehow got it into her head that I might also catch my father's disease so she packed me off to her foster sister in Allahabad for further studies. I'm certain that every month she also sent this sister a little something extra, over and above my expenses. My father passed away two or three years after I left for Allahabad, but I finished my education there and only then returned to my native Lucknow. And now, for the past several years, I have merely been roaming around, living off my mother's wages like my father before me. If I have done any work at all, it hasn't gone beyond lighting a lamp at my father's grave every Thursday. All the same, I had felt good about my life.

The night of the riots, in trying to answer the third question, I saw this life of mine, this life about which I had felt good, play out before me over and over, each time in exactly the same way, until I began to feel anger toward myself and pity for my mother, both of which, the anger as well as the pity, grew worse, especially when I arrived at our door and found out from the neighbors that my mother, draping her burqa around her, had ventured out looking for me the minute she heard the news of the riots and hadn't yet returned. They had done their best to stop her, but she paid no heed to anyone. It occurred to me that she must also have been subjected to the same questions, "What's your name?" "Where do you live?" and "What do you do?" I was about to set out in search of her but the neighbors forcibly held me back. Mother had extracted an oath from them that in the event I returned before she did and attempted to go out looking for her they wouldn't allow me to. The neighbors were asking me about the riots but I evaded them by saying that I didn't know anything. And that was indeed true. I was worried about Mother and wasn't about to be stopped by the neighbors, but I stopped myself thinking that if she returned while I was gone she would set out searching for me again. So I went inside the house. In the courtyard my meal was laid out covered with a tray on a *chowki* and a neighbor woman sat near it waiting for me. Mother had also asked her on her oath to make me eat as soon as I got back. I asked her to leave. I had no urge to eat even though I was feeling terribly hungry, so I washed my hands and mouth and sat down near the tray. Just then Mother returned.

Outside, the neighbors had already informed her that I was back, safe and sound. Nevertheless she entered the house weeping and wailing as if she was being brought in to look at my dead body. And when she reached me she did everything a mother would do on finding her missing son. I realized then that she still thought of me as a small child accustomed to holding on to his mother's hand as he walked. I also realized that I was grown up and yet there was only one way I could answer "What do you do?"

From the time she fed me until the time she made me lie down on the bed while she patted me, she kept touching me again and again as if she wasn't certain I had come back home in one piece. I was now lying quietly and had started to feel sleepy, while

Mother sat nearby scrutinizing me. After a while she asked, "Did something happen?"

"No, nothing," I answered. "Why?"

"Nothing happened along the way?"

"Nothing at all," I said. "Why do you ask?"

"Did someone say something?"

"No."

She continued staring at me, and then said, "From now on I won't let you go out anymore."

At that point I said, "From now on, Mother, I won't live off your earnings."

That very night Mother had her first bout of coughing.

Without telling my mother I started to sneak out looking for work, but I didn't know the first thing about how to find work. I just roamed around as I used to and then came back home. After a few days when I went out I didn't even remember that it was to look for work. But I no longer enjoyed roaming around. Gradually I started going out less and less, or rather I should say more and more, because now I stepped out several times a day, only to come back shortly thereafter, go out again, return again. . . .

Around that time, one day I saw Mother holding a very fine piece of some white cloth close to her eyes and embroidering an exceedingly delicate vine on it with white thread. I sat down on a *chowki* close to her and said, "Mother, don't hold the cloth so close to your eyes. It'll ruin your eyesight."

"It's already quite weak, son," she said. Then she had a mild attack of coughing.

"You've started to cough a lot too."

"It comes and goes," she said, "but it's the breathlessness at night. . ."

"Isn't there any medicine . . ."

"There is," she said, "and I take it. It helps too."

Obviously it wasn't helping, or perhaps she wasn't actually taking it at all. One day I brought the subject up again, "Mother, your cough isn't getting any better."

"Really it has. It only flares up during the night," she told me, and then, after a pause, she asked, "It doesn't disturb your sleep, does it?"

No, it didn't disturb my sleep. One night, though, I woke up in the middle of a dream. It was dark. I couldn't recall my dream. I tried but I couldn't. I turned over in bed and was about to go back to sleep when I heard the muffled sound of Mother's coughing. A wave of drowsiness swept over me, followed by a second wave, but the sound of coughing persisted. I opened my eyes wide and strained my ears. The sound was coming from the courtyard. I sat up in bed. The courtyard was illumined by the faint light of the stars, but Mother couldn't be seen there.

"Mother!" I called out for her, "What are you doing in the courtyard?"

I could only hear a string of coughs in response. I got out of bed and walked out into the courtyard. She was sitting on the ground next to the well. I approached her and called to her. Then I bent down and looked closely. She was coughing away with a corner of her *dupatta* rolled into a ball and tucked into her mouth, while her body jerked about fitfully in silent spasms. I sat down near her.

"You've been coughing for a long time," I said. "Why didn't you wake me up?"

She was in no condition to reply. I helped her up and brought her into the *daalaan* [hall]. Then I made her sit on her bed and tried to rub her back. It took some time before her breathing began to ease. She asked for water and after sipping it she said, "Why did you get up?"

"I had a dream," I told her. And I began to remember it, but only dimly.

"Go back to sleep," she said. "I'll sleep too."

"I dreamt that I was eating my meal and you were sitting in front of me fanning me."

She broke into a laugh. "You call that a dream?" she said, and at the same time I said, "Mother, teach me to do chikan embroidery."

She looked at me with some concern and said, "No, son, you'll ruin your eyes."

"Then teach me some other work," I said, "or find me a job somewhere. How long will I have to live off your wages as Father did?"

She remained silent for some time and then said, "Well go back to sleep now. I'm feeling sleepy too."

Then she lay down and pulled her *dupatta* over her face.

The minute I got up in the morning I started pestering Mother, totally forgetting that I was myself behaving like a child who wanted to hold his mother's hand while walking. She listened quietly to my repeated demands until I again said, "How long will I, like Father ..." and her face turned red. But she only patted me on the cheek and said very gently, "What's this, boy, why have you suddenly become an enemy of your father?"

"Enemy, not at all, Mother. But haven't you suffered on account of him?"

"What have I suffered? It's he who suffered. What man enjoys feeding himself on his wife's wages? In his time he earned well and provided for me. When he stopped earning ..."

"I don't recall ever seeing him earn any money."

"What have you seen anyway, son," she said, suddenly on the verge of tears. "What comfort was there that that departed soul didn't give me?! And all that he did for you too!"

"For me?" I asked. "What did he ever do for me?"

"He was planning to send you to England."

"England?"

"To study," she said. "But he couldn't. So you may say what you will now."

She again seemed to be almost on the brink of crying and remained silent for a while.

"England …"

"Even before you were born he had made it plain that if it was a boy he would send him to England for an education."

"England … Do you even know where England is?" I asked.

"Why would I know," she said. "He used to say it was some sort of college across the seven seas."

"Did he even have any idea how much money it would have cost?"

"Why wouldn't he know? He did the calculations after talking to many people."

"And how much did it come to?"

"How would I know how much it came to. It was a huge sum—that's all I know."

"Then?"

"Then what? That brave man of God didn't loose heart. First off he sold the properties in Rustam Nagar and Shah Ganj."

"He sold off two houses?"

"Houses? They were more like ruins," she said. "Next he borrowed as much money from his office as he could. Some money came from selling my jewelry."

"He even made you sell off your jewelry?"

"Well, he'd set his heart on it."

"What about your heart?"

"His wish was my wish. But it did hurt me to see those preparations. Our only child and this trip across seven seas …"

"OK, OK, where did all that money go?"

Mother remained quiet. Her prolonged silence prompted me to ask, "He blew it all on the lottery, didn't he?"

"No. The lottery came only after he had no money left … I

used to give him money for the lottery."

"So where did he lose all his money?"

"He never did tell me that, nor did I ask. But this much I know, he wasn't involved in anything bad."

After that she lapsed into a silence which made it seem inappropriate to query her further. So I too became silent. But when she got up to go to the kitchen, I stopped her. "OK, what happened next?"

"Nothing happened. His respiratory ailment completely incapacitated him. Whenever he had an attack of asthma, it seemed as if he had stopped breathing. His office retired him on a pension before the end of his term of service."

"How much did he get from his pension?"

"God knows. I never got to see any of it."

"So he squandered his pension too?"

At this her face again turned red.

"What's this you're saying, 'He squandered it. He squandered it.' He was not a man to squander."

"So then the pension …"

"He sold it off to pay back the loan he'd gotten from his office. Well, call it squandering if you must."

"What office did Father work in?" I asked.

"It had a long English name; I never could remember it."

"What was his position there?"

"That too had an English name."

She again didn't say a word for a long time. Finally I said, "OK, tell me more about Father."

"What shall I tell you?" she said. "When he returned after selling off his pension he just stayed in the house for two days without touching food. He was dead set on ending his life. Only after I swore to him on my oath that you would die if he did that, did he come to his senses."

"And then?"

"Then what? I picked up a needle the very next day."

"Did you know chikan work?"

"Already from when I was little."

"Who taught you?" I asked realizing that I also knew next to nothing about my mother.

"My *phuphi-amma*," she replied. "She used to embroider as a hobby. I learned it for fun. But it gave me a skill, otherwise I'd be sweeping floors or washing dishes in any and everyone's houses."

Then Mother told me that she had herself taught chikan embroidery to several poor girls who had later started to work for wages. When Father became indigent these very girls came to help. It was through them that Mother also started to get work from an embroidery wholesaler in Goal Darvaza. She praised the wholesaler, "The Lala is a good man. A connoisseur of fine quality work. If he likes the workmanship, he pays extra."

Then she went off on another tangent and kept talking about this and that for a long time. I had no idea that she could talk so well. Lost in listening to what she was saying, I forgot how we had started off on this conversation. But she hadn't—of that I'm certain.

2

I ventured out of the house even less now. Most of the time I sat idly and, without really paying attention, I just looked at Mother perched on a *chowki* working away at her embroidery and coughing every now and then. Sometimes when she was seized by a fit of coughing, I rushed to her with some water or rubbed her back. She recovered in a short time and took hold of her needle again.

One day as I was rubbing her back gently, my eyes fell on some lengths of cloth piled up beside her and I said, "Mother, you really shouldn't work so much."

"It's coarse work," she said, "it doesn't take much time."

I looked at the colored pieces of rough material again. I also noticed that she had embroidered large flowers on them with colored threads. Up until now I'd only seen her embroider on very soft, fine material with white thread. I picked up an embroidered red ochre piece and asked, "What kind of embroidery is this? Before you used to …"

"I can't handle delicate work anymore. My hand shakes. And my eyesight isn't what it used to be." She drew a deep breath and continued, "In the beginning my work was exported to England."

"England?"

"My work received high praise there, though not my name. The Lala says that even now specimens of my old work are sent to him asking for more of the same."

"But this …" I said picking up another piece of faded material and examining the flowers on it.

"Just ordinary work," she said. "Whatever happens to be popular."

"Who would wear it?"

"Why, people wear it a lot, men as well as women."

"I never saw anyone wearing it."

"There's a lot you haven't seen. Next time when you go out, pay special attention."

She removed my hand from her back and picked up a piece of material and her needle. Holding the piece very close to her eyes she studied the traced pattern for some time and then started to stitch along the pattern. I watched the same pattern emerge in colored thread. I looked at her and found her looking at me, while her needle followed along the printed design. I looked at her again; she was still gazing at me.

"Mother, you embroider without looking at the pattern?"

"I've looked at it already."

"But you've looked at it only once."

"What's the need to look at it over and over," she said. Then she said again, "It's coarse work."

I sat quietly watching her work. She was really embroidering quite fast. After she had finished a piece she immediately picked up another, brought it close to her eyes and examined the pattern, and then she let her needle run along it. She kept up that way until it was late at night. She picked up the finished work, counted the pieces a few times and put them to one side after neatly folding them. Then she picked up the unfinished pieces, counted them as well, and kept looking at me for some time. Afterward she said, "Aren't you sleepy?"

"I am," I said. "You go to sleep too. It's rather late."

"There are only a few pieces left to do," she said, "I'll finish them and then go to bed."

"There are quite a few. Leave them. You can finish them tomorrow."

"They aren't that many. It won't take me long," she said, and then said again, "It's coarse work."

Her needle got going again. For a while I watched a big maroon flower with five or six petals begin to take shape on a piece of cloth. Then I lay down on my bed and, perhaps immediately, fell asleep facing the wall.

A few times my sleep was interrupted briefly by my mother's coughing, from which I concluded that she was still awake and working and it was not quite morning yet.

When my sleep broke, well into the day, I saw that Mother had fallen asleep right there on the *chowki*. One of her hands was lying on the unfinished pieces. I guessed that they were more or less the same number as when I went to sleep. I went close to her and looked. Her needle was stuck at the very top of the piece in the fourth petal of the maroon flower. I grabbed her shoulder and shook it gently. She always woke up at the slightest sound so I looked at her intently. I couldn't tell whether she was asleep or unconscious. When I began to shake her shoulder vigorously she started and opened her eyes.

"Are you all right, Mother?"

"I'm all right," she said. "Don't worry, I'm all right."

"Did you feel unwell during the night?"

"No … yes, a little …"

Just then she suffered another coughing spasm. I rushed and brought some water. As I was giving it to her I noticed that her hand was trembling badly.

"Here, let me hold it for you," I said and helped her drink the water. Then I helped her onto the bed and sat down close to her head. After a while she started gasping for breath and sat up. I tried to lay her down again but she made a sign with her hand telling me not to. About noon her condition improved a little. Every few minutes I asked her how she was feeling, but she seemed to have lapsed into silence. She barely answered yes or no. One time I asked her, "Mother, would you like something to eat?" and she shook her head no. I hadn't eaten anything myself since morning and was feeling hungry.

"Do eat something," I said to her.

She shook her head no and remained silent for a long time. Then, suddenly, she said in a loud voice, "Call Husna."

"Husna?"

"You know where she lives?"

I didn't even know who Husna was. I was hearing this name for the first time. Meanwhile Mother had another of her coughing bouts. I started to rub her back but she moved my hand away and said haltingly in between fits of coughing, "Husna … You don't know her house?… the one that has the peepal tree … the one between the firecrackers and the incense sticks …"

She thrust her head between her knees and started to cough. I was worried about leaving her alone in this condition, but when she lifted her head and found me still there she said in a louder voice, "You didn't go?" and I sensed such desperation in her voice that I immediately stepped out of the house.

I knew where the firecracker shop was located in the Chowk. I had seen it there ever since my childhood. But I had no idea that beyond it there was another shop where they sold incense sticks and that a lane separated the two shops. It was a fairly wide lane that twisted and turned far into the distance, with an abundance of houses, all more or less crumbling, on either side of it. It was perhaps their crumbly state that made the lane look rather wide. Not a single tree could be seen anywhere. I proceeded along the lane's meandering course until I saw the crown of a peepal tree behind two houses. A few moments later I found myself standing before a fairly wide wall with loose bricks. The peepal tree was growing through this wall and its widely spread roots were holding the wall together tenaciously. Not far from the roots was the house's half-open door. I knocked with the door ring a few times. A man's voice said from inside, "Coming."

The voice seemed somewhat familiar. As I was trying to place it, the thought of my mother's condition at that very moment intervened. Standing at the door I was also struck by the thought that I hadn't left her with a neighborhood woman to watch over her. I remembered her breathlessness, the hacking coughs that shook her body, her trembling hands. I was about to rush back home when, behind the half-open door, I noticed a woman standing in the dimly lit *devrhi* staring at me. I looked in her direction; she took a step forward and pushed on the open panel of the door leaving it only slightly ajar. Then I heard her say, "Who is it?"

"Is this Husna Sahib's residence?" I asked.

"Yes, it is."

"Might you be …"

"Yes, what is it?"

"Mother is unwell. She's asked for you."

She kept staring at me for a while from behind the door. I felt as though she hadn't quite understood me. So I said, "She's having immense difficulty breathing and her cough … She's also shivering. She's asked for you to come quickly. Perhaps …"

I stopped. She still said nothing and I wondered whether she had understood me at all. I said, "At the moment, she's all alone at home."

She said slowly, "I was just giving Father his food. Please go back, I'll be along soon."

I hastened back without waiting for her to turn around.

Mother still sat with her head tucked between her knees. She was still experiencing some difficulty breathing but her hacking had stopped. Sensing my footsteps, she lifted her head.

Sitting down near Mother I said, "Well, I've informed her. She'll be here soon."

"Poor girl, she must have been alarmed," Mother said to herself, and then she asked me, "She didn't come with you?"

"She was serving her father his meal."

"What else could she do!" Mother said. "Her father is an invalid."

"Mother, who is Husna?"

"She's a nice young woman," she said. "She does needlework. A while back she came to take lessons from me."

"From you?" I was surprised, for no reason at all. "How come I never saw her here?"

Mother wanted to say something—perhaps "Well, what have you seen anyway"—but stopped short. Then she said, "You were in Allahabad at the time."

"And what's wrong with her father?"

"Paralysis of the legs, poor soul," she replied. "You used to be quite fond of buying his toothpowder."

"What toothpowder?"

"The same, Ladlay's Badshahi Manjan [Royal Toothpowder]."

"Ladlay?" I asked, much surprised. "Is he still in Lucknow?"

"Worse than a corpse. Both of his legs have shriveled up."

Just then there was a sound at the door and Husna entered. Since the veil of her burqa was raised, I recognized her. I marveled at the fact that she had arrived so expeditiously. Mother blossomed the minute she saw her. "Come, daughter, come!" she said. "I knew you'd fly over to me."

She proceeded slowly toward the *daalaan* and I climbed up the stairs to the rooftop.

Watching the kites soar lazily in the receding afternoon sun I was struck by the realization that it had, perhaps, been years since I had bothered to lift my head and look up. At the moment, the clear blue sky and Ladlay's name carried me back to my childhood, to a time when, besides the acrobats, the jugglers, and the man who caught only the most bizarre animals, there was also this Ladlay who drew me to the Sunday market at Nakhkhas. He would spread out a sheet by the side of the street and stand next to it. On the sheet, some fifty or sixty herbs were neatly laid out in small open-mouthed bags, and behind them, on the closed lid of a small box, were several rows of big and small bottles containing Badshahi Manjan. Ladlay himself stood behind his wares. He was a stocky man with even white teeth. Within a short time buyers would gather around him. Then he would speak. A strange excitement and grandeur swept over him when he spoke; nonetheless the speech itself never changed. For the first few minutes he spoke in English, or in some kind of gibberish he had cooked up himself but which nonetheless sounded like English to those who didn't know any better. Then he would tell the people that he had studied in England and that, if he wanted to, he could become a Deputy Collector of Revenues that very day, but he preferred making his toothpowder to working as a Deputy Collector. And then, tapping each of the bags in turn with his cane, he described its contents with great facility, telling the effects of the ingredients and the incredible hazards that attended the effort to collect them. Next he picked up two bottles of his Badshahi Manjan and, clinking them together, explained how his toothpowder contained all those ingredients and how its recipe was kept well guarded in the Royal Treasure House. Seriousness was so mixed with jocularity in his speech that people had a hard time deciding when to laugh and when not to. I used to be a bit frightened of him, nevertheless I eagerly awaited the moment when, just before launching into his sale's pitch, he would press a thick copper coin between his teeth and nearly bend it over with his thumb. Then he would pass the bent coin around for everyone to see. Some customers made vain attempts to straighten it. Eventually the coin was returned to Ladlay who would press it between his teeth as before and flatten it out. Thereafter the sale of the toothpowder would begin. I bought a small bottle of the stuff every second or third Sunday, used the powder regularly, and tried to straighten bent coins.

After a while my enthusiasm for the market waned. The market also was no longer what it used to be and I had stopped paying attention to whether Ladlay still sold his toothpowder there. Then I was packed off to Allahabad. When I returned to Lucknow after finishing my education I did go out once or twice to the Sunday market, but now it had become unbearably crowded. Finally I quit going past the Nakhkhas because its bazaar got in the way of my aimless wanderings.

I had forgotten this market of my childhood and it's many attractions, including Ladlay, long ago, but at this moment, when kites were calling out and circling slowly in the blue expanse of the sky, and downstairs Ladlay's daughter was talking with my mother, I could vividly see that market and Ladlay standing in it— why, I could even see the coin that he had bent between his teeth.

It was late afternoon when Mother called to me from downstairs. I went down and took a seat beside her. She was sitting on her bed and looked more or less well. The pieces of embroidered material were gone from the *chowki*, replaced by a tray of fresh, warm food.

"Eat," Mother said, "I've starved my son today."

"That ... Husna ... she's left?" I asked.

"The poor girl cooked all this and then went home."

Going over to sit on the *chowki* I said, "You come too. Or shall I bring the food over to you?"

"No, she had me eat before she left."

After a couple of morsels I realized that I was eating Mother's cooking. When I couldn't hold back any longer, I asked, "Did you also teach Husna how to cook?"

"What a perfect guess," Mother said feeling pleased. "Yes, when she used to come for embroidery lessons ... I told her, 'Daughter, why not learn cooking too,'" and then Mother said again, "What a perfect guess."

"Why? I can pick out my mother's cooking from a thousand dishes."

Mother laughed softly, and then recalling something she said, "Tell me, what exactly did you say to Husna?"

"Just that you weren't feeling well."

"And?"

"And? Yes, that you'd asked for her."

"And then you took off without telling her who you were?"

I realized my mistake.

"Yes, now that you mention it," I said. "She didn't ask me. And besides I was in a hurry to get back home."

"You shouldn't be so jittery, boy."

"Then how did she ..."

"She figured it out herself and came over."

I had the feeling that Mother had brought this up just to have me ask a certain question, so I put that question to her, "But how did she recognize me?"

"From your shirt," Mother said, rather proudly.

I looked at my shirt. It was quite worn, but Mother had embroidered a very intricate floral vine on it herself, not a single stitch of which had loosened from its place even now. I ran my hand over the vine and asked, "She recognized your needlework, didn't she? But what made her think I was ..."

But the answer dawned on me before I had even finished

the question. There was only one way a man of my modest means could be wearing a shirt with such fine embroidery and that was if he was the son of the one who had done that embroidery. It was a matter anyone could figure out and so Husna had too.

Mother looked at me intently and started to say something but stopped. When I was done eating, she said, "Put the dirty dishes by the well. I'll wash them."

"No, let me," I said, standing up. "Where are your dishes?"

"She did them and put them away," Mother told me. "And listen …"

I stopped on my way to the well.

"Yes, what is it?"

"She'll come again tomorrow at noon. Try to be here."

"Why?"

"She has some business with you."

"With me?"

"Yes. She wants you to read something for her."

The next day Husna came to Mother a little after noon. I got up and went toward the well. The two talked by themselves for quite a while and then Mother called me.

She was lying on the bed. Husna was sitting near her on the edge of the bed. She looked my age, or maybe a little younger. She had regular features and her face bore a faint resemblance to her father's. Observing all this in one glance, I pushed aside the piece of embroidery on the *chowki* and sat down. I also noticed that at some point Mother had embroidered all the pieces left over from yesterday and that some fresh pieces to be embroidered had been added. Just then Mother said, "Here," and she held out a sealed envelope toward me. Sitting on the *chowki,* I also extended my hand and took hold of the envelope, flipping it back and forth to look at it.

"It's sealed," I told Mother.

Mother looked at Husna. She made some sign, and Mother said, "You may open it. Her father has given it to her."

I opened the envelope. On the cream-colored paper inside the following was written with a broad-tipped pen:

This document is on behalf of Ali Muhammad, alias Ladlay, son of Ali Husain, alias Dulare Navab, resident of Peepal Tree House, Chowk, City of Lucknow. Though of sound health, I have grown old, an age when a man begins to feel closer to death. I am, therefore, leaving this testament.

Let it be known that I earned my living in weekly markets. I sold Badshahi Manjan in three separate markets; Pahari Oil for pain, injury and impotence in two; and performed magic acts in one. On the seventh day I rested.

I have only one daughter, Musammat Husna, who will become 30 this winter. She was going on 15 when my legs became useless and now, for the past 15 years, she has been supporting me through her earnings from chikan embroidery. Inasmuch as she is my only child, whatever I own legally belongs to her. However, the purpose of this document is not to reiterate this fact, but to declare that nothing from my belongings kept in the wooden chest are to be given to my daughter. Nonetheless, every single one of those belongings must be shown to her so that she will know what she has not received.

Signed, Ali Muhammad, alias Ladlay, written in his own hand.

After I finished reading the document I looked at Husna. "This is his will."

"Will?" she asked, a little taken aback. Then she thought of something, looking perplexed.

"It's about his belongings."

"His belongings?" she asked looking at Mother, and became even more perplexed.

"Read it aloud," Mother told me.

I started to read out loud. Coming to the Pahari Oil I hesitated a little, then, skipping it, I continued to read on. After I'd finished, I folded the sheet and put it back in the envelope. I gave the envelope to Mother and then walked over to the well in the courtyard. I was marveling at the fact that this piece of writing belonged to the man who used to sell Badshahi Manjan at Nakhkhas and who used to frighten me a little. I also felt a desire to see the contents of the wooden chest that Husna was not to receive, and to see Ladlay writing something.

I saw Husna leaving. I stood up, but just as I was going over to Mother a couple of neighbor women came in, so I again sat down at the well. The neighborhood women had started to call on Mother more frequently the past several days. They helped her with the household chores. Mother seemed well now but her hand trembled quite a bit. Even so, when I came over to her after the women had left, I saw her sitting in bed embroidering. She glanced up at me once and continued with her work. I thought she would want to talk about Ladlay's will, but she didn't open her mouth at all. After watching her pass her needle through the piece for some time, I said, "Mother, your hand is trembling badly."

She didn't respond. I sat down near her on the *chowki*. For a long time I looked at the embroidered pieces, flipping through them until sunset arrived. Mother bundled the pieces and, after putting them aside, she looked at me. "Today is Thursday," she told me.

"I know," I said. "Where are the matches and the lamp?"

On my way back from the cemetery I roamed around for a while before going home. When I did get back I saw that Mother had already gone to sleep and that my meal was laid out on the *chowki*. Shortly after eating, I also went to sleep.

3

Mother had already finished all the pieces well before noon the next day. She cooked food, gave it to me to eat, and then said, "Son, will you do something for me?"

"What?"

She bundled up the pieces, gave the bundle to me, and said, "Take this to Husna. She'll take it over to the Lala's."

"I know where the Lala's shop is. I can take it over," I said.

"No, no," Mother interjected hurriedly. "You take it to Husna. She has to also get some fresh work for me."

"I can bring that too."

"The account also has to be settled," she said, and then she again said, "Listen …"

I listened to her. Once again I went to the Peepal Tree House and tapped on the door with the knocker. Again the same male voice said, "Coming."

But it was a very old woman who answered the door. She peered at me as though trying to recognize me. Without trying to recognize her I said, "I've brought this stuff over."

"What stuff?"

"Chikan embroidery," I said. "It's to be taken to the Lala's shop."

"All right, wait here," she said, and went inside. Returning shortly she said, "Come in, he's calling you."

The small *devrhi* led into an unpaved courtyard. There was a thatched roof on one side, a *daalaan* on the other, and a scraggly hedge of henna on the third. Behind the hedge were two small, rusted tin roofs with curtains of sackcloth hanging from them. The woman led me into the *daalaan*. There, after so many years, I saw Ladlay.

He was half-lying and half-sitting on a bamboo-framed bed. I didn't notice any significant change in him except that his hair, entirely black before, now had the reddish gloss of dye. I glanced at his legs but they were covered with an old blanket.

"Sit down, Mian," he said after acknowledging my greetings. "Put that thing over there."

The old woman took the bundle from my hands and put it on the wooden chest in the corner of the *daalaan*. Then, pointing at a *chowki*, she said, "Make yourself comfortable, brother."

I sat down on the *chowki* and looked at Ladlay.

"Bitya has gone to the hospital," he informed me. "She said that you would be coming. Do you want to leave a message for her?"

"Just that she should bring back fresh work," I said, "and that the account ..."

"I'll tell her. Everything will be taken care of," he said, and then he told the old woman, "His mother taught our Bitya chikan embroidery."

"Don't I know that?" the woman said. "I took her there myself several times."

"You're absolutely right," Ladlay said.

He chatted with me for a while, mostly about the art of chikan embroidery and my education. He spoke softly and calmly, and his conversation was very refined. I realized that I couldn't converse with such polish. Finally I got up to leave.

"Bitya's been gone for quite a while," he said. "You can wait a while longer if you like. She should be back any minute now."

"No," I said. "I have a lot of work to do."

Before he could ask, "Mian, what do you do?" I said salaam and walked out of the *daalaan*, his voice trailing after me, "Please do give sister my regards."

I was feeling pleased with myself for having evaded Ladlay's question. But by the time I reached the Chowk it occurred to me that he should have asked me that question when he was inquiring about my education. A few more strides down the road I became convinced that he already knew the answer to that question. Husna must have told him. "But who would have told Husna?" I asked myself, and then answered myself, "Mother, obviously."

Sorry for myself, I felt angry toward Mother. By the time I reached home, I had made up my mind to have it out with Mother. I'd even decided how to proceed: "Mother, what's this? First, you don't let me do anything, then you go about complaining to the whole world that I don't work."

But I didn't get a chance to carry out my plan. Mother had died shortly before I reached home. Perhaps she'd been struck by paralysis, or maybe it was a heart attack. Before dying she was only able to tell a neighbor woman where she kept the money.

4

Everything that followed from that point on seems like a dream. I vaguely remember that women gathered inside the house and men outside, and that I was doing whatever I was being told to do. I had taken the money from the place Mother had indicated and, without counting it, had given it to one of the men. Accompanying the bier to the cemetery, the fog lifted briefly from my mind and I complained that Mother was not being buried next to Father. I was told no empty space could be found around his grave.

Starting the next day, women began to visit my house to offer their condolences. Most of them were burqa-clad women who did chikan embroidery. I didn't know any of them so I just sat quietly on the *chowki* while the neighbor women talked with them. I had no interest in their conversation, but it did surprise me a little that so many women knew Mother and that the news of her passing had reached them so quickly.

The neighbors sent me food for the next three days. Husna also showed up on the fourth day with several women in tow. After talking with the neighbor women for a while, she came and stood near me. I kept sitting with my head down for some time and then I lifted it up to look at her.

"Please go over to the Lala's shop," she said. "He's asked for you."

"He's asked for me?"

"He said it was something important. Besides, some money matters need to be settled."

"When is he at the shop?"

"All the time," she said, and after a pause, "I tried to come that day, but …"

Without caring to finish the sentence, and pulling her veil back over her face, she left along with the other women.

That night food was sent over from someone's house but I sent it back. I recalled that on the day of Mother's death I had taken out her money and handed it over to somebody and he had returned the remainder when we got back from the cemetery. He had also accounted for the expenses, but I hadn't paid attention. I took that money out from under the pillow and I had just started counting it when a neighbor woman came in with the food I'd returned. I had played in her lap as a child and called her Khala [Aunt]. It was she whom Mother had asked to swear on her oath the night of the riots to make sure that I ate my food. Now the same Khala was asking me to eat on my oath. I said I would eat in the bazaar, but she considered all bazaar food poison. We kept going back and forth for quite a while. At long last I pulled the money out from under my pillow, gave it to her and somehow made her agree that she would arrange for my meals with that money in the future. She left, but only after I'd eaten. For the first time since Mother's death I felt a sense of ease and, because of it, I felt my loss of her more fully.

The next day I went to see the Lala.

It was a big shop with two doors. The Lala's two sons were minding the business. There was a constant flow of workers, male as well as female. The Lala sat a short distance away from these people on a low *takht*, with a bolster behind him. He was a very immaculate old man. His eyebrows had started to turn grey. In front of him he had a small box with a bundle of papers on it, which he was rummaging through. I went and stood in front of him. After a while he raised his head and gave me a look. I greeted him and said, "You sent for me."

The Lala glanced at me a few times sizing me up, then with great courtesy he said, "Come, brother, come. Come over here."

I took a seat near him on a corner of the *takht*. He told me that he had heard of Mother's death from Husna, adding, "What can I say, brother, it's like my hands have been chopped off."

He talked about Mother for quite a while and praised her work. He also asked me about the details of Mother's illness and her burial. And then he turned his attention to the papers. After some time he raised his head and said, "Yes, I did send for you. For one thing, I wanted to settle the account." He removed the papers from on top of the box, opened it, took out some cash and putting it in front of me said, "These are her earnings from the last few days before she died. Put it aside, but count it first brother."

It was not a large sum by any means. I picked it up and counted it. The Lala signaled for me not to leave, meanwhile taking from the box another sum wrapped inside a handkerchief. He held it out to me.

"No, Lala," I said, getting up. "I have money."

"This too is your money, brother. I'm not giving you anything extra," the Lala said. "She saved some money with me now and then in your name. It was not possible to save any at home so she asked me to put something aside from her wages."

I looked at the handkerchief, then at him. "But Lala, this seems like too much."

"Small sums add up to a lot eventually," the Lala remarked. Now listen carefully to what I'm going to say." He pointed at the handkerchief, "Take some time to get over your grief. When the money begins to run low, come back to me. I'll give you work."

"Lala, I don't know embroidery," I said, "Mother didn't teach me."

"We'll have somebody teach you," he said, "or we'll find you some other work. You have to do something or other now. And we also need somebody we can trust."

Then he became lost in thought. I was unable to decide whether to stay or leave. Meanwhile the Lala started again, "It was just like a game. Sometimes I would say, 'Sister, put your son to some work. How long will he roam around idly?' Sometimes she herself would ask, 'Lala, find some kind of work for my son. How much longer will he have to stay idle?' But whatever work I suggested she considered demeaning. I would respond by saying, 'It's just this kind of humble work that makes one rise. How long did I myself have to comb through the lanes lugging a huge bundle on my shoulder and a yardstick in my hand? And didn't my throat become hoarse from hawking?' She would say, 'You're absolutely right, Lala. But the boy's father was planning to send him to England. Now if he were to go peddling in the streets would that give comfort to a departed soul in his grave?'"

The Lala kept repeating such things for a long time. Perhaps he had gotten into the habit of talking a lot. Finally he tired and I got up. He picked up the handkerchief and handed it to me. Asking me to come closer, he patted me on the head and then ran his hand over the embroidery on my shirt. "We won't get to see such fine work anymore," he said, his head bowing in respect and remaining bowed for quite a while. As I turned around to leave, he lifted his head and said, "All right, brother, go now and get over your grief."

After my visit to the Lala's, I started to light a lamp on Mother's grave every Thursday along with Father's. The rest of the time I just wandered around. At that time it was the only way that I knew of getting over my grief.

5

Without even opening the Lala's handkerchief, I handed it over to Khala next door. I told her emphatically not to forget to let me know when the money was about to run out. I asked her about the money every few days and each time she said that there was still plenty. She would also give some account of the expenses for food, never failing to round it all off with, "An amount the size of an ant's egg, that's how much you eat. What expenses could there be."

This prompted me to laugh, and then I'd go out to wander around some more.

One Thursday I was returning home via the Chowk. Thursday was the day the bazaar remained closed and there was nothing for me to see there. But as I passed by the firecracker shop my feet began to slow down. On the wooden board at the front of the closed shop sat Ladlay, all alone, his feet dangling. I thought he wouldn't be able to recognize me so I kept walking, but when he saw me he shook his head in such a way that I had to stop. I greeted him and asked, "How are you?"

"Just so," he replied, then he pointed at his legs.

Above the board he looked like a fairly stout man, but below his waist his emaciated legs hung down from the board like a pair of dried up sticks. Although Mother had told me about his condition, it was still painful to look at him now. I was at a loss for what to say to him, so I just stood quietly gazing at him while he stared at his sturdy staff which was leaning against the board.

"I learned about sister," he spoke after some time. "I wanted to be part of the funeral procession, to be present at her burial."

"No, how could you have gone in your condition?"

"We are indebted to her for her many favors," he said and then, out of the blue, he popped *that* question, "Mian, what do you do now?"

So you're asking me this *now*, Ladlay? I said in my heart, and simply lied to him, "I'm working at the Lala's."

I had even thought of what I would tell him if he asked me about the kind of work I did. Instead, he asked, "What do you do at home?"

"I fret," I answered. "That's why I wander around all day long."

"Yes, walking around must distract you a little," he said. He didn't ask when, precisely, I worked at the Lala's if I spent my entire day wandering around.

"How are you?" I asked again.

"I'm the same as before, but Bitya has left us," he said and hung his head.

I couldn't grasp his words right away. Before I could ask him, he volunteered himself, "She had come down with jaundice."

I sat down beside him on the board.

"When did this happen?" I asked. "No one told me."

"Who could have gone to tell you," he said and became silent.

There was so much I wanted to ask him but didn't know quite where to begin. So I thought it best to stay with him a while longer and then take my leave.

When he saw that I was about to leave, he started to say something, but stopped. He tried again and stopped again. I, too, stopped in my tracks.

"What is it?" I asked.

He kept scratching the head of his staff with his fingernail, then proceeded hesitantly, "Mian, will you help me a little?"

This was bound to happen, Ladlay—I said in my heart. But I had no money on me at the moment, so I said hesitantly, "Yes, what is it?"

"I've got some stuff. Will you keep it at your place? Just a small box. It won't take up much room."

Saying this he slid down from the top of the board. I leaped to help him but by then he had already planted his elbows on the board. With his elbows still in that position he grabbed his staff and, lowering himself ever so slowly onto the ground, sat down on his haunches. His henna-dyed head rose slightly above his dried up legs as he started to move forward in that position. I was standing behind him, watching how his head and shoulders swayed by turns to the right and to the left, like someone inebriated. To see him move this way was even more painful than seeing him sitting on the board. Perhaps he knew that too, for when he reached the opening of the lane he stopped, twisted his neck and said, "You go on ahead; I'll be there shortly."

I felt relieved and started to walk fast until I reached the Peepal Tree House and stopped at the door. After quite a while I saw him coming. He was very out of breath by the time he reached me. He sat on the door's ledge for a while and then said, "I've put you through a lot of trouble, Mian."

The door was closed. He pushed on one of the panels with his shoulder. The door creaked faintly and opened. He put his staff to one side and picked up his withered legs with both of his hands, placing them on the door ledge as though they belonged to someone else. For a moment I actually thought that he would stand up, leaving the legs and the staff lying on the ledge. Instead, he grabbed the staff and, still moving along on his haunches, entered the *devrhi*. He turned back to look at me and said, "Come on in, Mian, I won't keep you long."

I had not seen Husna in this house, but nonetheless I felt her absence. The *chowki* in the *daalaan* resembled the one on which Mother used to sit and do her embroidery. Ladlay was sitting on the floor, one of his hands resting on the *chowki*.

"I'm giving you a lot of trouble, Mian," he said, starting to inch his way toward a big wooden chest sitting in a corner of the *daalaan*. When he had come near it, he put his hand on the lid and looked at me. The lid came to slightly above his shoulder. I asked, "You want it opened?"

"Yes. I'll try."

It wasn't possible to lift that heavy lid unless one stood at one's full height. So I moved forward and opened it.

"Look inside. Do you see bottles on the right hand side?"

"Yes, they're there," I said. "Shall I take them out?"

"May you live long."

The chest contained plenty of other stuff as well. There was a large enamel bowl filled with such unsightly-looking creatures as snakes, scorpions and chameleons, carved out of some dark-colored wood. Long-bladed knives, chains, cooking pots and the like lay on another side. I had seen this kind of paraphernalia with those who put on magic shows at the Nakhkhas. These things also reminded me that somebody used to sell Magic Oil in the same bazaar. That man also kept the same types of scorpions and snakes in an enameled vessel, all drenched in the Magic Oil. But I, like many other people, took these creatures to be alive and thought that the Magic Oil was actually squeezed out of them. The seller also made this claim.

I took out all the bottles of Badshahi Manjan and set them in front of Ladlay. The bags of herbs could also be seen inside one open bundle. I took the bundle out carefully and set it beside the bottles. Ladlay gave me a surprised look, and then, saying "May you live long," he undid the bundle fully, removed a few bags and looked at the mildew that had formed on the herbs. He shook his head in disappointment. Then he put the bags back into the bundle and tied it securely. When I was returning the bundle to the chest, I spotted the copper coins, some of which were still bent. I took the coins out and gave them to Ladlay. Placing one bent and one unbent coin on his palm he thought for a while, then extended his palm toward me and said, "Put these back too, Mian, I don't need them either."

After closing the chest I turned toward him. He quickly counted the bottles and then said to me, "I've really put you through a lot of trouble today."

"No, it's all right," I said, and then asked, "So you want me to keep these bottles for you, is that all? And their case?"

"The case is up there. I'll have somebody bring it down for

me," he said, pointing at the wall in back of the chest.

As quickly as I had recognized the bottles of Badshahi Manjan, I also recognized the small case that lay on a shelf several arm's lengths above the chest.

"I'll take it down," I said.

Since the chest stood in the way, I found it difficult to reach the case with both hands, so I pulled on the case with one hand while supporting it from below with the other and managed to bring it down. I put it in front of Ladlay. He wiped it with his hand and removed the lid. It was filled with what looked like snippets of cloth. He stared at them in silence for a while and then took them out, putting them on top of the chest's lid until the case was empty. He was now putting the bottles in the case, one by one. I gave a fleeting glance at the bits of cloth. Nearly every one of them had some chikan embroidery on it. I picked one up and examined it. A delicate floral design, neatly embroidered with white thread, appeared at the very top, with some half a dozen copies of it embroidered by a novice's hand below. One after another, I picked up pieces of cloth and gave them a look. They all had specimens of different chikan embroidery. Each with a sample by a master hand at the top, followed by its crude and not-so-crude copies. I stared at them in silence and then I became aware of Ladlay's presence. By then he had already placed the bottles in the case and had put the lid back on, and he had been gazing at me for God knows how long. When I looked at him, he lifted up one hand and reached for the cloth cuttings. Then he tapped the lid of the chest and said, "Maybe we should return them to the chest now."

Sitting the way he was, he struggled with one hand and managed to lift the lid just a little while he attempted to sweep up the cuttings with his other hand.

"Here, let me do it," I said, lifting the lid some more and putting the cuttings into the corner of the chest vacated by the bottles. Then I turned towards Ladlay. Resting his elbows on the floor behind his dried up legs which were stretched out in front of him, he was half-sitting and half-lying and seemed to be dozing. I asked him, "Is that all?"

"Nakhkhas is closer to where you live. Every Sunday I'll come and pick this up from your place and bring it back in the evening. But if it would inconvenience you too much …"

"No trouble at all."

"So then, I'll bring the case over to you by this evening."

"You don't have to," I said. "I'll take it along."

"No, Mian, it doesn't look nice that you should carry my burden."

"It's not that heavy," I said, picking up the case. "I can hardly feel it."

"I'm really very embarrassed, Mian."

"What's there to be embarrassed about?" I said. "All right, you're sure there isn't anything more you'd like me to do?"

"How much I've troubled you today," he said, gathering his outstretched legs with his hands, and then he sat down supporting himself with his staff.

"Well then," I said, turning toward the courtyard. "I'll be at home on Sunday."

"Hang on, Mian. I'm coming too."

I stopped and asked, "Where do you want to go?"

"Just as far as the door, to see you off."

"No need to. You stay here. I'll see myself out."

It occurred to me after I came out that I hadn't offered him my sympathies over his daughter's death, but at the same time it also occurred to me that he himself hadn't given me a chance to. So I didn't turn back.

After depositing the case under Mother's *chowki* at home, I headed straight for the Lala's shop, but, it being a Thursday, it was closed. I returned home. After that I only went out to go to the cemetery.

The next day I went to the Lala and told him that I was pretty much over my grief. The Lala took me into his employ the same day. When I inquired about my work, he said he'd let me know later.

Ladlay didn't show up on Sunday. He didn't show up the next Sunday either. I waited for him the whole day. In the evening I went over to his house. The lower latch of the door had a padlock on it. When I asked his neighbors, I was told that he was seen going out last Sunday morning and that he had not come back since. They had made inquiries about him here and there, but nobody had the foggiest idea where to look for him.

No one tried very hard to look for him either. By and large his neighbors were almost certain that he had gone to some other city and must be begging there.

Weather Vane

1

Our weather vane, which looked partly like a fish, partly like a bird, had quit showing the direction of the wind long before, yet it stayed on our rooftop till my father's end. Now and then my father was asked why, since it no longer did its job well, it wasn't taken down, but each time he replied that it belonged on the rooftop, and if not there, where? Sometimes he added that it was the emblem of our house, and that this indeed was its true function, for who needed to know the wind's direction anyway?

Well, I did. I was fond of kite-flying. But I didn't need the weather vane. During the daytime I often looked up at the colorful kites sailing in the sky. With a glance at any one of them, far or near, I could tell which way the wind was blowing. I could also tell things the weather vane could not: whether the wind was gentle or strong or uneven. In the evening when it got dark the kites were brought down, and the sky looked somehow desolate. From then until morning one might, of course, need the weather vane to learn the direction of the wind, but when the time for kite-flying was over, why would I want to know the direction of the wind?—and even had I wished to, the vane could not be seen in the darkness.

Sometimes after watching a kite in the sky I would glance at the vane and notice that it was pointing the right way.

Whenever I saw all the kites aloft in the hot afternoon sun move slowly in one direction, I would suspect that the wind was changing direction even as it blew, and I'd have an impulse to look at the vane. At such times, slowly, as if involuntarily, but quietly and effortlessly, the weather vane would turn right or left and stop in the direction the wind blew. When that happened, I'd go up to the roof for a closer look.

On one such occasion I heard it make a sound for the first time ever. I drew still closer to it, but now it had come to rest in the wind's direction and was soundless. I looked at it for a long time that day, and from quite close. It had looked like an animal—part fish, part bird—from a distance. Now, up close, its form bore no resemblance to a bird; it looked entirely like a fish, but its maker had fastened it to its anchor in such a way that it evoked a bird perched on a treetop. It had side and tail fins like those of a fish, but from a distance they could be mistaken for a bird's outspread wings and tail, making it appear at an idle glance to be simply a bird, and not a fish at all; perhaps this was also because its business was with the wind and not with water. Distance also made it seem delicate and slim, but now, on closer examination, it looked rather heavy and ungainly. No doubt it had been constructed to endure all manner of intemperate weather and wind.

I had been staring at it for a long time, and just when it had become clear to me that it was only a fish, the thought crossed my mind that it was in fact a bird that had by some strange process turned into a fish. Precisely at that moment my eyes caught sight of a kite flying in a straight line in the direction the vane was pointing, and I sensed that the gently blowing wind was again changing course. Involuntarily my eyes returned to the vane: it was still pointing in the earlier direction, quivering slowly. I pushed it gently in the direction of the prevailing wind, and as I did, again heard it make a feeble sound. I couldn't determine which of its components was making that sound, nor did I realize then that its inexorable decline had already begun, for my attention was fixed on the sound itself, which seemed vaguely familiar to me, though I was having difficulty recalling where I'd heard it. My eyes probed the vane all over. By now it had stopped wavering and had aligned itself with the wind's path.

After that I noticed several times that it was not pointing accurately, and each time it occurred to me that I should tell Father that our weather vane was behaving erratically. Since it did work accurately at times, however, I didn't mention it, but now, the minute I got to the rooftop I would first look at the vane and then search the sky for a kite to determine which way the wind was blowing. Usually the wind was blowing in a direction other than the one the vane indicated. Now and then, though, the wind changed its course and started blowing in the direction indicated by the vane. On those occasions it occurred to me that our vane was not bound by the wind, but rather that the wind was bound by our vane. Strange thoughts came into my youthful mind in those days, the strangest being the notion that not only could the vane turn itself in the wrong direction, it was also quite capable of turning the wind in that direction.

Finally, one day it came to rest in a direction no wind had ever blown. The season of hot, gusting winds had arrived, and the time for flying kites was over. The wind early in midday had started to turn hot and I could feel the sensation of it on my body, although it had not become so strong that I could determine its direction merely by this touch. Even then I really didn't feel a need for the weather vane. I ran downstairs, took a sheet from my stationery supplies and picked up a shard from the broken clay water jar lying in the trash in the courtyard. By the time I returned to the rooftop I had ripped the paper into round pieces, which we called *tikkals*, and pressed them together into a small wad. Standing near the vane I placed the shard under the wadded paper and tossed the entire lot straight up. The shard rose some distance, projecting the wad along with it, then halted in midair for an instant before falling back down alone. The *tikkals* also remained immobile for a second, then scattered everywhere. Just at this moment I heard the shard hit the back end of the weather vane, making a hollow sound, and my attention was diverted from the *tikkals*. The faint vibration in the vane was just dying out. I gently rubbed the back part of the vane with my hand, exactly the way one pats a child after an injury, or an animal when one is pleased with it. And then I looked up. All the *tikkals* were moving in a single direction, from west to east, tossing and turning in the air. At last they disappeared below the rooftop.

I looked at the vane. It was fixed in a different direction from that of the wind. I made a feeble effort to move it, but it had jammed in its position. I tried to move it the other way, but it didn't budge. When I tried to turn it with some force, it again emitted a faint sound and vibrated, and I feared that if I applied more force I might break off a piece of it, or the vane itself. I had drawn back a little and was gazing at it when I heard a voice.

"Why—is it broken?"

A girl was standing on the rooftop of the house that abutted our own. The wind made her diaphanous *dupatta* ripple ever so gently. Her eyes were fixed on the weather vane. Then she looked at me. This girl, and others from the neighboring houses, came up to their rooftops in good weather and talked among themselves in hushed tones. Sometimes one would have a few girlfriends with her. At such times they all talked and laughed loudly. They also looked at our weather vane and pointed it out to each other. I paid more attention to my kite-flying than to these girls, although their voices always reminded me of the cacophony of the little birds that twittered at roosting time in the evening amid the vines covering the low walls of our courtyard.

This, however, was not the time for girls to appear on the rooftops. Seeing this girl standing all alone on her roof in the dead, barren stillness of the noon hour, staring at the weather vane, gave me the inescapable feeling that one of our family secrets had been divulged. Meanwhile she asked again, "Broken?"

"No," I said. "It works all right."

"Oh?" she said, looking at her *dupatta*. "But the wind ..."

"The wind is blowing wrong," I said before she could even finish.

She stayed on a while longer, gazing wistfully at the vane, then she turned around, picked her way slowly over to the stairs on the other side of the rooftop and climbed down.

I thought I might now inform my father that the weather vane had stopped working. But I decided against it, thinking to give it another few days, perhaps. Now, though, I did make several trips to the rooftop every day and, finding the vane always turned in the same direction, came back down. I made it a special point to visit it early in the day. I stared at it until the sun got stronger and the air warmer. Sometimes as I watched I began to doze off, only to be quickly roused by some sound or other nearby. Once I heard some rustling sounds, looked up, and saw the sky filled with soaring kites of different colors, as on certain festival days. I observed this crowded assemblage with interest for a while, then remembered the weather vane and looked back at it. It had oriented itself in the direction the kites were flying. I glanced up at the sky. The kites were moving slowly to the right. Then I looked at the vane; it too was moving slowly to the right. Just as I was about to sit down and inch my way toward it, a gust of hot air slapped me lightly in the face and I was startled awake. The sun had grown quite strong and the ground had started to heat up. I looked at the sky: not a kite anywhere, but I could tell that the wind was blowing west to east from the scorching blasts of its gusts. However, the vane was still stuck in that totally mysterious direction. I rose and went up close to it. The hot gusts of wind violently assaulting its right side seemed to be trying to knock it down from the roof, but it held its ground, like a stone statue, without even a slight shudder. At this I concluded with certainty that it was definitely broken. I hastened downstairs to let Father know. I was also feeling somewhat elated. It was the same kind of elation that children—even grownups, I can say now—feel when they come upon some special news, even if it's bad news, that they can relate to others before anyone else.

As I climbed down the stairs I remembered that in my dream I had also felt angry with the vane, but now, after waking up, I couldn't recall the reason for my anger.

I went straight to the reception room in the outer side of the house, where my father had taken up residence. He lay there reclining in a large rattan chair. Although I had observed him in this room and in this chair for a long time, I remembered the days when he used to live in the inner part of the house and would often be obliged to go to the reception room, because quite a few people came to see him. Many visitors still came to see him now, but at this particular time only my mother was sitting near him, and at first I didn't see her. I had just walked in from the bright sunshine outdoors and the room seemed to be filled with darkness. I couldn't even see the rattan chair, though I was certain my father was in it, and moreover that several visitors must also be present in the room. That's why I blurted out the news about the vane excitedly, almost as though I were making an announcement. I even volunteered that it had been stuck in the wrong position for the past several days, and that its parts had probably gotten jammed. Meanwhile the darkness in the room dissipated and I saw that Mother had her finger on her lips, asking me to be quiet. So I was. I would have stopped talking anyway because I'd already said all I wanted to say. I glanced at my father. He was lying almost flat in his chair, covered up to his waist with a sheet, his eyes closed, his tranquil face indicating he was sound asleep.

I was silent; still my mother again brought her finger to her lips, beckoned me to come near her and whispered to me, "He had a very hard time falling asleep."

Just then my father's voice was heard, "What happened? What's broken?"

My mother again gestured me to be quiet and whispered, "He's sleeping."

My father's face and closed eyes continued to reflect the same tranquility. Both my mother and I kept looking at him and then she said softly, "Are you busy?"

The season for flying kites being over, I had all the time in the world. I shook my head to indicate that I was free.

"Well then," she said, "sit by his side for a while. I'll be back soon."

I sat down near my father. Mother got up to go out but then she hesitated and turned around, signaling me to come to her and asked me even more softly, "Really, it's broken?"

I was about to nod when my father made an effort to turn over. This was very hard for him to do, and he needed help to accomplish it. His eyes opened a few times and then closed. Mother came to his chair and carefully helped him turn over, and he went back to sleep. Mother bent over and whispered into my ear, "Don't tell him that," and went out of the room.

I sat gazing at my father in silence. He was still stretched out, his eyes closed, his face tranquil. Lying with his eyes closed he asked, "Since when has it stopped working?"

Is he sleep-talking? I asked myself. Just then his eyes opened and a look of pain crept over his face. He was again trying to turn over. When I tried to assist him, he stopped me and said, "Wait until your mother's back."

"Shall I call her?" I asked, rising.

"No. She'll be along soon," he said, and then he asked, "Since when?"

I felt obliged to give him the answer, and was rather happy to have this obligation. I remembered the day the weather vane had begun to work erratically, how the wind had been changing course while the vane failed to move along with it. I told my father all that had transpired since that day forward. What I didn't tell him he asked himself: "You tried to fix it, didn't you?"

I flatly denied it. He kept gazing at me with his half-open eyes. I suspected that he didn't believe me, and I started to feel a bit guilty. And as a guilty person will, I was coming up with another lie when he said, "All right, but don't tinker around with it, and ..." he placed his hand on mine, "don't tell your mother."

He wanted to say something more, but hearing a sound at the door, he stopped. My mother had brought something for him to eat. Before she had reached his chair he gently pressed my hand and said, "Don't tell anyone."

The very next day he was surrounded by visitors, all of them talking about the weather vane not working properly.

2

As I have said, the visitors who came to see my father were numerous. They included some who were unfamiliar; they came once or twice and then I didn't see them again. Besides these changing visitors, there were also those who came to see him regularly, almost every day. If one of these showed up after an absence of several days, my father inquired after his well-being in a partly disgruntled, partly anxious voice. Even though most of them were residents of our own neighborhood and lived in houses close to ours, I rarely saw them out in the lane or street. However, I did see some of them on their rooftops, mostly taking sun in the winter, when I went to our roof to fly a kite. At those times they all wore ordinary domestic clothing, but when they showed up at our house they were dressed from head to toe in formal clothes, as if they had come to attend a party. My father, too, whenever a visitor was announced, went to the reception room not in his home clothes but fully dressed as if to receive a guest. But ever since he had made the reception room his permanent living quarters he had put aside this formality, preferring to pull a sheet up to his shoulders rather than change into formal clothes.

Often I had to escort the visitors to this room. Sometimes my mother also commissioned me to carry fruit drinks and such like to show the guests hospitality. At those times I enjoyed catching snippets of the conversation in progress, though I never could hear them well enough; I never really stayed there very long. All I knew was that they all, my father included, made exceedingly fine conversation and laughed heartily, although the minute I appeared they would hush up somewhat, and I would quickly leave.

That day, however, when I entered holding a tray of food all the visitors suddenly grew quiet and looked at me so attentively that I was disconcerted and, for no reason, began to feel guilty, although all of them, including my father, were smiling and looking at me the way kindly elders regard young people. After some time one of them asked, "Son, that thing on the rooftop, the thing that shows the direction of the wind ..."

"It's broken," I quickly told him, and then, embarrassed, I looked at my father, but he was still smiling. Gently, he said to me, "Tell them everything."

"Yes, Mian, from beginning to end," one of the visitors said.

And I told them everything I had already told Father, but not that I'd tried to correct its direction.

Silence followed and continued for a long time, until the smiles slowly evaporated from their faces. Then someone said to Father, "That's why we keep telling you to have it taken down."

In response my father gave the same explanation mentioned earlier. After that they started talking of other things and I left with the empty tray.

In the days that followed I heard the weather vane mentioned in that room many times. Gradually, though, it came to be mentioned less and less, perhaps because the number of daily visitors had also started to dwindle.

Before two winters had passed only a few visitors still came, and even that remainder thinned down to one or two at a time. In the end only a single visitor was left, and he came only sporadically. He had started to experience difficulty in walking. Someone from his house escorted him to our place, then returned later to help him go back. But even in those days this visitor was dressed from head to toe in the finest garb.

One day, while I was present, I heard this last remaining visitor talking once again with my father about the weather vane. He put the same old questions to which my father gave the same old answers. That day, for the first time ever, I butted into my elders' conversation and asked them something that had often crossed my mind, "Can't it be fixed?"

"Who'll fix it?" my father said in a despairing tone.

"Only he could have fixed it, son," added the visitor, even more despairingly, "who made it in the first place."

My father shook his head abjectly in agreement, then said, "Others will only make it worse."

The visitor nodded despondently, agreeing with my father. A long silence ensued, during which the two men seemed to be carrying on a nonverbal conversation, until the servant from the visitor's house showed up to take him home.

After he was gone, my father called me over to him.

"Give up worrying about *that,* son," he said, "worry about your mother instead. You do see, don't you, how she is killing herself caring for me."

Right then Mother, who had perhaps been waiting for the visitor to leave, walked into the room. She was holding a round brass salver in her hands. A brazier was set in the middle of the salver and some kind of oil was being warmed in a small vessel over the burning coals. The oil's aroma filled the entire room and it began to feel safe and warm. She placed the salver on the floor close by the chair, removed the vessel, holding it with the edge of her *dupatta*, and set it too on the floor. Father kept looking at her, and then he said, "You do all the work yourself; aren't there other people in the house?"

Without troubling to answer him, Mother removed the sheet covering his body and started to fold it.

3

Surely there were other people in our house, but my mother personally took care of all of Father's needs. She never complained of anything at all, so none of us ever imagined that she was killing herself. One morning, though, time went by and she didn't get out of bed. By afternoon her dead body was lying in the midst of all our relatives, from near and far.

That day other people in the house did everything for Father and kept the news of Mother from him. In the evening, however, instead of inquiring about Mother, he himself gave the news of her, adding, "I'd already foreseen it."

He didn't talk to anyone for several days. Various people in the house tended to his needs. Visitors had long since stopped calling on him. And no one came even when Mother died, or perhaps someone came but I didn't know about it. Now we made sure that a member of the household was with him at all times. I also went into his room several times during the day and stayed for quite a while.

One evening as the birds were twittering in the vines of our courtyard, I stepped into the reception room and found the last of the visitors with my father. Only with difficulty was I able to recognize this person, but I couldn't calculate how many days had passed since he had last come to our house. He was sitting in the visitor's chair rather precariously and one of the servants of his house, who himself seemed to need assistance, stood behind the visitor to keep him from pitching this way and that. This time around the visitor was wearing ordinary at-home clothes and it occurred to me that he used to sit on the rooftop of the house adjoining ours in the winter sun with a single cloth draped around his waist. Back then, though, I had not thought he was one of my father's visitors.

He was sitting in silence with his head bowed, his body rocking this way and that in uncoordinated motion. My father too was silent. It seemed neither was conscious of the other's presence. And I too was standing silently. As I continued gazing at the two of them I once again felt as though they were talking to each other without words. I was near the headrest of my father's chair, the visitor directly in front of me. His body was still shaking, the servant supporting him, sometimes with both hands and sometimes with one while fanning his head with the other as if shooing away flies. I looked closely by turns at the visitor's face, then at my father's and, with no evidence, began to suspect that they were on the subject of the weather vane. My suspicion became a certainty when all of a sudden my father said aloud, "Use? No use at all. All the same, it's not getting in anyone's way, is it?"

The visitor nodded over and over for a long time as if in confirmation. Finally, his old servant took him home, supporting him along the way; twice the servant himself staggered and nearly fell down.

By the time the rains ended everyone sensed that my father was not likely to last much longer. He was receiving more care now; his every need was diligently attended to. Whenever something was done for him he would bless all of us in a happy tone. But he also appeared to be thinking about something. I spent most of my time in his room now, watching him think. Sometimes his eyes were open fully and sometimes only halfway, yet he didn't seem to be looking at anything. Seeing him in this condition I thought sometimes that he was remembering Mother and sometimes that he was thinking of the weather vane. But his condition was deteriorating so rapidly that pretty soon I forgot about the vane and about Mother as well.

There were no longer any clouds to be seen in the sky. Still, without a cloud in sight, lightning would suddenly flash, prompting people to speculate as to whether it might rain. One night—it must have been during the last days of the waning moon—the silent flashes increased in frequency. I was in my father's room. Here it remained dark even during the day, but that night it seemed as though very strong lights were being turned on and off in unison. My father would appear, sitting in his chair, and then disappear in darkness. The experience of this light and darkness, which had quite pleased me in my childhood, now made the room seem as though captured in the throes of a terrifying struggle. My father was lying quietly. Suddenly I sensed that he was caught in the throes of death. I thought of calling to the other people in the house, but just then I heard his weary voice: "Who's up there?"

I drew close to him.

"Up where?" I asked, bending over him.

"Up on the roof," he said. "Someone is talking up there."

I strained my ears. It was quiet all around, with only the flash of lightning; I strained harder; now even I began to hear a faint sound. It was a little like the moaning that issues involuntarily from the mouths of very old people when they move. But it didn't appear to be coming from the roof, or from anywhere.

The faint sound was heard again, and I quickly remembered that a long time back it had come from the weather vane, once when the wind was changing direction, and a second time when I'd tried to turn it in the direction of the wind.

Lightning flashed again and I saw that my father was trying to hear that sound. I said, "I'll go up and have a look."

He didn't respond. I quickly left the room, crossed the courtyard, climbed up the staircase and came out onto the roof.

The weather vane could be seen sparkling intermittently a little distance ahead. In a flash of lightning it looked like a delicate object of pure silver. I walked up to it and looked it over. It was still locked in the same mysterious direction, without movement or sound. As I walked round it repeatedly, looking at it closely, I caught sight of a figure standing on the roof of the house adjoining ours, the face illumined repeatedly from the light of the flashes.

Some old woman in her declining years, or so it seemed. I was having great difficulty trying to make out who she was and was straining to get a better look at her each time there was a flash.

Finally I remembered that in the past she used to come up to the rooftop with her women friends, and even alone. Now she was alone, watching the weather vane from her rooftop and apparently oblivious of my presence. I also tried to act unaware of her presence and, taking slow steps, I climbed down the stairs.

In the room my father was still lying on the same side. I tiptoed in, but he heard my footsteps and asked, "Was anyone there?"

I told him that only the weather vane was up there. And also that it was quiet and hadn't changed direction. For a long time he continued lying on the same side in silence. Just when I had convinced myself that he had fallen asleep, he drew a deep breath and said, "Do see to it that it's taken down," and drew another deep breath.

I stared in the direction of his voice. The lightning had meanwhile stopped flashing and a cloud was thundering somewhere in the distant sky. I came close to my father and looked intently at his face in the dim glow of the only light burning in the room. He was sleeping soundly, the cloth lying on his chest heaving gently up and down.

After that, as we had all already sensed would be the case, my father didn't live much longer. He was entirely lucid until the end, and he even talked a little. Mostly he gave blessings to those who looked after him, expressing regret now and then that he was causing them inconvenience. As for the weather vane, he never once mentioned it. This didn't surprise me as much as the fact that he didn't even mention Mother. However, on his last day he did utter Mother's full name, including "daughter of …," but before he could say anything further, he died.

4

After my father's death I became preoccupied with household matters. During this period new levels were added to several houses in the neighborhood. This new construction surrounded my house to such extent that it was no longer possible to see the weather vane from the ground. I hadn't noticed it at first, but one day on my way home I came to the corner where my rooftop and the vane atop it had once been visible. The newly built upper story of a house blocked the sight of both of them. I went around and looked from different angles. The vane could not be seen from any of them.

After circling around unsuccessfully a few times, I returned home and went straight to the roof. The vane was still fixed firmly in its direction, without the slightest change in its appearance. Its drab color and clumsy shape made me wonder with surprise how it could have appeared delicate and silvery in that flash of lightning. Even so, it looked more charming at this moment than it had that night.

The next day a workman began tearing down the small platform to which the vane had been anchored. Before starting he had made it clear that he would take the vane down carefully, but he wouldn't be able to reattach it at the correct angle again. Upon which I had told him, "No reattachment will be needed." After that he had set to work, relieved.

He removed several layers of mortar from the platform, until the vane's anchor grew loose and began to wobble. As he continued to work, the man turned toward me and asked, "Do you have a place in mind for it?"

I hadn't thought about that at all. I made a quick decision and said, "On a high shelf or inside a big trunk."

"It'll get ruined lying around like that," he said, and then, after a pause, added, "I have a suggestion, if you'd agree to it."

And I accepted his suggestion.

5

Not as many visitors call on me as called on my father. These visitors keep changing, and they come only when they have something to ask me or I have something to ask them. When they first come, every visitor looks with curiosity, at least once, at the odd-looking fish resting on its anchor on the small platform built in a corner of the reception room. Its tail and its head are exactly the same height from the floor, which is why it looks flat sitting there on the tip of the anchor, and no one looking at it ever thinks that it's a bird whose business is with the wind. Everyone thinks of it as a decorative object so no one asks me what it's for. Nor do I tell anyone that it's our weather vane, which no longer works.

Custody

1

There's no longer anyone around now who can even tell what exactly was sold at Nauroz's Shop. It can be surmised though, on the basis of a few scattered oral traditions and some true or false stories, that when this town was just a small hamlet, Nauroz's Shop had already been in existence for quite a long time. Back then it was right in the middle of the community so the residents of the hamlet could pretty much buy whatever was needed there. If this was really the case, one might also surmise that it was the hamlet's only shop in those days.

It remained in operation for several generations, and in each generation the owner's name remained Nauroz. Even though he had a different name before taking over the shop, after taking it over everyone called him Nauroz, probably because the shop was called Nauroz's Shop. These people had some genetically inherited condition that caused every Nauroz to eventually lose his mind. When this happened to one Nauroz, another Nauroz took his place at the shop, losing his own mind in turn, followed by another Nauroz who worked there until he also lost his mind. This continuing streak of madness was considered to be the result of some curse. People who believed in this sometimes got into spirited discussions about whether the curse was on the shop, the owners of the shop, or the appellation "Nauroz."

When a Nauroz would stop showing up at the shop, one knew he'd gone mad. But there was also one Nauroz who clung to the shop even after losing his mind, with the result that within a few days the shop itself began to look crazy. I belong to the time of that Nauroz.

At first, nobody suspected that that Nauroz had gone mad. Although, if they had given it some thought, it wasn't something that was hard to figure out, because, in a matter of just a few days, the shop's condition became such that when it opened one day it would be chockful of clay toys. The next day it would be filled with domestic birds, and it was selling their meat on still another day. One would see herbal plants on one day and piles of firewood on another. But instead of suspecting that something was the matter with Nauroz's mind, people became fascinated by the changing merchandise, indeed to such an extent that they started betting among themselves about what item was likely to be on sale the next day when the shop opened. Only when this fascination had spread like an epidemic did some people, who had repeatedly lost their bets, suspect—the suspicion itself spreading like an epidemic—that Nauroz had gone crazy. Then it became a routine that people would gather outside the shop every morning and, when it opened and its curtain was lifted up, they would distribute among themselves whatever merchandise could be had and they would leave whatever they thought its price was on top of the high *takht* with heavy posts, in a corner of which Nauroz sat huddled.

One day, when the curtain was lifted, Nauroz couldn't be found anywhere. The *takht* was empty and two baby girls, who hadn't yet learned to sit properly, were playing with two clay balls on the floor. Naturally, this became the talk of the town. And also, naturally again, neither the girls nor the clay balls, which were perhaps their toys, were considered the shop's merchandise. So, it could be said that that was the first day Nauroz's Shop had nothing at all to sell.

After searching unsuccessfully for Nauroz people began to look for somebody who could take care of the girls because, so far, they had remained unclaimed. People also looked for a new Nauroz. The absent Nauroz did have a brother, but he was already mad and, according to some, mad since birth. Even so, he was brought in and repeatedly made to sit on the shop's *takht*, but, each time, he fled the minute the opportunity presented itself, finally disappearing altogether one day as his brother had done earlier. During this time the girls stayed with me because I used to live above Nauroz's Shop and one of the staircases to my place started inside the shop. Also, nobody else agreed to raise them.

And, although the shop was no longer in business, people had meanwhile also started calling me Nauroz. Then, one day, I took stock of the shop.

The shop became visible immediately upon reaching the last bend in the road which ran along the edge of the jungle by the ruins. In place of a door it had a heavy curtain that was raised onto two bamboo poles like a canopy during business hours. At that time, from a distance, it sometimes looked like a child who had just woken up and was yawning, and sometimes it looked like a ferocious animal opening its mouth before making a sound. I was interested in both of these similarities and occasionally, in moments when my mind was wandering, I would think about them.

The shop's floor was somewhat lower than the ground outside. The space inside the shop was much bigger than that of any other shop in town. Its high walls had compartments and shelves in several places, or thick wooden pegs and heavy iron hooks. There were also many crisscrossing rope webbings that were tied to these hooks. Bamboo poles and chains hung from the rafters with hooks on either end. In many places the floor also had recessed compartments of various sizes that had been reinforced with bricks and then covered over with fitted boards. Brass rings were attached to these boards for lifting them up. There were also brass rings in quite a few places on the unpaved floor, but there were no compartments beneath them. I pulled these rings up one by one and examined them closely but detected no movement around them. Just foolishness—I thought; then I counted these pointless rings. Could it be, I wondered, that their number corresponded to the number of generations that had run Nauroz's Shop? I examined the entire shop again. Wall compartments, floor compartments, pegs, webbings, bamboo poles and chains suspended from the ceiling, all manner of empty jars and baskets lying about on the floor—they all revealed that the shop had seen many generations, but they gave no clue as to what object or group of objects was, in fact, sold there.

I sat down on a corner of the *takht* with the heavy posts that the last Nauroz used to sit on before his disappearance. Although bereft of saleable merchandise, the shop still looked so full that it was impossible to move about in it freely. As I continued sitting on the corner of the *takht*, I felt that all the objects scattered around me were more precious than the merchandise that had been sold here. But I would not, I resolved, let a single one of these objects be sold, at least not as long as I'm called Nauroz. Meanwhile, I remembered the original intent with which I had come to examine the shop. Once again I looked at each and every object and finally felt assured that there was nothing here that could possibly harm small children. I climbed the staircase inside the shop returning to my place where both girls had by now woken up. The minute they saw me they both started pushing themselves toward me, but without making any noise.

They had now learned to sit. In fact, for several days already they had even started to crawl forward a bit as they sat, only to fall down after going a distance of one or two lengths of the hand. I sort of liked the way they tumbled over silently and remained silent after falling. I sometimes sat them up and started to back away slowly, snapping my fingers. They would crawl forward with their eyes fixed on my hand and eventually tilt to one side and fall. This was my only game with them up to now. After playing with them for a little while I would pick them up and carry them downstairs to the shop. There, I sat them on the unpaved floor and, all of a sudden, they would come to life as though a fish's young had been released into water. After pushing their tiny bodies toward everything at first, one started off in the direction of the jars while the other aimed for a basket. They only went a short distance and then both toppled over on their sides, picked themselves up again and moved, then again fell back down. This time though, as one of them tried to raise herself, her eyes fell on the hooks hanging from the ceiling. In trying to reach for them she fell on her back on the soft dirt floor. I picked her up and sat her down. Then I brought a basket over to her. The other girl had come upon the ring handle of a board and was trying to eat it. I sat her beside the basket too and one of them got involved with it. At that point I looked at them closely. Their faces and bodies were so similar that they could be considered twin sisters. The thought struck me that I might have given water, etc., twice over to just one of them on several occasions. Only after a close and protracted inspection could I perceive some slight difference in their features, but what stood in the way of identifying each of them individually was their eyes. Their eyes were absolutely identical.

These belonged to a race I wasn't familiar with. I even thought that eyes such as these were only seen in paintings, although, unlike the eyes in a painting, soft lights seemed to glimmer somewhere deep inside of them. After watching them for some time it occurred to me that I had absolutely no connection with these girls and I had been made responsible for them for no reason at all. As a result, some of my habits had been changed and certain routines had pretty much been done away with. I realized that because of these girls I had had to stop going to the jungle, or even observing it sitting inside my quarters. So I thought, in fact I more or less decided, to keep them at Nauroz's house, which I could see clearly from my place. This was a small, old, but strongly-constructed building that stood a little ways from the shop and it was where Nauroz had lived with his brother. I'd never gone there, and even Nauroz himself had never spent much time there. I remembered him. As long as he had remained of sound mind, he had routinely closed the shop at sundown and walked off toward some place outside of town. He would return late at night, sometimes even the next day, empty-handed or with some merchandise for the shop. Besides his brother, he had no relatives, at least not in this town where he had his shop. His dealings with the townsfolk didn't go beyond what was required by the business, and with me they were even less. Nevertheless, I looked over his accounts now and then, and he had given me the space above his shop to live in. He sometimes wandered in there of his own accord, but it never seemed that he had come to see me, so I didn't attempt to talk with him much. Still we did converse a little and then he addressed me as Saasaan, informing me that that was my family name. He always took a place near the window that stood directly above the entrance to the shop. If he spotted an approaching customer from there, he immediately got up and went quickly down the inner staircase, arriving in the shop before the customer.

My own favorite place to sit was by this same window because the trees in the jungle by the ruins were clearly visible from that vantage point.

I sensed a faint glimmer of those trees before my eyes and realized that I had actually been staring at the girls' eyes this entire time. They had stopped playing with the basket and were feeling frightened watching me staring at them so intently. When I straightened up, they started to crawl toward me with halting steps, their frightened eyes still glued to me. I felt that even though they were frightened of me, they still wanted to rush over to me. I took a few steps backwards; they started to crawl faster. Before they tumbled over, I lunged forward and picked the two of them up together. Their tiny hearts were racing. I succeeded in making them smile, but only after a long time.

2

I had no experience with raising children. Nonetheless I was raising them, somehow or other. At first I had thought that the people who lived in the area around the shop, whom I knew quite well, would help make my job easier. Because I read and wrote for them, they cared for me a lot and were also quite mindful of my needs. But when I brought up the subject of the girls around them a few times, they took off in other directions.

One day a nice breeze was blowing so I took the girls out as far as the bend in the road. After playing with them on the soft grass at the edge of the road for a while I was taking them back when I saw four or five important townsmen standing in front of the shop's curtain. I asked about a few ordinary things, to which they gave cursory answers and then became silent. They remained silent for quite a while. Then one of them, without pointing at the girls, said, "Nauroz, don't bring them out."

"Why, is something wrong with that?" I asked.

"Not really, but ..." he said, "Who knows who they are."

"Why," I asked, "couldn't he have had daughters?"

"Daughters?" he said. "Then why did he abandon them?"

"He had gone mad."

"So does every Nauroz, Nauroz. But even a mad man ..."

After that all of them stared at me for a long time without speaking.

"Even so," I said finally, "is there something wrong with bringing them out?"

"Who knows who they are?"

"No one has come forward to claim them?"

"None at all," he said. "But does that mean there isn't any claimant?"

"I'm taking care of them," I said, "all by myself, and I think their claimant is Nauroz."

"Which Nauroz?"

Several answers came as far as my lips and stopped. All of them, perhaps expecting an answer, had their eyes fixed on me.

"All right," I had to say, "From now on I won't bring them out."

That very day I removed the curtain from the shop's entrance and installed a regular door in its place, making doubly sure that it could be closed from both inside and out. The townsfolk helped me a lot in this, just as they always had in everything else.

After making sure the door was secure I decided, first of all, to make a visit to the jungle by the ruins.

I used to go there fairly regularly, almost daily, before Nauroz's disappearance. I did this to survey the interior of the jungle, but mostly I ended up just enjoying the sights of the ruins, though not completely, since they couldn't be seen clearly because of the tremendous density of the trees. The trees' serpentine growth along the stone balconies that were drooping over dilapidated columns made it well-nigh impossible to determine the true form and character of their crooked trunks or their cracked bark. The vines, running recklessly here and there, going up and down trees, brought to mind children playing in the garden of a home and prompted a person to touch them involuntarily. Sometimes these vines seemed to be laughing and crying without even breaking the silence of the jungle. Dense

straw bushes, sprouting from the dirt which stuck to the surface
of the rocks, soared higher and higher, while the aerial roots of
ancient trees seemed in need of help, struggling to find a way to
the soil through the crevices in the rocks.

It was impossible to gauge the dimensions of the exterior
of the jungle from this vantage point, but the window above
Nauroz's Shop where I sat—and Nauroz as well—did offer a clear
view of the jungle's treetops, so there one could get some idea of
the jungle's outward form, at least someone who had also seen the
jungle from the inside while wandering through the ruins.

This wasn't a real jungle, just a cluster of old trees and wild
bushes growing through the crevices of the ruins' massive walls,
whose exact height or depth it was impossible to ascertain.
Wherever the crown of one tree was found, the root of another tree
started up in a crevice nearby. More trees grew in the lower area,
taking on bizarre forms in order to escape from the shade of the
trees growing in the areas up above. These lower trees went straight
up for some distance, then bent to one side and continued along
parallel to the ground, and then straightened up again after passing
the perimeters of the shade. To the eye, this multi-storied jungle
looked like the garden in a scenic photograph that had wrinkled in
several places. When the wind blew quickly, the fluttering sound of
paper, like the pages of a book being riffled, could be heard. But
when the wind changed into a dust storm, the sounds of the jungle
also changed, frightening the townsfolk at night. Strange noises rose
and fell in the fluctuating gusts of the storm and a man could, if he
used his imagination, find similarities to other sounds. Perhaps the
townspeople did just that. Why, without trying even I heard cackles,
sobs, laughter, cries of joy and pain, reprimands and laments in the
sounds of the jungle on several occasions while I was sitting by the
window above Nauroz's Shop.

Sometimes, right in the middle of these sounds, suddenly a
sound as if somebody was screaming something could also be
heard. This may have been the sound of large limbs snapping and

their barks splitting. At least I thought so. But people spun stories about that sound. These stories had been circulating for generations and were perhaps as old as Nauroz's Shop. Each story invariably ended with the sound definitely being heard just before the onset of madness in a Nauroz. Nobody could ever figure out what the sound said, but it was rumored that every owner of Nauroz's Shop understood it sometime or other, after which he stopped taking care of the shop and went mad, or went mad and stopped taking care of the shop.

However, this sound was not heard by the Nauroz of my time—the one just prior to me. Several times, of course, the sound was heard and no Nauroz lost his head, but the townsfolk maintained that this was the first time a Nauroz had ever lost his head without the sound being heard. Perhaps this was why people at first didn't think that he had gone mad.

That day I didn't enjoy my excursion in the jungle and came out rather quickly, yet it was evening by the time I reached home. When I went down the inner stairs I found the shop dark and still. I strained my ears and detected the sound of breathing. Standing by the staircase, I snapped my fingers a few times and strained my eyes to see two tiny blurred figures crawling toward me. A short while later I felt the touch of their slender fingers on my shins. Before long their arms were wrapped around my knees. And so, holding on to me, they stood up for the first time ever.

In a few days they'll be running around, I thought, and carried them upstairs. From that very day I started to have them sit with me by the window. The season of strong winds had just set in. With their painting-like eyes they could see the trees of the jungle swaying from side to side and they felt happy hearing the flutter coming from them. When, however, the wind became a gusting dust storm for the first time, they became frightened. But I didn't take them away from the window. In a little while they started to listen to the strange new sounds of the jungle with even greater interest. Apart from those occasions, I usually kept them down in the shop and listened to them play, laugh or shout from my quarters. When their noises started to grow faint, I understood that they were feeling tired. I would then go down and bring them up. Watching me with the twinkling lights of their eyes, they would soon fall asleep.

They slept through and didn't wake up until very early in the morning. Well before that I would go downstairs and open the shop's door fully. After making sure that the fresh breeze outside had filled every corner of the shop, I would close it securely. Then I would bring them downstairs, where there was nothing to harm them.

3

Those days were such that I began to think they would never change, nor even the seasons, although now, on the far side of the jungle, where the sky met the earth, a dusty greyness appeared in place of the twilight red, and, at times, the entire sky had a dull muddy color. Somewhere high up the gusting storm left small silent flashes of lightning in its wake. I looked at them and thought of them as a common occurrence because in Nauroz's Shop everything from top to bottom remained intact.

But late one evening when the sounds of laughter and playing had grown progressively fainter and finally stopped, I padded quietly down into the shop and stood by the staircase snapping my fingers. Without straining my eyes I saw the fuzzy shapes crawling toward me, felt a touch on my shins and then a grip on my knees, and I bent down to pick both of them up together—but only a single body came into my hands. I extended one hand and groped around, thinking one of the girls was just running away from me as a game. I then turned the lights on in the shop and I knew immediately there was only one girl there. I searched for the other like a madman. I stuck my hand in the empty jars, turned the baskets upside down, lifted up the boards over the underground compartments, and even tugged on the rings which I knew for a fact had no compartment underneath. I looked at the ceiling and the hooks hanging from it, and three times I climbed the staircase which I myself had come down in the first place. The shop's curtain was rolled up in a corner. I unrolled it and spread it out on the floor, tapping on each of its folds. Finally, I shook the shop's door, only to discover that its panels were not closed tightly. I didn't remember closing the door that morning, or even opening it, but it was open now.

They were just here, I thought. I went out of the shop and started walking straight ahead. It occurred to me that I had left the door wide open. I scurried back. By the time I was halfway I had already begun to convince myself that I would find them both there when I got back. However, I only found one of them sitting there looking at me. Her eyes were heavy with sleep and she appeared to be waiting for me to tuck her in. I picked her up, brought her upstairs and laid her down on my bed. I started patting her clumsily as though I wasn't trying to put her to sleep but rather to wake her up by shaking her vigorously. Even so, she soon fell asleep watching me. I looked at her closely for a moment and then, after covering her, I went out. I had only walked a few steps when it struck me that I had again left the door open. I turned on my heels, closed the door securely, and started off.

I stopped at the bend. Here, the road curved sharply to the right and continued on to other small towns. On my left, the jungle's entrance looked like a crumbling black wall. I had walked some distance along the road when I imagined that I heard a sound in the jungle and, without thinking or planning, I just plunged into that maze of rocks and vegetation. Never before that evening had I ventured into the jungle at night; it was pitch dark inside. I heard a sound like the fluttering of paper. The entire jungle reverberated with it, and it didn't have any significance. As I was thinking of getting out of there, the wind developed into a storm and sounds inundated me from all sides. Somebody said something loudly somewhere quite far away, and all the other sounds immediately grew louder. In the middle of all these sounds, I repeatedly imagined that I heard the sound of a child, but sometimes this sound came from on top of the crowns of the trees growing at the highest elevation and sometimes it appeared to be flitting through the rustling bushes. I was hearing quite a bit more besides. I just kept climbing up and down the piles of rocks as I made my way pushing aside the vines and shoving the bushes apart. Meanwhile, at some point I suddenly realized that the dust storm had passed and the jungle was quiet. I also stopped and stood in complete silence for a while.

There's nothing here, I finally told myself as I peered out into the darkness here and there. In the distance the jungle's entrance appeared like a big bluish blob. I came out, stared down the road that headed toward other small towns for a while, and then I headed back to the shop, but I stopped near it. It wasn't yet late at night so I turned toward the streets of the town and knocked on the door of whatever house I found in front of me. I gaped at the residents of the house with suspicion, queried them insanely, and, by midnight, had earned the displeasure of the entire town. My own displeasure was no less. When I mentioned at the very first door that one of the girls was missing, I was asked, "Which one?"

After that everyone asked me the same question. In answer I grilled them with senseless questions and then pushed on to the next place after making them terribly unhappy. Finally, the important men of the town stopped me at one place and asked me the same question: which girl had disappeared? and then they started to grill me. They also said that I shouldn't have left the girls alone in the shop in the first place, at which I said, "They weren't alone, I was."

They looked at me the way someone looks at a madman. Then they tried to make me believe that I hadn't been negligent and that, therefore, I shouldn't let it bother me. At this I looked at them the way someone looks at a madman. I did give them some answer or other to every one of their questions, but when one of them, who had been especially kind to me, said, "Nauroz, you shouldn't have been suspicious of everyone like this," I remained silent. And when another man said, "And as far as suspicion goes ... well, we too can ask what you did with her, can't we?" Still I remained silent.

Whatever they said subsequently, I didn't respond. They interpreted my silence in different ways and talked a lot trying to put me at ease. Nevertheless, I continued standing there in silence. At last, the kind man stepped forward, almost embraced me, and said, "Perhaps this had to happen, Nauroz. And ... in a manner of speaking ... look at it this way: only *one* has disappeared."

"Only one ..." I said, "but which one?"

Naturally, he had no answer, and yet he was about to say something, but, before he could do so, I freed myself from his grasp.

"I've been out here for quite a long time ..." I told him in a tired voice, then returned home.

The only girl was sleeping on my bed as before. I spent the rest of the night watching her. I became convinced that the one who had disappeared was exactly like her; so I couldn't tell, even with one girl sleeping right in front of me, which of the two had, in fact, disappeared. This question was gnawing at me in a million different ways, but the question of which one was the one who was still with me, bothered me even more. While I was still grappling with these questions morning dawned. The girl began to squirm and I became busy taking care of her.

For the next three days I kept her near me constantly. For three days the townsfolk dispatched men to other small towns. For three days these men kept coming to me again and again to look at the girl so that they could describe her to others, and the girl kept clinging to me looking at the outsiders. On the fourth day I noticed that her face was changing: it had become longer, her eyes had become larger than before, and the lights deep inside her eyes now appeared dimmed. She remained absolutely silent at all times, unwilling to let go of me even for a minute; in fact, one of her hands continued touching my body even when she slept. Sometimes a faint sob escaped from her lips, as if she had been crying for a long time, although I had never seen her cry, and I wondered whether the other girl might also be in the same condition. Thinking such things I went down the stairs and out onto the road at night, peering everywhere without feeling any curiosity. Soon I heard the sound of crying upstairs. But when I got back, stomping up the stairs, I found her still asleep and silent.

4

Those days, which I thought would never change, had changed. And now, to me, these days, these new days, didn't seem likely to ever change. I remembered what the kind man of the town had said, "The disappearance of a child is far worse than its death, Nauroz."

I hadn't said anything in response, but I could tell now why it was so. There were times when I longed for the news of her death to arrive, and there were times when I only wanted to hear that she was alive. I could see that the one who was still with me had gradually begun to wither away.

At last, when a strong desire to do something had arisen inside of me, although I didn't quite know what to do, then, late one night, Nauroz turned up.

He had concealed himself inside of a big blanket and couldn't be seen clearly in the darkness. He knocked gently at the shop's door three times and softly called out Saasaan to me. I peered at him from the window and then went down and opened the door just a little. He didn't come inside. When he sat down on the ground a short distance from the threshold, I realized that it was pointless to try calling him in, so I sat down near him on the threshold.

"One disappeared," I informed him as soon as I sat down.

After that, without asking him anything myself, I told him everything: from the moment when my groping hand had found only one body inside the shop, to the moment when Nauroz, wrapped in the darkness of the town's night and a big blanket, sat down on the ground outside the shop—I didn't neglect telling him anything.

Nauroz heard me out in silence and remained silent for quite a while after I was finished. Then he said, "You aren't willing to give her up." And, without waiting for my answer, added, "And she isn't willing to stay with me."

Then a tiny body slipped under my arms.

"She looks a little sickly," Nauroz was saying, "but she'll get better living with you, and with the other one."

"You took her, Nauroz?" I couldn't say anything else.

"You guarded her well, but ..." he stopped and touched the door, "it isn't good for doors that are usually closed to be left open one day."

He drew a deep breath, passed his hand over the door, and said, "That's why a curtain always hung over the entrance."

"I've saved the curtain," I told him, then asked, "Shall I get rid of the door?"

"No," he said, feeling terribly distressed, "it's already installed."

"Go now," Nauroz said, "take her to her."

I stood up, and said as I was leaving, "Don't go yet, Nauroz."

"I'm here."

The girl pressed against my chest was sound asleep; nevertheless, I heard her sob faintly. I walked quietly upstairs and laid her down on my bed too. The other girl was crying in her sleep. I patted her gently and placed each girl's hand on the body of the other. Suppressing a desire to stay there and watch them for a long time, I went down to Nauroz. He had stood up meanwhile and was rubbing his hand over the door. When he saw me he turned around and started going away slowly. I lunged forward and caught up to him and he stopped.

"How is Brother?" he asked.

For a while I struggled with whether to answer his question or not and then said, "He's disappeared too."

"They didn't search for him?"

"No."

He started walking again with slow steps. Seeing that I was walking along, he touched my shoulder and said, "All right, go back to them now."

Knowing that I wouldn't get an answer, I still asked him, "Where did you go, Nauroz?"

He kept walking forward without saying a word. I asked, "Where do you live?"

I realized that this was more or less the same question, and Nauroz didn't answer this one either. Instead, he started walking faster. I again rushed forward, caught up and walked alongside of him for some ways.

"What are they to you?"

"Merchandise," he answered in one word and then became quiet.

"Who was their mother?"

"They don't have a mother."

"What was she to you?"

"Merchandise," he again replied with the same word and became quiet.

Will he keep this up forever? I wondered, and asked, "Why did you abandon them, Nauroz?"

"Why, you were there, Saasaan?"

"Saasaan," I repeated, and told him, "My name is now Nauroz."
His feet slowed down.

"Two Naurozes at one time …" he said thinking something and said faltering, "Then one of them has to be crazy."

I realized without a shred of doubt that he hadn't lost his mind, but just then his tone took on a wild quality, "Go back!" he howled, "What you've installed and forget to close is open."

I grabbed his hand, "Nauroz, if I need to see you urgently …"

"At the mouth," he answered, again with a howl, "sometimes and only …"

"You live in the jungle?"

"In the jungle, only … humans don't live in the jungle."

He jerked his hand free and concealed it under the blanket. I clung to a corner of the blanket and asked like an obstinate child, "Why did you abandon the shop, Nauroz?"

"It was time to become mad," he answered, and the blanket was no longer in my grasp.

He was walking so fast now that I couldn't keep up with him. I also remembered the shop's door that had been left open and I spun around and went back, walking more or less as fast as Nauroz was.

Both of them were sleeping, with the hand of one resting on the other. I bent over them and watched them for the longest time. Now their two faces looked different to me, but even that night, very little of which was left, I couldn't figure out which one of them had disappeared. The faint sound of their sobs was also identical.

"Where did you find her, Nauroz?" the kind man asked.

"By the ledge of the shop's door," I answered.

"Surely somebody had kidnapped her," he said, "but then why did he bring her back?" He started to think of something.

"Perhaps he couldn't keep her amused."

"Children aren't kidnapped to be kept amused, Nauroz," he said and went off still lost in some thought.

That was the only conversation concerning the girl's return that I had with the townsfolk, although I had feared that I would get tired of responding to a barrage of questions and eventually having to repeat myself over and over. I had imagined that the stream of visitors coming to see her would continue unabated for several days, leaving me little time to attend to the needs of those tiny patients. But no one besides the kind man turned up at the shop, and the girls recovered so expeditiously that I was truly amazed. Before long everything was back to the way it had been, except that I no longer opened the door to let some fresh air in. I looked out the window at the jungle as before and I also brought the girls to the window for longer stretches of time. They mostly played downstairs in the shop as before, while I, in the comfort of my quarters upstairs, listened to them laughing and screeching.

I not only took strolls through the town, I also headed off to other towns, and roamed around in the jungle as well. Many times, I went to the mouth of the jungle at midnight and returned only after going some distance into it in the dark. Nauroz had said that humans didn't live in the jungle, but in this one, by the ruins, I didn't even see an animal, and yet I suspected that Nauroz's place was there somewhere. I even tried to search for him several times during my daytime strolls, but I never did find traces of anyone living there. I did, however, develop some ideas about the ruins during these searches.

At first I had thought that these were the ruins of some large building, but now I was absolutely certain that they were from some hamlet that, without having been visited by any heavenly or earthly disaster, had been progressively deserted over the course of time. Later on, the pressure of the growing trees had shaken its foundations and hidden most of it, and various dust storms had rocked the trees violently, causing the hamlet's remains to crumble. How long it might have taken, I didn't try to guess because I couldn't stir up enough interest in me for these lifeless ruins, and I didn't try to imagine how they might have looked in their original condition. I didn't even slow down when I passed by the crumbled walls, drooping columns, and piles of rubble. One day, though, quite a distance in from the mouth, I mistook one of the small ruins for Nauroz's Shop.

The parapet wall of an elevated passageway arching over the depressed ground had become so twisted that, from a distance, it created the illusion of an open mouth. I walked over to it quickly. The passageway seemed rather dark; I called out softly, "Nauroz!"

A feeble echo of my voice was heard from inside the passageway, and I entered it. There was absolutely no trace of anyone living there. The area of uneven and unpaved ground was more or less about the size of Nauroz's Shop. The natural round- and oval-shaped pieces of stones were strewn here and there. I carefully evaluated everything and made sure there was nothing there that could harm children. The thought occurred to me by chance that, if it became necessary, I would bring them over here. After that I came out of the jungle.

That day there was a small fair going on near the road that ran right in front of the shop. In one area some shows for children were taking place. I noticed these children were laughing loudly and calling out each other's names. One of these groups was singing some song over and over in their less than perfect language. I could vaguely understand some of the song's words. As I listened, a thought suddenly crossed my mind, but I couldn't decide whether it was merely a suspicion or if it was a revelation, so I left the fair's shops behind and went toward Nauroz's Shop.

They were now running around inside the shop, the impressions of their tiny feet forming and dissolving and forming again all over the dirt floor. I didn't have to snap my fingers to call them to me.

Hearing the sound of my footsteps, they themselves came and stood at the base of the staircase. I bent over to look at them and went up a few stairs backwards. They tried to climb the stairs too, using both their hands and their feet, and one of them fell down softly on the ground. I picked them up.

I'll have to install a barrier here—I thought, and started climbing up. At the top of the stairs I halted. And one here too—I thought again as I stood the two of them on the floor. Then, placing my hands on their shoulders, I talked to them for the first time, the kind of talk one does with children, but instead of saying something in response they merely laughed and clung to me as they looked at me again and again. I called out the names of several common, everyday objects that were around and they kept laughing and holding on to me.

This is the limit, I told myself.

I used to listen to their sounds coming from downstairs, but I never thought about the fact that they were just prattling, not really saying anything. I rummaged around and eventually located the two clay balls that were found in the shop with them. They had been fashioned by baking fermented grey-colored clay and they were much lighter than their size suggested. It seemed that, if they were dropped, they would bounce on the floor for a long time. I twirled them around and inspected them. All this time the girls' eyes remained fixed on my hands. I maneuvered the balls on the floor in front of them for a while. Then I rolled them from side to side, and both of them immediately became interested, more interested than they had been in anything up until then. I raised the barrier at the top of the staircase and, leaving them to play with the balls, went over to sit by the window. Pretty soon they started to make laughing and screeching sounds and I thought about those sounds.

They could imitate sounds. Just about every sound of the jungle during a dust storm, and also that other sound of someone saying something in a loud voice, could be distinguished in their shrill sounds. Then I realized that they were also uttering some meaningless word-like sounds. I got up and went to them. Whenever they uttered such a sound, I showed them one of the objects that was around and repeated the name of it over and over again myself, and I also let them say it. I did this so much that before long, when I uttered the word, they would look at the object and repeat the word themselves.

In a matter of days they'll start talking to me, I assured myself as I sat them on the bed. They were happy and insistent on continuing their verbal word game, but I went on looking at them wordlessly.

Suddenly one of them let herself fall backwards on the bed and then closed her eyes. Her lips opened and closed two or three times. I bent over and looked at her. Her lips opened and closed again. I placed my hand gently on her head, and she, her eyes still closed, uttered in a slightly heavy voice, "Saasaan."

Then she opened her eyes, sat up, and looked at me, laughing innocently and mischievously. I stepped back a few steps and looked at her. Then I came near her, placing my hand on my chest and saying, "Nauroz!"

Without shaking her head no, she said, "Saasaan!" and looked at me laughing as before.

"Nauroz!" I said again, pointing at myself with one finger, "Nauroz, Nauroz!"

She lay back on the bed again, shut her eyes and repeated, "Saasaan! Saasaan! Saasaan!"

Her voice sounded somewhat like a moan, and she had her hands folded over her breast, just as I did when I slept. Sleep came over her even as I watched, still her eyes opened just a little and then closed, and I heard her drawn out whisper, "Saasaan."

It was a brief sound and a soft whisper, but to me it seemed as if the wind was howling accompanied by all the other sounds heard among the trees of the jungle.

5

It appeared as though I was the slow-witted pupil of two tiny female teachers. In naming objects and remembering those names they were so quick that I couldn't keep up with them. Still, just like the moves of a game learned by a new player hover in his mind day and night, so too their voices echoed continually in my ears, even when—in fact, even more so when—the two had gone to sleep. Just before falling asleep, one by one, each would shut her eyes and utter in a prolonged whisper, "Saasaan."

Afterwards, until they opened their eyes and broke into laughter, I would continue to feel that, instead of two tiny girls, two small women lay before me.

After they had fallen asleep I tried to remember the names they had spoken and I jotted them down on a piece of paper. Then, looking at the paper, I memorized those names. Slowly the number of pieces of paper was increasing and in my free time I nearly exhausted myself poring over them.

Meanwhile, I had stopped paying attention to other sounds. But one day I heard a loud, unfamiliar voice under the window, "Is this Nauroz's Shop?"

The voice of one of the townsfolk came from a short distance away, "It surely is, but it doesn't sell anything now." And then this voice also moved under the window.

The first voice mentioned a couple of everyday items, and the local man gave the names of several shops in town and directions on how to get to them. Then another voice said something softly in an unfamiliar language and the first voice said, "Up there, in the window, there was a girl just now."

"There are two," the local man pointed out, "Nauroz's daughters."

The unfamiliar voices exchanged a few words with each other, after which the first voice said, "And their mother?"

"I haven't seen her."

"When can one meet with Nauroz?"

"He's gone away somewhere. He had become mad."

"Does he have a relative?"

"I don't know much. The other shopkeepers, perhaps they would know."

The unfamiliar voices again talked to each other, and the first voice said, "Who's raising the girls?"

"Nauroz ... I really don't know much, please ask the shopkeepers. Come, I'm going that way."

Then all the voices receded into the distance and disappeared. Just then the girls, who had been silent up until then, attracted my attention toward them.

I couldn't quite figure out the conversation that had transpired below. I decided that it was accurate to think that that conversation, any sentence of it, or rather any word of it, was totally without significance. Nevertheless, that day, at midnight, I found myself at the mouth of the jungle. After staring at its howling darkness for what seemed like an endless stretch of time, I returned home. I was back at the jungle's entrance again the following night, waiting in vain. The third night I prolonged my stay trying to hear something. I felt the entire jungle was filled with some sort of fanciful hissing sound. This was not the sound of wind; it wasn't the sound of any kind of movement at all. Perhaps then, the sound of the ruins—I wondered, and I felt as though what I had in front of me was not the mouth of the jungle but some eye, and the ruins, hidden in the darkness, were staring at me through its black socket. Even so, after going through the futile exercise of staring into that hissing darkness, I returned home.

On the fourth day, about mid-afternoon, I stepped out. When I was returning, after wandering aimlessly along the straight road, my eyes fell on the open door of Nauroz's house. It usually stayed open and from a distance it looked like the door of an empty house. However, that day I spotted people moving around inside. I'd never seen them in the town before. Two or three were also pacing about outside the house. They glanced at me briefly; the real focus of their attention was the shop, which they were looking at up and down, up and down, over and over. This may have been the reason why, when I started to climb up the outer staircase to my place, I felt several eyes creeping along my back.

The two were waiting for me. As soon as they saw me they leaped toward me and, in order to please me, started doing all the things that only children can do; I too did all the things a grown-up can do only to please children and no one else, which don't necessarily indicate his own pleasure. But I didn't let them go anywhere near the window, although I myself did go to it several times. Each time I observed that a strong, steady wind was bending the trees of the jungle to one side, and one eye or another in Nauroz's house was glued to the window.

Today I'll find him no matter what, I decided, even if I have to set up fires in half the jungle. But I was still asleep after midnight. I was awakened by a knock at the shop's door. I waited for a while for someone to call out, then I got up and looked down from the window. I recognized the blanket-wrapped Nauroz and went downstairs. He held my hand gently and let go of it, turning around to go. I closed the door securely and started walking behind him, leaving some distance between us.

His stride was chaotic and uneven. Had I not firmly resolved to see him, I would probably have hesitated to go with him. I noticed that in spite of the uneven strides he walked along soundlessly. I started to walk carefully, my own strides becoming uneven in the effort. If anyone had seen us then, he surely would have wondered who we were and why we were out at that hour.

Such an observer, I concluded, wouldn't have been likely to think anything good about us, and I wasn't thinking anything good about Nauroz either.

Meanwhile the mouth had appeared. The space inside looked a little brighter to me even though there were no signs of morning. Nauroz grabbed my hand and entered the jungle. Bending along several curves, we passed by a row of crumbled columns, arrived at a hexagonal platform, and halted. A small pile of wood was burning in the center of the platform, giving off the scent of some medicinal oil and sending up curls of smoke.

Nauroz gave me a look.

"Both are OK," I told him. Then I said, "Some people have arrived at your house."

"They are my relatives," he said, "foster relatives."

"Have they come looking for you?"

"No. They've come after making sure that I've disappeared."

"Why have they come?"

"That they will tell themselves," he said, and then asked, "Is Brother with them?"

"No," I said, "but maybe he is. I didn't see him."

"Also some very old man?"

"I haven't seen him either," I said, feeling embarrassed without cause.

Nauroz sat down on the edge of the platform. I too sat down, a little ways from him. In the dim glow of the fire I observed a trace of madness on his face, although it was also apparent that he was living in hardship and shadows of that flitted across his face every now and then making it appear as if his madness had vanished.

"They haven't come to the shop yet, have they?"

"Well, yes they have," I said, "three days ago."

"Three days ... No, those must be some other people," he said. "They must have come to buy something."

"Yes, they had some things to buy," I said, "but they also wanted to see you."

I gave a full account of those unfamiliar sounds, in as much detail as I had done earlier when I reported the disappearance of one of the girls. Nauroz listened to everything with his head lowered. Even after I had finished, his head remained down for quite a while, until the night came to its end. I was waiting for him to say something, but he was thinking, who knows what. A strong odor of burning wood was wafting from the platform. I looked that way. Thick smoke was rising from the platform. Soon the smoke burst with a soft noise, and flames leaped upward. I felt as though we were sitting inside of a deserted place of worship. The flames arched over to one side and a loud rustling sound was heard. I lifted up my head and saw that the tall peaks of the trees were being buffeted about so much that I could often see the increasing blueness of the sky between them. After quite a long time I looked at Nauroz. He was still sitting in the same position as before and the light from the burning wood was beginning to grow dim.

"Nauroz," I called out to him softly.

"They are different people," he said. "They've come from some distant place. They're not bad. They've come for the ruins."

"Why did they want to meet you?"

"They have come to learn something about the ruins. And now they want to know more—perhaps everything."

"But why did they want to see you?"

"They've also come to learn something about the race that built these ruins ... or rather, that built the buildings whose ruins these are."

"But why did they want to see you?" I asked again; at the time I couldn't think of any other question.

"Both belong to the same race," Nauroz said in a soft voice. "Haven't you looked at their eyes?"

I remembered how lights glimmered in their painting-like eyes. Then some other questions came to my mind.

"Who was their mother, Nauroz?"

"She had the same eyes," he whispered.

"Who was she?"

"She is no more," he said, a wildness appearing in his tone, "I've already told you."

"What was she to you?"

"I've said that too."

Then he looked at me with tremendous goodwill and placed his hand on my shoulder. "She is no more," he said it again. "Her people too have all perished, except for the two who are with you."

"Why have your relatives come?"

"Perhaps those ruins-people have made it to them."

"To them ..." I checked myself.

Nauroz took close stock of me. He was completely visible in the growing light of the morning. In appearance he usually looked absolutely like a madman, but in that light, with his eyes lifted upward, he looked more like the sage of some untamed nation, and exactly in the manner of a sage he said, "One must endure everything." And then the wildness returned to his eyes and the howl to his tone, "Because one has to endure everything."

He began to look very tired. I suspected that he hadn't slept for several nights. Still I asked him, "Your relatives ... would you like to see them?"

He didn't answer.

"Will I have to talk with them?"

Nauroz remained silent.

"Shall I tell them about you?"

He continued to sit silently. I called out to him softly, "Nauroz!"

Still he didn't open his mouth.

I stood up and walked over to him. He got up too. He repeated, without any wildness this time, and entirely like a sage, "One has to endure everything."

He turned, and I didn't even suspect that this was the last time I was to hear his voice. He wrapped the blanket around himself securely and walked away with a perfectly even stride toward where there was, perhaps, another exit from the jungle.

I too turned around after he had disappeared and walked out of the jungle.

6

Shortly after my return, although it was still quite early, I was informed that Nauroz's relatives had arrived and a meeting had been called, in which I too had to participate, to settle the matter of his house, shop, and other effects. I hadn't had a full night's sleep for several days and could hardly remember, except for his last sentence, anything of my conversation with Nauroz in the jungle a short while ago, so this information didn't make any particular impression on me and I spent the time before the meeting taking care of the girls' needs and making them laugh a bit.

"We've abandoned hope of ever finding Nauroz," the kind man said to me.

"You won't find him anymore," I said without a shadow of a doubt, and I believed it just as fully in my heart.

"These people aren't at all hopeful either," he said, pointing toward Nauroz's relatives.

We were all gathered behind Nauroz's house and all those people were sitting leaning against the wall of the house. I couldn't make a good estimate of their number, but Nauroz's brother was among them. I looked at him for a long time. His face bore traces of wounds that had healed. Even though two burly men standing on either side of him held him tightly, something welled up inside of him that staggered his restrainers now and again.

Sheer power of madness, I thought, and the kind man, seeing that I was looking at them, said, "He's under the supervision of these people, and so is that one," he pointed at the man who sat in the middle of those men but a little ways from the wall.

He was a very old man, completely toothless and bald, and without eyebrows either. His eyes were so devoid of luster that it was difficult to know whether he was blind or not. He was counting something on his fingers, jotting something down on the palm of one hand with a finger of the other hand as he went along, and making a point of looking at the sky each time before making an entry. He was wrinkled from head to toe and even though I was looking at him with my own eyes, I was having difficulty believing that a man could be so old.

"He's an old Nauroz," I heard the kind man say, "from two generations ago."

I was somewhat amazed to see that he was sitting with absolutely no support. Sheer power of madness, I thought again.

"And if the present disappeared Nauroz could be found, these people would watch over him too," the kind man said, "as they should."

"Naturally," I said.

I had guessed that the kind man would be talking on behalf of those men, so I kept looking at him. One of the relatives moved forward and whispered something to him. He nodded in reply and said to me, "Now there's only the question of Nauroz's daughters."

"How can anyone say they are Nauroz's daughters?" I said.

"But no one has come forward to claim them."

The answer came to my lips but stopped there. The kind man, finding me silent, said, "After all they must be related to someone in some way."

"They are merchandise from Nauroz's Shop," I said.

"And Nauroz's Shop—whose property is that?" one of the relatives blurted out unexpectedly.

"Anyway," the kind man made a sign to the speaker with his

eyes and then informed me, "they have decided to close down the shop; this decision too is theirs to make now."

"Naturally," I said again.

"Now a decision has to be made about the girls, Nauroz."

"My name is Saasaan," I said.

"Ah, your family name," he said, feeling a little melancholy, "I know. Anyway, now the decision about them ..."

"The decision about them too is the right of the relatives," I said.

"You've taken good care of them. They are all grateful to you."

"They are kind."

It seemed that he was finding it difficult to know exactly how to proceed further. Even I, because of lack of sleep, was beginning to feel weary. Since he had been kind to me all along, I said, "They were given to me temporarily in the hope that Nauroz would turn up. Now his relatives have rights over them, and their further upbringing is also the responsibility of his relatives. If they like, they can take them right now." I didn't feel surprised that I had said it all so easily. "But they aren't accustomed to seeing anyone other than me." I said that just as easily. "If they had been allowed to go out with me ..." Perhaps there was a slight tone of displeasure in my voice.

The kind man moved forward and embraced me. "They'll get used to it," he said. They're still very young. After all, they became accustomed to you, didn't they?"

I quietly freed myself from his grasp, and he said, "We think they should first be kept at Nauroz's house, and then ..."

"But for two days, at least, no one should go near them."

"Absolutely. These people will stay somewhere else during that time. Whatever you say will be done," he said and tried to embrace me once again, but I left.

I made several trips up to my quarters, each one from inside the shop, collecting their playthings and the other items they needed and then I carried those over to Nauroz's house. This took longer than I had expected, perhaps because I checked out Nauroz's house a little on each trip. It was constructed entirely of stone and was very sturdy. The ceiling and walls of the shop and my quarters, on the other hand, had become decayed and didn't look like they would last long. The thought struck me that I should have kept them in the house from the very beginning. Then I went and brought them over too.

As I had expected, they became happy when they saw the new place and so many other new things at once, and they became so engrossed in playing that they didn't even notice that I was leaving and closing the door behind me.

The big dust storm also struck the same day. A few of the townsfolk were expecting its arrival for several days already. They were weather experts and they could, just by looking at the color of the sky and the pattern of the winds, predict even the time of ordinary dust storms. The past two or three days I was also noticing how in the lightening and darkening dusty-colored sky, the sun sometimes looked faint yellow and sometimes it was as white as the moon; how the wind stopped blowing, then suddenly picked up with a gust restoring the blue to the sky; how the wind then moved erratically, as if stumbling every step of the way, and then the sky turned dusty. But I didn't know, nor did anyone tell me, that these were the signs of a big dust storm.

After closing the door of Nauroz's house, I walked slowly until I came to the bend. At the mouth of the jungle I saw a vehicle of some new style from which baggage was being unloaded. Besides small tents and other essentials, the baggage included tools like the ones used for measuring land and timber. Two men from a neighboring town were giving directions to the laborers who were doing the unloading. Watching all this without much enthusiasm, I moved on. I was taking slow strides and I had no idea how far I had gone until my feet began to ache. Only then did I realize that I had walked all the way to the outskirts of the next town and that sundown was fast approaching. The breeze had stopped completely and, partly because of the stagnant air and partly because of my having walked without interruption for quite a long time, I began to feel hot. I turned around and started walking back, but it soon became very difficult for me to walk at all. I flopped down on the grassy area by the edge of the road and I might have dozed off there were it not for the fact that, with the first blink, it felt as if somebody had pushed me to one side. Startled, I opened my eyes. There was no one around. Must have been a dream, I thought and stood up. I had walked only a few paces when somebody gently pushed me sideways. I realized that it must be because of the wind, which was blowing in gusts. Suddenly it started to blow faster and faster. I was moving forward without putting much pressure on my feet. I knew now that I was in the path of a dust storm and it was no ordinary storm. The mouth of the jungle and, from there, my home were not very far, but the wind suddenly changed direction and my feet strayed off the road. Then the wind changed directions several times and the dust also began to rise so it became difficult for me to keep my eyes open. I had no idea how far I had walked along with the wind nor how many directions I had gone in. Sometimes the wind gusts swirled downward and then spiraled upward with such violent force that it became difficult for my feet to stay on the ground. It seemed as if those dreams in my childhood, the ones in which I soared like a bird, would come true that day. Just then the gusts let up a bit. I heard the sounds of the jungle, some branches crackled, and the smell of medicinal oil wafted into my nostrils. The wind changed direction again and the smell disappeared.

My back struck against something hard and I saw that I had come to the place, a short distance from the road and on the other side of a small, grassy slope, where a series of dry, flat-topped low hills began. The road lay in front of me and, parallel to it, the breached wall of the jungle's outer trees swayed, appearing as though it would collapse any minute. My fatigue had vanished. I continued on, ascending one of the hills. The force of the wind was lessened here because the neighboring hills were somewhat taller and the hilltop was shaped like a platform with a dip in the middle. Feeling safe from the storm's onslaught, I sat there and began to look at the road and the jungle as if I were a spectator.

Two small tents went rolling down the road with those measuring instruments caught in their ropes. After one of them had rolled some distance, it got stuck on something on the side of the road, while the other puffed up a little and was swept up by a large spiral of wind, disappearing in a whirl. Then my eyes fell on the carriage I had seen at the mouth of the jungle. It was moving along on its own in the middle of the road. Heading straight toward me, it faltered, as if trying to remember the way. It spun around in its place a few times and then went hurtling back in the direction it had come. Just then a violent gust of wind touched down near the carriage, causing it to swerve sharply to one side of the road and then leap to the other before overturning and somersaulting down the slope. Only one of its wheels remained on the road, spinning like a potter's wheel. Finally it too disappeared.

I looked at the jungle. I had never seen it from this angle and this elevation before. However, at that moment I was unable to determine its outward appearance because the jungle, along with everything in it, was in a terrible state of turmoil. Sometimes the treetops became flat and fluttered like green flags, and sometimes they separated into small clusters colliding with each other. Tall bushes were pressed down, allowing a clear vision of the ruins through the openings in the wall of trees. Sometimes it seemed that the wind had gone completely mad or was frolicking with children, sometimes that there were many different winds, all vying with each other for possession of the jungle's trees. The wind paused briefly, gathering strength, and forced itself up from the ground. Now it looked as though the hairs on the jungle's entire body had stood on end. This was just the beginning. Later on it sometimes felt as if the sky, like some hissing python, was trying to sweep up the entire jungle with its breath and devour it; sometimes as if the trees, like eagles, were about to snatch up the ruins with their talons and take off. But the ruins held their ground tenaciously, although quite a few trees with slender trunks and dense umbrella-like crowns were uprooted and flung into the distance, raining down the soil clinging to their roots. A gust of wind lunged toward me. Some of the dirt from the tree roots hit my face and the smell of medicinal oil drifted into my nostrils once again.

There were many kinds of sounds, but they were drowned out in the howl of the wind, the sound of which made me start to doze off, or perhaps lapse into unconsciousness. Before my senses were completely overwhelmed, I heard the sound of the houses of the town collapsing and a subconscious question surfaced in my mind: how did I end up on this hill and what was I doing there?

7

The heat of the sunshine woke me up. After a while the fog lifted from my mind and I began to remember everything. The ruins, covered over by greenery in some spots, were spread out right across from me for quite some distance. Here and there small trees stood motionless in between the ruins, as a gentle breeze flowed smoothly and soundlessly through their branches. I glanced at the ruins. It was difficult from such a distance to distinguish between the broken stone columns and broken off or stunted tree trunks.

Had these buildings been intact, I thought, they would now have looked like the site of a terrible disaster. Then I descended the hill, and it didn't take me long to reach the town. Coming to the last turn in the road, I saw that the mouth of the jungle had altogether disappeared, but up ahead Nauroz's Shop could be seen with its mouth gaping wide. But, before going there, I first went around the town and talked with people. Although the damage to trees and houses had been enormous, most lives had been spared, except for a few cattle. This was because the area had always lain in the path of dust storms and people were well prepared. At the moment almost everyone was busy making temporary repairs to their houses and clearing the paths. I just strolled through, and then started back.

Nauroz's house showed absolutely no sign that it had been affected by the storm at all. Its door was still closed, exactly the way I had left it. I went to the front of Nauroz's Shop. Its door had been plucked off its frame by the wind gusts, although who can imagine what kind of gusts they were that the door, instead of falling inside, was lying outside the shop. Then I inspected my quarters.

They were there all right. But it seemed as if somebody had picked them up and then put them back in their place after shaking them about violently, so now they looked like an unsightly turban plopped up on top of the shop's head—scarcely livable. I tried to remember what all had been there. Just then I felt the touch of a palm on my back.

"There has been damage everywhere, Saasaan," the kind man was standing beside me. "Mercifully, lives have been spared."

He stopped, looked at me, and then continued, "And mercifully too, those people had left here before the storm hit."

I glanced at the closed door of Nauroz's house and then at the kind man.

"Where they come from is not in the path of storms," he said, "so they were quite apprehensive. They aren't used to strong winds. They would have left much earlier but they were delayed somewhat on account of that old Nauroz. He didn't want to leave. He said that he wanted to see the big dust storm. And you know how difficult it is, Saasaan, to make a mad man agree to something."

"One has to become a little mad oneself to do that," I said, and then I asked, "How did they bring him round?"

"Who knows? They had taken him off to one side," he said. "Then there was also some delay because of the stupid women here."

I wasn't particularly aware of the women's presence in the town, so I asked rather inquisitively, "The women—how so?"

"When they saw your ... when they saw the girls they stirred up quite a fuss saying that they wouldn't let them go. And women, you know ... Anyway, they started to cry and wail. You weren't here and ... how shall I put it? ... well, it seemed like a small earthquake had struck before the dust storm."

"I was out at the time," I said.

"Yes. We did come to call you."

He peered at my face for a long time, then grabbed my hand and led me into the shop. Here, no trace of the storm could be seen. Even the dust, still moving about outside, had not reached here. Who knows what kind of wind that was, I wondered, or what kind of shop this was? I turned to the kind man. He pushed down on both of my shoulders and made me sit on the *takht*, then he took a place beside me himself.

"At their place they'll cheer up the girls in a few days," he started. "They've been taking care of two mad men after all, it won't be too difficult to manage two little girls. In fact, they had tried to cheer up the girls while they were still here, but when they found out ..."

He stopped. So far he had been simply informing me, but now he asked me somewhat dismayed, "Saasaan, you didn't even teach them to speak?"

"They speak," I replied, with a little dismay of my own.

"Your name, but nothing else."

I didn't say anything.

"They don't even know how to say the names of things. But never mind. They'll teach them themselves." He said that as if to reassure me.

Afterwards, for a while, he looked at the jars, baskets and other things that lay scattered around, then his eyes glanced at the dirt floor and he abruptly got up. "Let's go out."

"They've left the shop for you," he said. "They acknowledge your good deed. As for the upper part, we'll fix it up for you, enough so that you can live in it."

"I also had my papers there," I said.

"They went flying out the window," he replied. "But they were all picked up. They're safe with me."

He looked at the shop's open mouth for some time and then said, "There's no merchandise in the shop, but whatever there is, it's yours. Now they only want …"

"What do they want now?" I asked.

"That you won't go to their place to see the two until they have completely forgotten you."

I remained silent. He waited for my reply for some time, and then lapsed into something resembling a bout of melancholy.

"OK, I'll come back some other time," he said in a weary voice. "A lot of work needs to be done and we're short of men as it is. I'll bring over your papers."

He turned around to leave and said on his way out, "They're very small right now. They'll forget everything in a few days. Those people—they've promised to send for you themselves later on."

8

The tiny girls must have forgotten everything. Tiring of my papers, I sometimes lift up my head and think: no one has come to call me so far, nor has there been any news.

I bend over my papers again.

Epistle

My days among the dead are past.
—*Robert Southey*

Aanha ke kuhan shudand-o-iinha ke navand
(Those who have turned old and these—who are new)
— *'Umar Khayyam*

"Respected Sir,
Through your esteemed newspaper, I would like to draw the
attention of the appropriate authorities to the western sector
of this city. I feel compelled to say, with great regret, that
today, when large-scale development is taking place in the city
and the residents of every other sector are being provided the
most modern facilities, the western sector remains deprived
of even a water supply and power. It looks as though this city
has only three sides. When, after a long period, necessity drove
me to the western sector recently, I found it in exactly the
same condition as in my childhood."

1

I had no personal need to go there but I felt obliged on
account of my mother. Years ago, at the onset of old age, she
had lost her ability to walk, and later she nearly lost her
eyesight. Her mind had also become muddled. In spite of
her infirmity she would call me near her three or four times every

day and she would feel around my whole body with trembling hands. Actually it had seemed to her from the time I was born that I wasn't healthy. Sometimes she thought my body was too cold, sometimes too hot; sometimes she thought my voice had changed; and sometimes that the color of my eyes looked different. Because she belonged to an old family of hakims, she had come to know the names and treatments for many illnesses by heart. Every few days she would declare that I was suffering from some new ailment and then insist on treating it. During the early days of her infirmity it happened a couple of times that I became engrossed in some work and forgot to visit her in her room, so she managed, God knows how, to drag herself to the door. After more time had passed, when her remaining vitality had also ebbed away, her physician kept me away from her for one whole day just to test whether she had any strength left in her arms and feet. She also remained unmindful of me, or so it seemed. But when, hearing her moan softly late at night, I rushed to her, I saw that she had traversed about half the distance to the door. Her bedding, which she had started to spread out on the floor ever since the death of my father, had been dragged right along with her; or rather, it seemed that it was the bedding itself that was dragging her along toward the door. When she saw me she tried to say something but fell into unconsciousness from exhaustion and remained in that state for several days. Her physician acknowledged his mistake over and over again, expressing regret for putting her through this ordeal, because, following this episode, my mother's sight and mind both became impaired, until, gradually, her presence and absence became one.

A long time has passed since even her physician died. Recently, though, when I woke up one night, I saw her sitting on the floor near my feet, groping around my bed with one hand. I quickly sat up.

"You …" I said, looking at the web of protruding veins on the back of her hand, "… have come here?"

"To see you … how are you feeling?" she said, haltingly,

before a daze came over her.

I got out of the bed and sat down beside her on the floor, staring at her for a long time. I tried to recall my earliest image of her face as it was preserved in my memory, and for a few moments that face appeared before my eyes. Meanwhile she emerged from her daze a bit. Attempting to help her rise slowly, I said, "Come, let me take you to your room."

"No," she said with enormous difficulty, "first tell me."

"Tell you what?" I asked, in a tired voice.

"How do you feel?"

Actually, I hadn't been feeling well for a few days, so I said, "I don't feel well."

Contrary to my expectation, she didn't ask me for the details of my illness; instead, she only asked, "So did you have someone examine you?"

"Who should I go to?"

I knew what answer would be forthcoming. The one she always gave immediately and in a sharp tone. This time, after a long silence, she did say the same thing, but with tremendous sadness and a little despair, "Why don't you go there?"

I used to go there with her in my childhood. It was a family of old hakims who were close relatives of my mother. Their house was very large and several families lived in its different sections. The head of all those families was a Hakim Sahib, hardly known in the city, but who nonetheless commanded a group of patients from neighboring villages much larger than any of the renowned doctors in the city.

A lot of celebrations took place in that house, and my mother was invited specially to them; often she took me along as well. I used to watch the strange ceremonies that took place during those celebrations with tremendous fascination. It also didn't escape me that great deference was shown to my mother there and that a wave of happiness swept over the entire place the minute she arrived. For her own part, she never neglected to show proper courtesy to one and all. She called the younger members present, and those her own age, over to her, but went to the elders herself, and everyone accepted her judgment in the family disputes that frequently arose there.

There were many people there, but I remembered, as though through a fog, only the face of Hakim Sahib, and that perhaps only because there was a slight family resemblance between him and my mother. What I do remember clearly, though, is that women, men, and children of all ages used to be present in that place and that my mother, surrounded by them all, appeared to me like a flower in the midst of so many leaves.

Now, though, with her withered face turned toward me, she was trying to look at my face with her sightless eyes.

"Your voice sounds hoarse. Avoid eating oily foods," she said, and then said again, "Why don't you go there?"

"There ... I won't even be able to recognize anyone there."

"You will, when you see them. If not, they'll clear it up for you."

"It's been such a long time," I said. "I don't remember how to get there anymore."

"You'll start to remember when you set out."

"How?" I said. "Everything must have changed."

"Nothing's changed," she said. She again began to drift into unconsciousness, still she managed to say one more time, "Nothing's changed," and then she became completely unconscious.

I sat supporting her for a long time. I tried to recall the way to that house by imagining the days when I had accompanied her there. I also tried to remember the layout of the house. All that

came back to my mind was the mound—known as Hakims'
Perch—straight across from the main entrance. And yes, also that
Hakims' Perch was located on the western side of the city, that it
had a few bushes and unpaved graves, and that the last signs of the
city ended by the time one reached it.

I picked my mother up in my arms, just as she once used to
pick me up in hers, and felt as though I had paid back some of
what I owed her. And even though she was entirely unconscious,
I said to her, "Come, let me help you to your room. Come
morning, I shall definitely go *there*."

I woke up the next morning a little after sunrise, and some time
after I woke up I set out from the house.

2

I hadn't passed through the western side of my own neighborhood
in a long time. Now as I did, I noticed a lot of changes. Mud
houses had become brick houses; vacant compounds had turned
into small bazaars. A warehouse for lumber had sprung up on the
ruins of an old tomb. None of the faces I was familiar with a long
time ago could be seen. However, I did meet several people who
knew me, and I knew some of them, though I didn't know they
lived in my own neighborhood. I also spoke to them, just the usual
pleasantries, but I didn't tell anyone where I was headed.

Soon I had left my neighborhood behind. Then I came to
the grain market and left that behind too, and then the medicine
and spice market. Paved roads ran on either side of these markets
and stretched far into the distance, with temporary snack shops
and drink stalls along the way. However, on the road I was now
walking on I could see potholes straight ahead in several places,

and further down it turned completely into a dirt road. Even though I didn't remember the way, I was sure that I was walking in the right direction, so I kept going.

The heat of the sun had become stronger. By now even the traces of the dirt road had disappeared, but it could still be imagined between the two crooked rows of dust-covered trees. Suddenly the rows disintegrated in such a way that nothing of the road was left except a vague hint, splitting in five directions like the fingers of a spread out hand. Here, I wavered. It hadn't been long since I had left the house; I was certain that I wasn't too far from my neighborhood. Still I stopped and tried to figure out the way back. I turned around and looked. Dust-covered trees stood everywhere on the uneven terrain. I had imagined the dirt road between the rows of these trees; perhaps the rows themselves were the creation of my imagination because now I couldn't see them anywhere. In my estimation I was proceeding along a straight road, but I had often experienced how seemingly straight roads turned this way or that imperceptibly, throwing the wayfarer completely off course. I was convinced that this far into the journey I had already detoured several times and if I didn't find some trace of the road I simply wouldn't be able to make it back home on my own. However, at the time I was more concerned with Hakims' Perch, which appeared to be nowhere in sight, than with how I'd get back home. Although trees were everywhere, they were so scraggly that no sizeable portion of the ground was hidden from my view. But the ground to my right, sloping upward far into the distance, was so dotted with thick bushes, practically fused into each other, that it was impossible to see what lay on the other side of this slope.

If there was anything, it had to be on the other side—I thought, and set out in that direction. And I was right. The instant I emerged from a large tract of overcrowded bushes I saw a single-story house made of small brown bricks rising before me. This was not the house I was looking for. Nevertheless I proceeded straight toward it. A nameplate, most of its letters nearly obliterated, hung on the door. It was quiet inside the house, but not the kind of quiet to be found outside of deserted houses, so I knocked three times at the door. After some time there was a slight sound of movement on the other side of the door and someone asked, "Who is it?"

What would be the point of telling that, I thought to myself, and said instead, "I seem to have lost my way; is Hakims' Perch somewhere around here?"

"Hakims' Perch ... Where have you come from?"

This was quite irrelevant. I felt a bit annoyed at having my question answered with a question; but it was a woman on the other side and she spoke gently and sounded extremely polite. She was holding on to the slightly ajar door, but just lightly. Her fingernails were painted orange. A faint memory crossed my mind. Just then the door opened a tad bit more and in the span of a second I caught a glimpse of a smallish, dimly lit *devrhi*, the courtyard beyond it, and the sun falling on a few branches of the pomegranate tree growing in one of its corners. In the next second I vaguely remembered that Mother used to stop briefly at this house too. But I wasn't able to also remember the people who lived here.

"Have you come from some place abroad?" the voice came again from behind the door.

"No," I said, and explained to her who I was. Then I said, "I've come this way after a very long time."

After a lengthy pause I got the answer, "Please go to the back of the house. You'll see the Perch straight across."

The heavy voice of an old woman arose inside the house, "Mehr, who is it?"

I thanked her formally and went to the back of the house. Up ahead a number of hills, large and small, could be seen, their disorderly rows once again giving the impression of a road. These hills were just big mounds of earth, but slightly away from them bushes could be seen on another mound. I looked closely at this other mound: signs of mud graves were evident among the bushes. The whitewash on some of these graves glistened in the strong sunlight.

3

The house I was looking for was behind the Perch, and I had to go halfway around the Perch to reach it. Standing in front of the massive, old wooden main entrance, I thought for quite a while about how to announce my arrival. The wood of the door was quite thick and somewhat damp; nothing could be gained by knocking at it. Still I tapped three times, but even *I* couldn't hear anything. The thought crossed my mind that the house was probably deserted. I gave the door a gentle push. Both of its panels turned smoothly on their hinges and opened, unfolding before me a spacious *devrhi* with a small door on its opposite end. This second door was wide open but a curtain of double-layered sackcloth hung over the entrance. I walked over to the door. Now I could hear people inside the house talking. I knocked and a voice called out to someone, "Go see, somebody's at the door."

At that point my mind became crowded with thoughts. Who all lives here? What should I say to whom? What reason should I give for my visit? How shall I make them recognize me? The urge to walk away came over me, but just then a woman's curt voice asked from behind the curtain, "Who is it?"

I gave her my full name.

"Who have you come to see?"

I had only one answer to this. "The Hakim Sahib," I said.

"The *matab* [dispensary] is on the other side. Please go there. He's getting ready."

Her voice had begun to fade away with the last of her words so I said quickly and a little loudly, "Please tell those inside."

The voice again came close, this time markedly less curt,

"Where have you come from?"

Here, again, I introduced myself. Then I paused, mentioned my mother's name, paused again, and gave the name my mother was called at home, saying that I was her son, and then hesitantly I gave the pet name that used to annoy me in childhood. I went through all this in a rather haphazard manner and the woman behind the curtain relayed it somewhat more coherently to someone there who had asked for it, whereupon the voices of the women talking inside became louder and faster for a bit. I heard them repeat my mother's informal name and my pet name several times. I was hearing both of these names again after a long time. I became convinced that if I kept hearing them for a while I'd no doubt begin to recall the entire layout of this house along with all its dwellers; in fact, the image of a spacious courtyard had already started to take shape in my mind. Just then, the sackcloth curtain moved toward me with a rustle and then rose upward, allowing the front wheel of a bicycle to emerge from behind it. I stepped to one side and a boy walked into the *devrhi* holding on to a bicycle. He greeted me and went out the front door. I stood waiting silently. After a while muffled sounds rose from behind the curtain, followed by a few ducks that came into the *devrhi*. The disorderly fashion in which they were moving clearly indicated that they had been shooed out of the house. They waddled toward the front door, quacking among themselves. Meanwhile nothing was heard from inside the house for some time. I became tired of standing in the *devrhi* and began to imagine that the silence that wafts from deserted houses was pouring out from behind the curtain continually in an attempt to engulf me. Just then somebody on the other side of the curtain said, "Please come inside."

Pushing on the double-layered curtain, I stepped into the courtyard of that house.

4

In my childhood I had seen any number of houses with large courtyards, with double and triple *daalaans* [halls], spaces that could be called halls but without doors, overhanging balconies, and wooden arches. This house wasn't any different; I still couldn't recall having frequented it. Stopping in the middle of the courtyard for a few seconds, I noticed that every part of the house was occupied. In several small open halls without doors women were straining their necks and peering at me with curiosity. I tried to guess where the mistress of the house was most likely to be found and proceeded straight to the hall where big lanterns hung from its high arches. A large *chowka* made of wooden boards sat on the floor with heavy-looking canopied beds on either side of it. The beds all had sparkling, freshly-washed sheets, still crisp with starch. An old lady sat on the *chowka*. I greeted her without knowing who she was. She smiled, showered me with blessings, and said, "Son, what caused you to wander in here today?"

It occurred to me that this question was not intended to be answered, so with as much courtesy as I could possibly muster I inquired after her health. And she said, "Why, you'd hardly remember now, but when you came here as a child you just wouldn't want to go back home."

Then she recounted many occasions when my mother had to stay on for days because of my insistence.

"And even then you left here crying," she said, wiping her eyes with the edge of her *dupatta*.

Meanwhile, women continued assembling in the large hall from different parts of the house. Most took the initiative and introduced themselves. I was not one to grasp convoluted relationships; still I tried to look as though I recognized every woman who introduced herself and already knew how we were related. The women's hair was heavily oiled and combed, and all of them were draped in coarse cotton *dupattas*, some seemingly dyed at home. Each one had a collection of stories about my childhood. I was shown a guava tree at the edge of the courtyard from which I had taken a fall and been knocked unconscious, causing my mother to fall unconscious too. When the subject of my pranks came up, I found out that not a single woman present had escaped becoming the target of one of them.

I realized that I hadn't spoken a word for quite a while. Perhaps they were now waiting for me to say something since the hall had become somewhat hushed. I swept my gaze around and saw a few girls sitting on one side of the *chowka*. When I asked them about their studies and what other things they did to occupy themselves, they blushed and started to edge closer to one another, while somebody else answered on their behalf. At some point three boys had come in and they were sitting at a distance from the girls. I talked to them about a few things I thought might interest them, but I had no idea what their interests were. The boys seemed stupid to me, the girls ugly, although I did like the way the girls drew back from modesty. I was fishing for some topic of interest to the boys when a rattling sound was heard at the door. The boy with the bicycle had returned holding in his hands something wrapped in newspaper cones which had begun to ooze oil. He looked at the hall and made a sign. Promptly the girls got up and left. Shortly thereafter sounds of their laughing and of the clanking of china rose from a part of the house nearby. I sensed a vague resemblance between the two sounds; I also suspected that they were imitating the way I talked.

How long had I been sitting in this hall? I tried to guess. Just then a door opened to my left and I saw Hakim Sahib standing behind the reed screen that was hanging in front of it. I recognized him instantly. He was trying to adjust the angle of his cap. Then, turning his face toward the screen, he started groping for something in his pockets. I saw another door behind him with a crowd of peasant men and women near it.

"Listen everyone! I'm coming in," he announced as he lifted the screen.

"You may come in now," the mistress of the house said. "Look who's here—recognize him?"

By now Hakim Sahib had walked into the hall. I quickly got up and greeted him. Repeating my whole name softly he said, "Mian, you've changed so much. If I had seen you elsewhere, I wouldn't have recognized you."

For a while he recounted some of the things that had happened in my childhood and also told anecdotes about my father's unwavering deference. Meanwhile a maidservant walked in with a rather long brass tray of snacks. I glanced at the delicate china plates. Most of the foods on them had been bought from the bazaar, but some items were also homemade. Hakim Sahib pointed at the tray and said, "Now don't let ceremony stand in the way." Then he said to his wife, "All right then. I'm going to be late getting to the *matab*."

After that he went back to his room.

"The *matab* keeps him so busy," the mistress of the house said apologetically. She also said something more, but I may have dozed for a moment. When I became alert she was the only one left in the hall and curtains of some coarse material were swaying in two of the arches. Only the arch in the middle was still open and the lantern hanging there swayed, sometimes to the right and sometimes to the left, in the wind. I looked in the direction of the reed screen. Near the door that was behind it, Hakim Sahib had his hand on the pulse of an old peasant man and seemed to be lost in thought. I turned toward the mistress. She too had dozed, but the muffled sound of girls' laughter coming from some small hall nearby made her sit up alert.

"Has Mehr come?" she asked herself, and I saw a faint trace of anxiety sweep over her otherwise contented face for the first time. Just then the curtain drawn over the right arch moved to one side and a young woman entered the hall. I gave her a fleeting glance. She was dressed in an orange sari made of some wrinkle-proof fabric and she wore nail polish of the same color. The mistress turned toward me, "Do you recognize Mehr?"

I again glanced at the young woman's face. She was wearing a faint shade of orange lipstick. I answered her greeting by shaking my head as if I recognized her, just as I had for the other women. I was about to look at her more closely when some girl called to her softly from behind the curtain and she went out of the hall.

Hakim Sahib still had his hand on the old peasant's pulse and the mistress had again begun to doze. I got up. The mistress looked toward me with half-opened eyes, and I said, "With your permission, I'll go now."

"So you want to go?" she asked in a heavy voice, and suddenly I remembered something.

"That ... scary room ... is it still there?" I asked.

"The scary room?" she said thinking, and then she recalled with a melancholy smile, "Once you locked Mehr up in that room." The melancholy in her smile deepened. "At least you remembered something of this place."

"Is it still there?"

"It's there all right. Over there, the door by the *devrhi*. It's not much. The kitchen used to be there before. The walls are black from the smoke. Has a door that opens to the outside. Must be open. The latch doesn't fasten anymore."

"I'll let myself out that way," I said, raising my hand to say good-bye, and turned toward the courtyard.

"Do come sometimes as you have today. Back then you came almost daily," she took a deep breath and her voice trembled a little, "Time has made such a big difference, son."

Her lips were still moving, but I walked across the courtyard and went through the door adjoining the *devrhi*.

5

There was nothing unusual about the room. The ceiling and walls were coated with soot. But that hadn't made it overly dark. A large hearth, fashioned from wet clay mixed with chaff, stood on one side, but it had become dilapidated. In front of me I could see a vertical shaft of light.

Must be the door opening to the outside, I told myself, and coming close to the shaft I peered through it. I could see Hakims' Perch straight across. I felt the cool touch of the dangling iron latch on my forehead and pulled it toward me. One of the door's panels opened. I let go of the latch; the panel slowly closed on its own. I did this a couple of times, recalling how opening such doors and then watching them close on their own used to be my favorite pastime as a child. I pulled both panels toward me simultaneously and went out.

A few moments later I was in back of the one-story brown brick house. Hakims' Perch and the bushes and graves on it could be seen more clearly now. I sensed that something was missing there and immediately the thought occurred to me that I had not gone to the top of the Perch to have a look. At the very same instant I recalled something else. I turned back around and walked up to the top.

There were more graves than I had imagined, but the dense patch of straw, which was believed to harbor an ancient snake, had disappeared. Those who claimed to have seen the snake said that hair had sprouted on its hood. Children used to play near the straw patch, and I even used to hide inside of it, but the snake had never harmed anyone. Perhaps that's why it was widely believed that the snake had stood guard over the Hakim family for generations. By now the image of the partly dry, partly green straw patch had been completely resurrected in my memory, but what I couldn't remember was its precise location on the Perch. The place where I suspected it to be was occupied by several graves sparkling from the lime wash.

I kept looking at the main door of the house from the Perch. The desire to go and knock on it began to well up inside of me, and I even took a few steps in its direction, but then I stopped.

That would be an absolutely absurd thing to do, I thought, and started to come down from the Perch in the opposite direction from the house.

The way back was not difficult. I reached my home easily.

Lamentation

1

I have spent my life in fruitless diversions. And these days I spend most of my time wondering what, if anything, I have gained from them—which is my latest, perhaps final, perhaps even most fruitless diversion.

For years I knocked about the country, perhaps out of a desire to learn more about our cities, large and small. The upshot was that all cities began to look alike to me, except my own, and after the last trip I remained holed up in my house for several months. Then restlessness got the better of me and I set out again. This time I headed for the rural settlements. But I soon realized that they weren't much different from the cities, to me at any rate. I returned home and was for a long while haunted by the suspicion that I'd lost my ability to distinguish between things. I let the doubt grow inside me, but I made every effort not to let it show from my actions or words. When, however, I noticed that the people with whom I socialized almost daily had begun to give me strange looks, I set out on another journey.

On this journey I roamed the desolate areas of my ancient land. The weather there was harsh and the earth barren. There were no rivers anywhere near these areas, so they were practically uninhabitable for anyone used to rather more amenities. Still they weren't completely uninhabited. I also passed through areas that perhaps had never been home to anyone; they were merely immense stretches of uninhabited geography, which, in a vague sort of way, resembled the seas and, though unpopulated, somehow didn't look so desolate. Rather, it was the areas where humans had dwelt from ancient times that looked truly desolate. Across these immense geographical tracts they abruptly surged into view like islands and looked desolate precisely because of their human habitation. And just as these humans affected their habitats, so too did the habitats affect the humans, so much so that even in bustling cities one could identify them as wastelanders. At least I could, for I had spent the greater part of this journey roaming among just such folk.

These were small communities, each distinct from the other, or so they appeared to me. During this journey my main occupation was observing these communities and spending a few days with each. I was especially keen on this undertaking because these scattered human communities were slowly dying out. A sudden epidemic or a major shift in the weather pattern could easily wipe them out, and often did so. It even came about that on a second trip to the area occupied by a community I had visited some time earlier, I found it deserted and the area itself practically swallowed by the surrounding uninhabited geography. This was because the traces of habitation left by these communities tended to disappear rather quickly—or perhaps weren't even there in the first place.

I couldn't gather much information about these people, for although they could understand my language a little, I could not understand their variety of tongues. We mostly communicated through signs. But this didn't help me much either. Different communities expressed themselves through different signs, and sometimes the same sign denoted the opposite meaning in a different community. Where one community used a particular hand gesture to express happiness, the other used the same gesture to express sorrow. Where a nod of the head indicated "yes" for one, the other used it to indicate "no." Much time was thus required to understand their gestures precisely, and I never stayed long enough in any given community. Thus what little I was able to uncover about them simply could not be trusted, and by the time I returned I had already expelled from my mind whatever confused information I had gathered about them. The only thing that clung to my memory was the congregational lament of these communities, which although different in each place was nonetheless easily recognizable to me.

I cannot be certain whether it was merely a coincidence or whether in fact these people were prone to a higher death rate, but the fact remains that within a couple of days of my arrival in a community a death invariably occurred, which was announced by the wailing and weeping of the deceased's nearest or next nearest relatives. The other members of the community softly approached the bereaved, calmed them down, and left just as softly. Others occupied themselves with funeral arrangements. These out of the way, the members came together at a fixed time and place, in some communities after disposing of the body and in others before it, to perform a congregational lament. The lamentation of most communities began with an accusatory complaint against death and moved to a recapturing of the memory of the departed, steadily gaining intensity and tempo. At the lament's highest point, emotion would overcome everyone and their body movements, their voices, and, more than anything, their eyes, all came to reflect anger rather than grief. At times it seemed as though they had all taken some potent intoxicant. In certain places I too was obliged to participate in the rite. In such cases, while I would be busy crudely mimicking them, dumbly and without the least bit of emotion, the lament would come to an end, with everyone trying to comfort and console everyone else. And I too would be offered the same.

In some places women outnumbered men in the lament, in others men outnumbered women; but in one community their numbers were equal. This was the only community whose women I was able to observe, even touch, but only during this ritual. Short in stature and tawny in complexion, these women seemed to have been liberally endowed by nature in those parts of the body that made them women, so that they looked like the originals of those ancient statues and mural paintings, which, it is sometimes assumed, were fashioned by people who never laid eyes on a real woman, or at least not from up close, and certainly never touched one. The lamentation in vogue among this community went something like this: men sat on their haunches in a row on the bare earth, with women sitting likewise in a row facing them. Each man–woman pair would touch first elbows, then wrists, then slap each other's palms, then interlock their fingers, and then say whatever needed to be said; they would then separate and once again link their elbows and repeat their words. Their lament would repeatedly rise in a crescendo, then begin to fall, then rise up again, like the ebb and flow of the sea, until everyone's eyes were rolling back in their heads. Dripping with sweat, they all finished the lament in a faint, quavering voice and pulled away, panting slowly.

Three deaths occurred during my presence in that community. I participated in the lament for the first two. The third time, death claimed my own host, a decrepit old man. I had tried to treat him with the medicines I had with me, but he couldn't be saved. Not just his face, but even some of his mannerisms reminded me of my father, and I had tried to communicate this to him, partly through speech and partly through gestures. I have no idea what he had told the community about me, but a couple of the group who came to comfort and calm the bereaved made their way toward me as well, and even though I was silent, "calmed" me down. Their visit brought back the memory of the day my own father had died. The house resounded with the crazed wails of the women folk, while I was left to sit quietly by myself.

My host's death brought back to me the image of my father's face just as he lay dying; I then began to recall the face of my elderly host. After the funeral arrangements, when the men and women of the community began to line up opposite each other, I quietly got up and left for the neighboring uninhabited area. Once there I quickly decided to end my journey, and that very day I set out for home.

These days, as I mentioned, I spend most of my time wondering what I have gained from these diversions. Thus my life, the greater part of which has been spent lurching from one stimulation to the next, has for some time now been quite drab and monotonous. One day, though, a bit of stimulation did interrupt the monotony. The occurrence could be seen as something gained from one of my diversions, but turned out to be worse, I believe, than no gain at all.

2

That day early in the morning there was a knock at the door of my house, which opens onto the bazaar. I lazily got up and opened it. The local crazy boy, who lived in the neighborhood, was standing in front of me with a crumpled scrap of paper in his hand. As soon as he saw me he stuffed it into my hand and took off laughing. It was his custom to pick up any fallen item in the bazaar and then give it to others as a gift. He called it "prize-giving." The market folk begged him to give them such "prizes."

Well, I got a prize today without even asking!—I thought to myself as I closed the door and got on with the day's routine. I also wondered, as I did from time to time, why people considered this boy crazy. There was nothing really unusual about him except that he always looked cheerful and laughed at everything; still everybody thought of him as crazy, so I did too.

Shortly thereafter another knock came at the door. I opened it once again and there was the same boy. "They're calling you," he said, trying not to laugh.

"Who?" I asked.

"The ones who've come."

"Who have come?"

"The piece-of-paper-people," he said, then laughed loudly and sprinted off.

I closed the door and picked up the scrap that I had earlier dropped on the bed. The paper itself was old; it bore my name and address in my own hand and appeared to be from the time when I wrote very deliberately, making each letter with flourish and elegance. Those days came to mind, and with them the time I had spent wandering among the wasteland communities. All the same, I couldn't recall exactly where or when I had written this scrap, though I did remember I had in those days liberally distributed similar slips among the various communities I visited. This was the only way in which I had repaid their hospitality. I would emphasize, in our mostly haphazard sign language, that if ever one of them needed something done in the city, with the help of my handwritten scrap he should come to me straightaway. I was sure I would never see any of those countless slips of paper again. Now, though, ages later, one had found its way back to me; I had been apprised that some people, aided by this scrap, had come calling on me, even though the news was brought by one who was considered crazy by everyone, myself included. In the span of a few seconds all the communities I had visited whirled through my mind like dream images and then vanished, and I stepped out of the house into the bazaar.

It was time for the shops to open, but most of them were still closed. The shopkeepers, however, were present, standing in a group whispering furtively. When they saw me, they strode over to me.

"Who brought this?" I showed them the piece of paper.

Without saying a word they pointed at the nameless dirt path that sloped down toward the north, its mouth nearly blocked off by the bazaar's encroaching garbage dump. I looked where they pointed. At first glance it appeared as though the area beyond the dump was dotted all over with small garbage heaps, but a second glance revealed them to be a group of people who sat crouching on the ground.

"Who are they?" a shopkeeper asked me.

"Looks like some community," I replied. I was about to walk over to them when another shopkeeper asked, "Did you invite them?"

"No," I said.

"But it's you they want to see."

"Still, I haven't sent for them."

"All right, fine. At least get them to move their cart. It's blocking the way."

Only then did I notice the cart that stood in the paved street. A barrel had been cut lengthwise so that it resembled a small round-bottomed boat, minus the tapered ends. Or maybe it was in fact some discarded boat on which they had stuck a couple of wheels— huge disks cut from the round trunk of some old tree—making it usable on dry land. On closer inspection, I discovered that what I'd imagined to be a barrel was in fact a hollowed-out tree trunk with a big shapeless stone secured below it by a thick, coarse, tree-bark rope dangling so low it practically scraped the ground. Most likely it had been attached to stabilize the cart; all the same, two men were holding the cart on either end. Suppose they let go—I wondered absent-mindedly—which way would the cart tip, forward or back? Then I gave it an even closer look.

The inside of the cart was completely filled with rags. A woman stood bent over it, continually shifting the rags back and forth. Even though she was wrapped from head to toe in a chador, she appeared to be young. I had barely glanced at her and the two men holding the cart when I heard another shopkeeper ask, "Which community is it?"

I turned to look at the people who were squatting on the ground beyond the garbage dump. There were ten or twelve men in all, and so covered with grime that one couldn't tell the color of their clothes. Seeing them, not a thing came to mind; still I had no difficulty recognizing that it was one of the wasteland communities. I stared at them for a long time. They were all looking at me with indifference, and with every passing instant I was becoming more certain that I had never stayed among them. I couldn't understand how they had come upon my name and address. Once again I examined the scrap of paper. Just then they noticed that I had the scrap in my hand and a sudden surge of excitement swept through them. They exchanged a few words among themselves and quickly rose to their feet. Some dust drifted up from their clothes, and soon I was surrounded by them, as well as by the queries of the bazaar-*walas* who began by repeating their last question: "Which community is this?"

I told them that I didn't know these people, but they kept on questioning me as though they thought I was accountable for them. Their questions, however, were such that I could not possibly answer: Aren't they untouchables? There's been a rash of thefts in the city, do you think they are behind it? Where have they come from? Could they be beggars?

Now I asked: "Have they asked anyone for anything?"

"Well, not so far," I was informed. "When we arrived, they were showing everyone the slip of paper and asking how to find your address."

"In what language?"

"By signs."

"So?" I asked, "Did any of the signs look like they were begging?"

"But just *look* at them …"

"I *am* looking."

"And the cart …" said the shopkeeper with the loudest voice.

"I'm looking at that, too."

"…And who is this they're hauling around in the cart? Suppose he dies this instant—wouldn't they beg us for help? They're all tricks to swindle something out of us."

At that point I peered at the figure in the cart. What, until then, had looked like a lump in the pile of rags turned out to be the rider's constantly drooping head, which the woman was now and then trying to prop up, but it always just drooped back down. I went over to him. Just as the woman was propping the rider's head up once again with both of her hands, I heard their voices, all at once, and turned around to look at them.

They were touching my knees over and over again, saying something. Their speech sounded like a corrupted form of my own language—or its primitive form before corruption had set in—which was unintelligible to me. They would touch my knees and then point at the cart, their tone sounding increasingly like a plea. This made me wonder too whether they might perhaps be a pack of beggars after all. A few words to them and I was convinced that they didn't understand my tongue either. Given my perfectly flat intonation, they couldn't even guess at what I might be saying. Their own speech was varied in tone, but nonetheless I could easily sense that they were hugely afraid of something, that they had endured all manner of hardship to get here, that they were looking for some kind of assistance from me, and that all of this had something to do with the occupant of the cart.

All the while the woman kept arranging the rider's seat and supporting his drooping head. I edged closer to the rider. He was buried chest-deep in the pile of rags and his head was also wrapped in rags. The woman moved to one side and raised his head with both of her hands, turning it toward me.

I saw the inflamed face of a child before me. His eyelids were incredibly swollen. One of them was open just a crack and he was looking at me through the opening. The other completely shut, but it had been smeared with lime or some other white substance; in the center was a large iris painted with lampblack or some other black substance; this gave the illusion of an eye frozen in a stare of astonishment. I looked away from it and bent down to peer into the slit of the other eye. Hidden behind the matted lashes it radiated torment, entreaty, and disgust, all at once. I tried to look at his face from still closer, which seemed to create a series of waves in the rags. The rider jerked his face away. His lips drew back, exposing his teeth. From a distance he may have appeared to the shopkeepers to be grinning, but to me he looked like a sick dog with mean boys coming at it.

Rising behind me I heard the buzz of bazaar-*walas* and the shrill voices of the community folk, which led me to suspect that the parties had perhaps begun sparring with each other. I whirled around to look: Both parties were telling me something, but I couldn't understand a word. Just then the woman grabbed my hand and I turned toward her. She stuck her free hand into the pile of rags and rummaged through it, eventually pulling out one of the rider's hands all the way up to the elbow. I had three hands before me: my own familiar hand, its fingers interlocked with the soft, white fingers of the woman, slowly turning moist, and between our two palms the hand of the rider—small, withered, with motley strings of color hanging down between the wrist and elbow; dead, wrinkled skin showing through.

Her fingers throbbed in mine like a heart and my body quivered lightly. The rider emitted a sound, like the sick dog I had imagined.

One of the shopkeepers placed his hand on my shoulder and I turned toward him. "Tell them to move the cart," he was saying. "They're ruining our business. First thing in the morning these people …"

I turned toward the community folk. They were staring at me mutely. I made a sign for them to proceed westward on the straight road and they understood my meaning right away. The men who were holding the cart on either end easily turned it toward the west. The woman withdrew her hand from mine, put the rider's hand back into the pile, and supported his head as the cart lumbered forward with a rickety noise. The clan followed behind, holding their drab, dingy bundles and long clubs, while the shopkeepers and neighborhood folk—among them a few women and children—stood quietly arrayed on either side of the road. Hurrying ahead of the cart and leaving the line of shops behind, I came to the southern bend in the paved road and stopped. I turned around and motioned them to halt at the bend, and they kept coming along slowly. Dust was hovering around them like smoke. And then I saw it all at once. Everyone and everything in their aggregate seemed fragile and decayed and in the path of imminent disintegration. And yet, I thought, had it all not been so grimy, had the stone suspended from the cart had the slightest fineness to its cut, the whole parade might have been taken for a royal procession.

They came up to me and halted. Behind them some distance away I saw the shopkeepers return to their stores and the line of onlookers start to break up. Now I turned my attention to the clansfolk; they too perhaps surmised that I was now ready to listen to them in some peace. They started to speak in a relaxed manner. I could make out that they were trying to get across some details about the rider, but I was able to comprehend only one thing: the rider inside the cart was the last one. During my journeys among those small communities the meaning of the word "last" had been so frequently expressed to me in so many different tongues and through so many different gestures that I understood it immediately. Most everyone of this community too, after recounting the condition of the rider, touched my feet and solicitously informed me that the rider was the last one.

Absurdly, I felt responsible for them, and even more for the rider, and motioned for them to rest easy. They became silent and fixed their gaze on me; they gestured to one another to rest easy and in fact did so. I made a sign for them to stay put and wait for me. Then, walking quickly as if I'd be right back, I returned to my house.

The crazy boy was standing at the door and looked scared.

"Who are they?" he asked in a choked voice.

"They're the paper-people," I replied. "You didn't give them a prize?"

"Prize?" he asked, uncomprehendingly.

I patted him on the shoulder and said, "Run along, find a prize for them quickly. Then we will go visit them."

"No," he said, appearing more frightened than before.

"All right, go and play," I said. "I've got work to do."

"Who is that old man?"

"Old man?"

"The one hiding in the cart."

"He's not an old man," I said.

My mind had another jolt. Why had I supposed he was a child? He might just as well be an old man. I recalled his appearance. His face was swollen and there were wrinkles on his hands. I strained to remember his hand but what came back to me instead was the slowly moistening white hand of the woman, its fingers locked in mine, throbbing like a heart. I shook myself out of it and tried to recall the words and gestures of the community folk. All I could fathom was that he was the last one. The community's last child ... or last old man? The last emblem of some person or event? The last testimonial of something or some age? I felt increasingly confused. Perhaps I allowed myself to indulge in my confusion far too long, for when I did decide to go back and look again, the crazy boy was already gone and the afternoon was beginning to wane.

Leaving the garbage dump and the series of shops behind me as I moved ahead I saw them approaching me. The cart pulled ahead of them. The rider's face was resting on the side of the cart and the rags wrapped around his head had come undone in several places. The woman was repeatedly trying to climb aboard the cart, but each time one of the clan grabbed her and pulled her back. I heard their voices beneath the clatter of the cart. They were singing something. By turns each person chanted something, then others took up the last few words and repeated them in unison. They had lined themselves up in a row and their voices were gaining volume. One of the men stepped slightly out of the row and intoned something, and the others chanted it back. Then he stepped back and another stepped forward. His voice and the following chorus were louder than before. And now their hands and their bodies had begun to sway, almost as in a dance. Every now and then one of the men would step forward and intone some words; the others would join in and then shake their heads as if in applause. At least I took it to be a gesture of applause; in reality, though, I didn't know exactly what the gesture meant in this community.

Perhaps they didn't see me, even though I was well within their field of vision. As they moved forward, I found myself moving slowly backward, my ears tuned to their voices, my eyes fixed on the movement of their bodies. They were recounting some ancient tale whose hazy scenes were forming and dissolving before me like images in a dream. I saw a newborn child held tenderly in someone's arms. The child is learning to walk, he wobbles along, tumbles down, cries. He's picked up and pacified. He's running about, climbing trees, and falls asleep, exhausted. He wakes up, rubs his eyes with his palms; his eyes have turned red.

I saw many pairs of red eyes advancing toward me. They were all screaming "Last, last!" in unison, in a single voice, with a single gesture, and their throats seemed ready to burst. A terrible agitation had seized them and they all seemed crazed with anger. Then a kind of drunkenness came over them. A gentle cloud of dust rising from their clothes and feet slowly enveloped them. Behind the dust the woman once again propped up the face of the rider. The slit in his eye had closed, but the other white-and-black-painted eye was fixed on me in a stare of astonishment, refusing to close although utterly covered with grime. The cart bumped over a rut in the road, jolting the rider's head. A trace of reproach flashed in the eye, soon turned to anger, then slight inebriation, and then it once again fixed on me in a stare of astonishment.

Approaching the series of shops they quieted down and halted. They appeared utterly exhausted and oblivious to my presence. After a brief consultation among themselves they pointed into the distance toward my house. I turned and quickly walked back home. Just before reaching the door I turned to look back. They were pointing at me and telling each other something. They began to move ahead, straight toward me. I turned and walked away, stopping again only after I had left my door some forty or so paces behind. I turned slowly and looked at them; they seemed like a moving pile of refuse. Then they broke into disarray and hung their heads low.

For a long time I felt I had seen a spectacle I was not likely to see ever again. I experienced a faint remorse that I was not included in it.

All the same I also felt myself quite safe, for they were now descending the nameless dirt road to the north that sloped out of the city toward the wastelands.

Allam and Son

I know now—well, I knew even before—that a man, after reaching a certain age, begins to forget several thousand, indeed several hundred thousand things each day, but the realization that some of his memory is being lost takes several years to sink in. Because the store of memories is so large, even the continual disappearance of thousands and hundreds of thousands of objects from it scarcely inclines him to suspect, at least not for a while, any appreciable loss. And so, well before the term of my employment ended, I had already accepted that, although I wasn't conscious of it, I was forgetting quite a number of things every day. Then, in a fit of something resembling stupidity, I wasted a great deal of time launching fruitless efforts to remember everything I was forgetting. Then I made a concerted effort and managed to pull myself out of that fit. Not long afterward, I was seized by another, even greater, fit of stupidity during which I wasted my time calling to mind all the things that were still intact in my memory. This wasn't a fruitless enterprise, yet it didn't yield anything other than confusion.

While engaged in this activity my employment finally reached its end, leaving me plenty of time to waste. After I had frittered away an inordinate amount of time in this pursuit, it dawned on me that the amount I still retained in my memory was impossible to determine. I remembered a lot of things, hardly any of which were extraordinary. And even those few extraordinary things began to appear quite ordinary during an episode of weariness that took hold of me. Finally I gave up this pastime altogether.

Later my memory became even weaker. I no longer felt a need to remember what I was forgetting. Things that I recalled remembering quite well—people's names, their faces, details of past events, and many other big and little things—none of these could be recollected despite straining my mind. Right about that time, or maybe shortly thereafter—I can't say for sure—my memory even started to goof. I'd call one friend by the name of some other friend, or take an acquaintance that I was meeting after some lapse of time for another acquaintance, or mix the details of certain events in with the details of others. Often this created difficulties, but that didn't bother me too much. I was already expecting that to happen and was quite prepared to accept it.

But even in those days numerous memories of my childhood and adolescence remained fresh in my mind. The children in my household would eagerly listen to me recount the stories of those times in my life and marvel at how well I remembered things from so long ago. I knew that even in the waning years of life, when one tended to forget things that only happened a couple of days ago, the mind still retained memories of childhood intact.

At about this time I once fell ill when the seasons were changing. I ran a high fever for several days and the children were stopped from coming to see me. When I recovered I was told how I had rambled on non-stop in the delirium brought on by the fever. I was also told that, with my eyes closed, I mostly recounted the same stories of my childhood that the children insisted on hearing from me, except that I told those stories in much greater detail than ever before.

At that point I discovered that I also no longer remembered anything from my childhood.

That, I was not prepared to accept. So I went through a third fit of stupidity: I would have the children tell me the very same stories I myself used to tell them. When this didn't help, I worked my mind harder, trying to remember my childhood. When even that didn't help, I thought up another trick. Before I was taken ill some scene or other would occasionally flash through my mind, and it wouldn't take me long to remember which memory of my childhood it corresponded to. So now I would lie down at night well before sleeping time and close my eyes, emptying my mind, as well as I could, of all thoughts. Then I would try to see something in the darkness of my closed eyes. Usually this didn't work and I fell asleep during the exercise. But sometimes a faint blur of light appeared somewhere in that darkness and revealed some static image just for a moment. I was certain that these images were part of my childhood memories. Beyond this conviction, I wasn't able to get much else out of this pastime since, no matter how hard I tried, I just couldn't relate any image to its corresponding memory. Then again, the images were strangely vague: sometimes it might be a bullock cart parked under the dense foliage of a tree, its image rippling over a puddle of rainwater; sometimes a fakir with a small kettledrum in his hand; and sometimes large, copper-plated metal cooking pots on brick hearths in an unpaved courtyard half lying in sunshine and surrounded by canvas tents. There used to be many images of clothing, both men's and women's and of various styles, but the faces of the people wearing the clothing couldn't be seen, or maybe they became dim and faded away completely by the time my eyes reached them. This old-fashioned clothing was of an elegant style and shape, and usually of bright, loud colors, with pink, turquoise, yellow, and purple predominating, but never black.

However, one night, I saw a scrap of black cloth form and quickly disappear on top of slowly fading colorful clothing. This image returned to me several times that night and again the following night, though on the latter occasion the scrap of black cloth remained visible a little longer and I recognized it. This was also an item of clothing made by ripping about a hand-and-a-half long slit in a length of unstitched cloth. It was worn by putting one's head through the slit and letting one end of the cloth hang in front and the other in back. Sleeveless and open on either side, this attire was usually white and was reminiscent of the *kafan*, the shroud draped around a dead body. It was called *kafni*—even though those who wore it were very much alive—and it was only rarely seen.

The black *kafni* disappeared and then reappeared. This time I could see, unlike with the other clothing, a slight movement in it, as if the body of the one wearing it was quaking. Then, even before it had become dim, the image vanished altogether, and my body began to shake at about the same time. I waited a long while for the *kafni* to reappear, but it didn't, nor did any other kind of clothing.

After this the images ceased to appear. Now when I closed my eyes I couldn't even see a blank spot. And so, the game of watching images, which I had played over the course of several nights, ended and I once again resorted to going to bed only after sleep had completely overwhelmed my eyes.

I had no way left to kill time at home now, so I started going out again to stroll around or visit with friends and talk with them about this and that. This used to be my daily, or almost daily, routine, but ever since the start of the grievously erratic behavior of my memory—which often displeased my friends, and just as often led to my own embarrassment before my acquaintances and sometimes even exposed me to their ridicule—I had terminated it. However now, after my illness, when I started socializing with them again they would tell me stories of their own lapses of memory.

One day I was sitting with my friends. We were talking about errors that we had made in identifying people. Now and then we laughed heartily. Just then one of the friends said, "Well, it doesn't bother me as much when I mistake an acquaintance for a stranger. I usually get away by apologizing. But when I mistake a stranger for an acquaintance ..."

So then we started talking about that. Just about everyone

related a story of his own involving this experience. Some stories were pretty long and really interesting.

"Yes, something like that has also started happening to me quite often these days," a friend, who had been quiet for a while, said, "but this past week I had a very strange experience." He stopped, resuming a little later, "I saw this fine fellow off in the distance in the Old Market," he pointed at one of the friends, "only to find out when I got near that it was somebody else...."

"Let me tell you what happened next," the friend who had been pointed at said. "This other man also mistook you for one of his friends, and for a very long time both of you ..."

"At least let me finish," the first friend said. "Anyway, on coming closer I realized that it wasn't you, but after I had walked just a few steps I saw that you really were approaching—in the flesh, with this same exact miserable face of yours."

Suddenly I recalled that similar coincidences had happened to me many times, so many times that they couldn't be called coincidences; in fact, it never happened that I mistook a stranger for an acquaintance and then didn't see that very same acquaintance shortly afterward. If he took a while to appear I would begin to feel restless, but in the end I would definitely see him. This was the most extraordinary thing in my life, although I never did remember it during the time when I used to count the things that still survived in my memory.

My friends were still talking. Just about everyone had had such an experience, though not more than once.

"Yes," I said after hearing their stories, "something like that has also happened to me."

But I didn't recount any of my experiences. In a way, I sort of regretted that they had experienced something similar, even though it was only once.

Then our conversation meandered off to other topics.

A week later, I was roaming around an old market, which used to be called the Big Market, with a friend I had played with in childhood. Following a few days of close, stuffy rainy weather, bright sunshine had appeared, and the sky was absolutely clear. Just as we were talking about this change in the weather, or rather about the weather before the change, the sunshine began to fade and the atmosphere became even more dreary than it had been during the preceding days. Looking glum, my friend said, "Can't understand the way these clouds just wander in all of a sudden."

"Nor where they suddenly disappear," I said.

Just then I saw a bearded man clothed in black off in the distance coming toward us. Something snapped in my mind and the word "Allam" escaped from my lips.

I broke out laughing.

"Allam?" my friend asked.

"What—you've forgotten Allam?" I asked, although the fact was that I had only remembered him just then.

"Who can forget Allam?" my friend said. "Anyway, what makes you suddenly think of that poor soul?"

The man was drawing closer to us. When he was only a few steps away, I examined him more carefully. He didn't look at all like Allam. With the sleeves of his long loose black shirt rolled up almost to his shoulders and his big collyrium-smeared eyes, he looked a bit like the caretaker of a shrine. He swept past us. My friend was saying something and I turned my attention to him. He said the same thing over again, "Who can forget Allam?"

"I had forgotten him," I said.

"Don't tell me you've forgotten his little brat too."

"His son? Oh, that wolf? Yes, I remember him. He bit you."

"He practically took a snip out of my flesh—the miserable wretch! Here, look," he showed me the mark from the wound on his right wrist.

We began to talk about Allam. I remembered quite a few things about him myself, and about others my friend jogged my memory. But one thing that I made him remember was that Allam was always seen wearing a *kafni* made of some black fabric.

He used to visit my father now and then. If he found me playing near the gate of our house, he would call out to me from the distance, "Young Master, please inform the Deputy Sahib that Allam, the rascal, is here to pay his respects."

My father wasn't any kind of "Deputy" at all. He used to teach at the biggest school in the city. He maintained himself in the manner of high government officials in keeping with the grandeur of the school, and he always went out in his own carriage. That's why the residents of our neighborhood—mostly people of modest means with little education—called him "Deputy Sahib." When I would inform him about Allam's arrival he would come out on the verandah and he would talk to him for a long time, either standing out there or after ushering him into the outer reception room. He would also mention Allam to our family and tell us that Allam was his boyhood friend and also his classmate at school for a while. I found out from my father that Allam was the scion of a prominent and well-respected religious family in the city and that he was very clever in his studies but had fallen in with bad company. His continual disobedience and intransigence eventually drove his father to throw him out of the house and later to disown him publicly. After that his hooliganism got out of hand and he could usually be seen hanging out with a gang of crooks notorious throughout the city. These lawbreakers specialized in kidnapping women; and Allam, mixed up in their antics as he was, was sometimes dragged off to the police lockup because of his association with them. He would let this be known to us somehow or other and my father would get him released on his own recognizance. He would come straight to our place after being released and, seeing me playing at the gate of our house, he would always say the exact same thing: "Young Master, please inform the Deputy Sahib that Allam, the rascal, is here to pay his respects."

The odd thing about him was that he really didn't look like a rascal at all. He only looked like somebody mysterious, at least to me. His black *kafni*, his black sarong, and his thick round black beard made it difficult to form an accurate opinion about him. The way he looked, he could easily be taken for a harmless man, except that he always carried a small hatchet with him, its edge covered in a sheath of some black cloth. While no one may have ever seen the blade unsheathed, just about everyone knew that Allam carried the hatchet in order to defend himself against jungle animals, and this was precisely how it became known to me that there were jungles around my city.

He caught all kinds of animals in these jungles and brought them to the market. Perhaps this was what he did for a living. I would often see him standing in a certain spot in the market holding a rope tied around the neck or waist of a dozing animal while people crowded around him. I would join the crowd and gawk in amazement at each animal he brought there. One day I saw him there with a *bijju*—an animal that it is said digs into fresh graves and feeds on dead bodies and so is also called *qabar bijju*. In the same way, I saw my first hedgehog, which I found to be much smaller than I had imagined. Up until then I had only seen hedgehog quills, which are used for magic and for charms, in roadside displays set up by medicine men. I also saw many other animals, some of whose names I had heard and others whose names I had never heard, and still others whose names even Allam himself didn't know.

One day I saw him standing in his usual place with a length of rope coiled around his neck and its two ends dangling over his chest. I saw long scratch marks on his arms and his *kafni* was also torn in several places. He appeared very animated as he related to the people gathered around him how he had heard the slight sound of movement inside of a dark jungle cavern and plunged into it fearlessly. As he was trying to see in the darkness, some animal had suddenly pounced on him and, after mauling him, had disappeared behind one of the curves inside the cavern.

"So I headed back home too," he said, stroking his hatchet gently, "but on my way out I did tell him, 'Well, Mister, you got me today, but watch out, I'm coming after you one of these days and then I'll let you have it. For now, enjoy your cozy hideout.'"

And sure enough, the very next week a much bigger crowd than ever before could be seen gathered around him. From what the people in the crowd were saying, I gathered that he had actually captured *that* animal and brought it along. People were trying to figure out what kind of animal it was. When I tried to get through the crowd, I was stopped, and so was every other child who tried to get through that day. I went to one side and tried to get some idea what the animal looked like from the conversations that were going on. I was able to gather just this: that it had strange-looking claws, that it was dozing just like every other animal brought here by Allam, and that it was a female. Suddenly I heard screams. People began to fall over one another and Allam's voice rose above the stampede, "Hatchet … my hatchet!"

The stampede, and even more so those beastly screams, scared me so much that I immediately took off.

That was probably the last time that Allam brought an animal from the wild to the market. Later I saw him four or five times after long intervals wandering around all alone. Toward the end of this period his beard had begun to look scraggly and rather unsightly, and he had also started to totter a bit. He had also dropped his visits to us. New and more interesting people absorbed my attention in the Big Market. Now I was reminded of Allam only when I sometimes spotted his son along my way. He had grown up into a strapping youth and closely resembled his father.

He was my age and now and then he joined in with the boys I used to play with in my childhood. However, our group tried to keep our distance from him because he was quick to lose his temper, and when he did he would bite his adversary. God knows how the rumor had spread among us children that wolves carried him away shortly after he was born and that Allam had searched for him in the jungle for several years until finally he retrieved him. Some of the older boys in our group even went so far as to say, or rather, they actually claimed to have witnessed with their own eyes, that even after returning home Allam's son walked on all fours for quite a while and only ate raw meat. Another boy said that around this time imprints of a wolf's claws were discovered near Allam's house and Allam had started to keep a hatchet with him at all times ever since. We decided that the boys were telling the truth and so we started to fear Allam's son. However, I never had any fights with him. He himself avoided tangling with me, perhaps because he sometimes tagged along with his father to our house. Sometimes he also came alone and told my father in tears, "Father has been locked up."

A few years into his youth his beard had become quite thick and round and now and then he also wore a black *kafni*. Seeing him, one felt that old Allam had become young all over again. But he scarcely ever greeted me then; perhaps he went by me without even recognizing me.

After this a passing thought came to me a couple of times that I hadn't even seen Allam's son anywhere for quite a while.

I was feeling a sense of satisfaction that some parts of my memory had returned. I tried to remember other things from that period and, I must say, I did succeed nominally in my effort. Just then I suddenly realized that my friend had left me at some turning point in the road. I had been out for quite a while. I immediately headed back, partly because of the thought that my overlong absence would be causing everyone at home to worry and partly because the increasing darkness made it difficult for me to see distant things clearly. Just after I had gone past the intersection nearest to my house, I again saw the fellow who looked like the caretaker of a shrine—or should I say, I saw his outfit—standing on the other side of the road. Again I thought it was Allam and again I laughed involuntarily. Then I remembered

Allam's son and my laugh quickly faded.

The next day again I saw him standing in the same place. Although I was on the opposite side of the road, I tried to look him over a bit more closely in the light of the sun. He wasn't the same man who was clad in black and had eyes smeared with collyrium that I had seen in the Big Market the day before. During the next few days I saw him several times. He would be standing quietly, in the exact same spot, and glancing at the passersby. I also noticed that he was wearing a *kafni*. But when I passed by him closely a couple of times, he looked at me indifferently, just as he did at others.

Right about that time one of the children in our family told me that I talked to myself when I walked down the road. This was bad news and my family had, perhaps knowingly, kept it from me. I considered people who talked to themselves eccentric, and even beyond eccentric, irrational. I stopped going out so often, and when I did go out I kept wondering the whole way whether I was talking to myself. In doing so, I often lost track of my surroundings.

One day, as I was returning home, I had the sneaky feeling, after I had walked a little ways past the intersection, that I had just said something to myself. I stopped rather suddenly and started to think of what I had said. Right then I heard a voice coming from behind my back, "May you remain safe! May you remain safe!"

Then I heard the sound of something wooden drop. I turned around to look. The man in the *kafni* was coming toward me holding out both of his hands to greet me. But after taking just a couple of steps he staggered and it appeared as if he was trying to go in several directions all at the same time. Then he fell to the ground. Quite a few passersby rushed toward him and so did I. We managed to stand him on his feet but his entire body was trembling and in that state he mumbled, as if to himself, "Can't walk. I just stand." It seemed that he was beginning to drift into unconsciousness.

None of the passersby knew him, and none seemed to know what to do with him. Finally I said, "I know him. Please take him to my place."

Those people knew me. Several of them practically carried him to my house and I had them seat him in a chair.

After the people were gone I was thinking of something to say to him when, still sitting in the chair, he began slumping to one side in such a way that two legs of the chair lifted up off the floor. I lunged forward and caught him before he fell over. He also made some effort to steady himself and said, "I can't sit either. I can only stand or lie down."

There was nothing in the room which he could lie down on. I was thinking that I would have somebody bring over a cot from inside the house or spread some bedding right there on the floor. Meanwhile, he stood up, supporting himself on me. He straightened up and said, "Now let go."

His body quivered slightly, and I asked, "You won't fall down?"

"No. I'll just stand."

"If you'd like to lie down, I could have a bed …"

"No. I'll stand."

Slowly I let go of him. He did indeed stand in place without wobbling. Then, with a trace of pride in his voice, he said, "I can stand all day long. Just like this."

My problem, on the other hand, was that walking didn't tire me as much as standing, but I suppressed the desire to sit down in a chair and asked him, "How long have you had this ailment?"

"Oh, many years," he said indifferently.

After that he kept squinting his eyes and looking at the room over and over for some time. Finally he said, "It's changed."

"So have times," I said, and then asked, "How's your father?"

"My father—oh, he's been dead a long time."

"What did he die of?"

"Old age—what else?" he answered, again with the same indifference. He ran a sweeping glance over the room once more and said, "It's changed quite a bit. When I used to come here …" He changed the subject and informed me, "I don't see well either."

"Has this man already resigned himself to everything?" I

asked myself feeling rather envious of him. Then I asked, "Who had you come to the intersection with?"

"Oh, yes," he said with a start, as if suddenly remembering something, "she must have come to get me. She's probably feeling terribly worried."

"Shall I send someone to look for her?"

Just then footsteps were heard on the verandah and a boy from the neighborhood peeked in through the door and said to someone, "He's here all right. There, standing."

A woman wrapped up in a burqa was right behind the boy. The boy left. The woman stepped inside the room hesitantly. The moment she spotted my guest she said in a sharp tone of voice, "I was sick with worry. You'd better stay home from now on."

"What's the problem?" he said unfazed. "This too is our home." Then he pointed at me: "I'm indebted to him for many, many favors. When I was locked up in this business with you, he was the one who bailed me out." At that point the woman greeted me.

The sound of footsteps on the verandah was heard once again. The same boy entered, holding a hatchet, its edge sheathed in its cover. "It had fallen there," he said, handing the hatchet over to the woman. Then he left the room.

I stood silently for quite some time. He too was standing perfectly erect and silent, but his head was bowed and his eyes were closed. I looked at him closely and then I heard the woman say, "Please wake him. He falls asleep standing up, just like that."

I wasn't surprised. A *pahari* watchman in my neighborhood also used to doze off for a bit standing on his feet. He used to say that, for him, just a few snatches of sleep like that made up for an entire night. I looked at the woman. She seemed to be in a hurry to leave; still, I asked her, "Where's his son these days?"

"That's the source of all the trouble," the woman said. "He slept at home in his bed one night and in the morning the bed was found empty. Since then he goes out looking for him every single day. He can't walk, so I hold him and take him out. He stands for hours on end, sometimes on this street and sometimes on that. He even insists on going to the jungle. Now tell me, please, where can I find a jungle for him. A long time ago he used to go to the jungle and catch animals. Once some animal …"

He was still dozing, but now he woke up with a start and snapped at the woman, "What are you telling him? Doesn't he know already?"

The woman fell silent. I asked, "Where does he live?"

She told me that his house was in a lane behind my house and that more than half of it had already collapsed. It was reached by going through a number of narrow lanes. The woman described its location in detail, but I forgot it before I could memorize it. In back of my house there was a veritable network of narrow, dimly lit lanes, some of which were even covered by roofs. I had only heard the names of some of these lanes, covered or uncovered, and hadn't even heard the names of some others. I remembered what my father used to say: the lanes of our neighborhood are as twisted as the human brain is inside the skull, and a stranger caught in this maze can hardly hope to get out of it on his own. I was already feeling caught in this maze; or rather, my efforts to get out were proving unsuccessful. Just then the woman said to him, "OK, will you come along now? Don't you see, he's been standing so long on your account?"

"Thank you very kindly, very kindly," he said, making a parting gesture to me with both of his hands, and then, holding on to the woman, he started to hobble out of the room. Suddenly he stopped, felt around his body with his hand and said anxiously, "Hatchet … my hatchet."

"Here, I have it," the woman said handing the hatchet over to him.

I accompanied the two of them as far as the gate of my house. He was saying something as he was leaving but his voice sounded muffled. Perhaps he was blessing me too. All I remember are the words he spoke when he reached the gate: "I didn't see the Young Master. He must have grown quite a bit by now, God be praised."

The Big Garbage Dump

1

The Big Garbage Dump was located inside a building dating from royal times. It couldn't be said who owned it, or what its original purpose was, or precisely when it was converted into a garbage dump. All that could be said with certainty was that now it was the personal property of no one, that it was not built for the collection of garbage, and that no one had seen it in its pre-dump state.

It was difficult to even call it a building because what little could be seen now was something like a *daalaan* [hall] with five small passageways and with three serrated arches visible behind it. These arches were also so filled with garbage that only their uppermost serratures were left open, a yawning darkness apparent behind them at all times. New garbage was dumped in this very hall. Whatever had lain on the hall's roof and behind its arches had been used as filler for the main highway, which passed right above the building. It was the longest and the straightest thoroughfare, starting in the north, continuing for a long distance, and disappearing in the deserted areas of the south. In royal times, when the crowded neighborhoods located in the low-lying areas and those standing on the elevations were connected by narrow twisting lanes that rose and fell, one could not even imagine such a long, straight, and level highway right in the middle of the city.

It was built after the demise of the kingdom and extensive demolition took place to reclaim space in order to build it. All the residential neighborhoods—and they were large in number— standing in its path were torn down, and all the houses standing on the elevations were toppled onto those in the low-lying areas to ensure that the surface was perfectly level, so now the highway passed over them easily.

The demolished neighborhoods survived only as names in old writings and official documents, but many old neighborhoods that had not fallen in the highway's path still endured. All these surviving neighborhoods were located in the low-lying areas of the city and were connected by a network of new and old lanes. Some neighborhoods were situated in such low-lying areas that the lanes leading to them had been built in the form of broad staircases, and such was the narrow lane that came to its end in front of the Big Garbage Dump. The stairs always appeared wet, but nobody knew where the water that dampened them came from. The lowest staircase eased into a long lane that, although it eventually headed south, proceeded in a westerly direction parallel to the highway but a little lower than it. Some distance up ahead this lane merged with a paved road that forked off from the highway toward the west. Like the staired lane, this lane was also usually deserted. Even children, big and small, who created a ruckus from morning until evening playing in the other lanes of the area, didn't step into this one. Why, even their noise didn't reach here. The only exception was that at first light some grubby-looking kids, with large jute sacks slung across their backs and carrying sticks in their hands that had hooked wires attached on the ends, emerged from the two lanes and converged on the Garbage Dump. They poked through the garbage using their wire hooks to pick up plastic bags buried under the trash and then they deposited these in their sacks. The only other visitors to the lanes were the stray cats, dogs, and unwanted cattle that came to the dump foraging for food. Their numbers increased significantly after the leftovers from a banquet had been thrown out there, with crows joining in.

Just now, though, nothing fit for eating could be spotted, yet a gangly dog, half buried in the garbage piled up in the lowest passageway, was frantically trying to pull something out from underneath. It was jerking its body repeatedly and rapidly wagging its tail as it attempted to hold its ground firmly with its hind legs. As a result, some of the trash on the upper part of the pile had begun to slide down. Suddenly the wagging stopped. The dog shuddered slightly and, jerking its body forcefully one last time, pulled its mouth out of the garbage. But the mouth was empty. The dog backed off a few steps and barked repeatedly, snatching at the trash over and over. Then it quieted down and, with its neck hung in humble resignation, it climbed up the stairs of the lane and dropped out of sight. Moments later its piercing howl rose from near the last stair at the very top and a man with a muffler wrapped around his neck was seen slowly coming down the stairs.

Carrying his briefcase in one hand and pulling up the bottoms of his trouser legs with the other, he passed by three passageways of the dump, but at the fourth he began to shudder and came to a halt. Standing perfectly still for a few moments, he twisted his neck around and looked toward the dump. His body turned slowly and he took a couple of steps toward the stairs, but then stopped again. He looked first at one end of the dump and then at the other. His body turned around again and, walking briskly forward, he went into the other lane. He turned left and walked even more briskly. Suddenly his feet slowed down. He let go of his trouser legs and shifted his briefcase to his other hand as he proceeded slowly toward the lane's southern exit. The gangly dog's bark rose behind him. Perhaps it was back at the dump.

By now the man in the scarf was coming up on the small *paan* and cigarette shop located right at the lane's exit. Opposite it was the government office building that had no name and seemed in need of repair. He acknowledged the greetings of the *paan-wala*, glanced down the street in both directions, shook his head no, without there being any solicitations from the *paan-wala*, crossed the street and entered the office. The old attendant who was sitting on a long bench next to the door of the room on the left-hand side stood up immediately and greeted him. Taking the man's briefcase from his hand, he dutifully opened the door for him. Walking behind the man, he entered the room and cleaned off the desk with a rag that was draped over his shoulder. By then the man had already taken his seat behind the desk. The attendant placed the briefcase before him and said, "Sahib, it's very chilly!"

"Yes. The chill has increased somewhat today," the man answered. Then he said, "Rahmatullah, bring some water."

"Water, Sahib?" the attendant said. He wanted to say something more but didn't. Turning around, he went out of the room.

The man pulled the briefcase closer and placed his thumbs on the clasps. The jarring noise of both fasteners opening almost simultaneously was heard, followed by the muffled sounds of their being closed one at a time. He pushed the briefcase to one side and then removed his scarf and wiped his face with it. He looked at the attendant walking in with the water, took the glass from his hand and drank all of it, one mouthful at a time. He put the glass down on the desk and said, "Send Ghayas in."

The attendant picked up the glass and wiped away the wet spot with his rag. Just as he was going out the door, in walked a young man.

"Ghayas Babu, Sahib would like to see you," he told the young man as he went out. The young man greeted the other man and said, "It has really become quite cold, sir."

"Yes, yesterday already."

"Looks like it's going to rain too."

"Yes, already yesterday the clouds started to gather," the man said and pointed to the chair in front of him.

After the young man was seated, the man at the desk continued opening and closing the fasteners on his briefcase for some time. The young man looked at him with inquiring eyes and asked, "Sir, shall I send for tea?"

The man shook his head no. He snapped open the fasteners once more, lifted the flap and looked at it for a while, and then turned his attention to the young man. "I've brought the papers along," he said, patting the briefcase. "I've arranged them all in separate files. Now we need to make a list of the items. You may do it here or at home, your home or mine."

"Wherever you say, sir."

"First study them," the man said, pointing to a chair on the right side of the desk.

"Yes, sir," the young man said as he got up from his chair.

"They've really added up to quite a volume," the man said glancing at the files stuffed in the briefcase. "You'll probably need to make a fairly long list."

"Consider it done, sir," the young man said, and then he asked, "By when, sir?"

"Whenever it's finished," the man said. "You've already seen the papers, but ... you must study them. First of all ..." he pulled a file out of the briefcase, "these are complete now. Make a list of these first. Have a look at the papers on top too."

The young man took the file from him and opened it. He examined the papers that lay at the very top for a while and then said rather playfully, "Well, now nothing stands in the way of gaining possession. Congratulations, sir!"

"On gaining possession of a garbage dump, Ghayas?"

The young man felt a bit embarrassed. Placing his hand on the topmost paper he said, "But, sir, it wasn't a garbage dump." He lifted the paper in his hand. "This document clearly shows that the building belonged to your family."

"You probably haven't examined the paper carefully, Ghayas," the man said. "In fact, it was taken from another family and then passed on to us. Today, times have changed and that other family also has a claim to it."

The young man looked up and saw that the other man's eyes were fixed on him intently.

"But, sir …"

"Read it again, Ghayas."

The young man started to read, faltering. Meanwhile, the other man kept looking at him as his hands opened and closed the clasps of the briefcase.

"But, sir," said the young man after he had read the paper and was returning it to the file, "the members of that family … they're all gone."

"Try to understand the difference between 'gone' and 'disappeared,' Ghayas. Why are you forgetting your friend?"

"My friend, sir?"

"The one who disappeared …"

"Ayaz, sir?" the young man asked, and then suddenly became a trifle melancholy.

"He's the lone survivor of that family, just as I am of mine."

"But he's disappeared, sir."

"Try to understand the difference between 'gone' and 'disappeared,' Ghayas," the man said, emphasizing each word.

The young man sat speechless while the man took the file from his hand, slipped it into the briefcase and closed the flap. The young man pulled the briefcase ever so slowly toward himself. "Shall I take it with me, sir?"

"One other thing," the man said as he reached for the briefcase. He opened it and pulled out a bundle that was below several files. "Here, this is the list I started myself …"

"I'll look it over, sir," Ghayas said as he stretched his arm forward. But the man put the bundle back under the files.

"Listen, Ghayas," he said softly and fell silent.

The young man put both of his hands on the desk and leaned forward a little, "Yes, sir."

"I ended up going there again today."

Signs of concern began to appear on the young man's face.

"Why did you, sir …" he said, "when you know …"

"I wasn't thinking," the man said. "It was getting late. I'd become accustomed to taking the shorter route."

"So then, sir," the young man started, hesitantly, "today again ...?"

"Yes, a slight pain started."

"And that ... the shudder?"

"That too. It was the shudder that made me conscious that I'd wandered there," the man said nonchalantly, "Anyway, let's just drop it."

"Sometimes a shadow of doubt sweeps over the heart, sir," the young man said, "How many times have I asked you ..."

"OK, I'll have myself looked at by someone one of these days," the man said, again nonchalantly. "Here, the list that I made ..."

The man stopped midway as he was pulling the bundle slightly forward from under the files. He pushed it back and closed the flap. The young man looked at him questioningly. The sound of the fasteners snapping shut was heard.

"Listen, Ghayas," the man said once more, and then once more he remained silent for quite a while.

"Sir?" the young man finally said.

"He was quite close to you."

"Who, sir?" the young man asked, again feeling melancholy. "He was a childhood friend, sir."

"Did he sometimes talk to you about the Garbage Dump?"

"The Garbage Dump?"

"About living there."

"Near the dump, sir?"

"No, inside it."

The young man's sadness changed to surprise and then back to sadness.

"Why are you asking that, sir?"

The man played with the fasteners for some time. Finally he said, "Ghayas, I have this feeling that he lives there now."

"Ayaz?" the young man said. "Ayaz? Living inside the Garbage Dump, sir?"

"Did he say anything to you?"

"To me, sir?"

"Never mind," the man said nonchalantly as before. "We'll talk about it more fully some other time."

"Nobody can live inside the Garbage Dump," the young man said, perhaps to himself.

"How can you say that?"

The young man stared at the surface of the desk in silence. The other man shifted to one side of his chair. Pushing his body slightly sideways, he took out a bunch of keys from the pocket of his trousers and placed it on top of his briefcase.

"A few vouchers are still hanging from yesterday and need to be expedited," he told the young man.

The young man was now standing in front of the cabinet that stood against the right-hand wall. The faint clinking of keys colliding with each other was heard almost at the same time as the muffled voice of the man, "Never mind, Ghayas."

The young man turned around to look and then rushed over to the desk. The man's head was leaning against the back of the chair and his face was covered with heavy beads of sweat. Before long his body began to slump to one side. The young man moved forward quickly and steadied it. "Sir!" that's all he could say, two or three times. Bending forward, he peered into the man's eyes. Then he let go of the body and backed away suddenly. The man's body slumped forward. The young man again stepped forward and steadied it as he called out loudly, "Rahmatullah, quick, bring some water."

He peered into the man's eyes. His grip relaxed a little. The man's body began to fall forward and his head came to rest on the briefcase lying in front of him on the desk. Abandoning him, the young man darted toward the door, but halfway there he turned around and again tried to make the man sit properly in the chair. Meanwhile the attendant entered with some water. He stopped at the door looking at both men for a while, then he approached the desk. He bent over and looked into the man's eyes. "Sahib is no more, Ghayas Babu," he informed the young man.

But the young man continued trying to make the man sit properly. Perhaps he hadn't seen anyone die before that day.

2

I hadn't seen anyone die before that day. Looking at Beg Sahib's eyes I could see that he was no longer alive, but I couldn't bring myself to believe that he was actually dead. Rahmatullah was an experienced man. Before even putting the glass of water on the desk he told me that Beg Sahib was dead. Holding Beg Sahib's shoulders, he had lowered his head until it came to rest on his briefcase. The two of us just stood there looking at him for a while and then I told Rahmatullah that Beg Sahib had been talking as usual and had been quite all right.

"He wasn't quite all right, Ghayas Babu," Rahmatullah said. "I was already alarmed when he asked for water in such terrible cold."

I glanced at the head resting on the briefcase, so did Rahmatullah, then he said, "You stay with the body so I can go let other people know."

"No, you stay here. I'm leaving."

Rahmatullah gave me a somber look. "Won't you stay a while longer, Ghayas Babu? Other people will be here soon."

I hadn't thought about the other office workers. Before long I heard their voices coming from other rooms. Rahmatullah dashed out, said something to somebody and returned. Within minutes Beg Sahib's office was filled with people, and Khairat Khan was among them. Before coming to the office Beg Sahib used to stop at his shop without fail to savor a *paan*. It was Khairat Khan who had Rahmatullah's bench brought in and had Beg Sahib's body placed on it. The office people had laid him out on his desk.

It took me some time to explain the details of Beg Sahib's death to the others. I didn't mention anything about the Garbage Dump or about Ayaz, so there wasn't much left to tell them. Nevertheless, however much there was, I had to tell it over and over, and I also had to hear it all repeated back to me. This done, I went to Beg Sahib's house.

The news had already reached there before I did. Chairs were being set out in the lane across from the house. Neighbors had started to trickle in. Most of the people appeared indifferent to one another, and certainly to me. I myself was indifferent to everyone because I didn't know them. And yet I watched all of them as I sat in my chair. Some people seemed quite knowledgeable about funeral arrangements so they were deciding among themselves who would do what. Just then somebody said, "Leave that to me, but first shouldn't the body be brought from the office?"

"I think it'll be here any minute," some other man replied.

At that point I thought: what am I doing here? I came to give the news, didn't I? And the news has been given. Even so, I lingered a while longer. Finally I got up and went back to the office only to find that it was already closed. Khairat Khan was also closing his shop. When he saw me he said, "The body has left, Ghayas Mian." Then he pointed at the lane, "If you go this way perhaps you will catch up with it somewhere along the way."

I immediately stepped into the lane and, without considering that there was no point in rushing, I walked quickly until I came to the bend in the stairs of the lane. As soon as my glance fell on the Garbage Dump, my feet slowed down. The upper layer of garbage always changed yet it always appeared the same, and even now I didn't notice any difference. The animals and the brats who poked around for plastic bags never looked any different either. There were neither bags nor brats at that moment, but there was an emaciated dog that was doing its best to yank out an empty sweetmeat box stuck in the garbage. Just above the box, two baskets made from bamboo strips were beginning to become dislodged from their place. High above all of this, a few strands had slipped down from a pile of marigold garlands. One of the strands of marigold lodged on the dog's back and he was trying to get rid of it by shaking his body repeatedly, though most of his attention was focused on the box.

The hall was nearly filled with garbage, but the three arches in back of it were still slightly open at the top as usual. I peered into the darkness behind these openings for quite a while. I remembered Ayaz. And the days of my friendship with him. I also recalled that from the start he was my only friend. On exactly the same day, we had both entered a mediocre school run by the city administration, and we weren't just fellow-sufferers in this new calamity, we were also fellow-comforters. We received education—or rather punishment, to be more accurate—at this school for several years. Punishment because we had both developed the habit of skipping school. When we did that we sometimes went to the Garbage Dump and looked at all the cast-off items there. This refuse also included perfectly useable things that had been dumped simply because they had gotten old. We fought hard against the impulse to pick up such things and consciously trampled over them with the old, decayed garbage below sinking and rising beneath our feet. At the time we imagined that we were walking over bodies, dead and alive. We felt frightened and shuddered a little, but at that age we were eager to be frightened—this same eagerness sometimes drove us to sneak a look behind the dump's arches. I thought about the day when I stopped meeting Ayaz for some time. We had played hooky from school that day. Bored from roaming around our favorite haunts, we went to the Garbage Dump and stomped over piles of trash all the way up to the arches. I was standing near the middle arch when Ayaz stuck his head into the first arch and then pulled it back immediately, saying in a muffled voice, "There's somebody inside."

Fear and curiosity both enticed me to go over to that arch. But when I pushed him aside to peek in myself, Ayaz suddenly grabbed my legs from behind and jerked them up in such a way that I was plunged up to my waist, or perhaps the whole of me, into the trash behind the arch.

"Well, now you have to stay here forever," Ayaz said. Then I heard his frightened laugh, the sound of his running feet, and the echo of heavy vehicles as they moved along the highway.

Suddenly I realized that I was standing idly in front of the Garbage Dump, oblivious of Beg Sahib's death. I climbed up the wet stairs of the lane to the highway. It seemed as if it was going to rain soon. I started to feel even colder thinking that I would have to sit out in the open at Beg Sahib's. But I crossed the highway and descended into the lanes on the other side and soon found myself at Beg Sahib's house.

The body had already arrived and the lane was filled with people, including not only our own office staff but also the staffs from other offices of the administration.

3

On the fourth day I went to Beg Sahib's home to return his briefcase. I used to go there even before I was employed because Ayaz used to live there. But back then I stood at the door and called him out. We would then go for long walks and when we returned I would say goodbye to him, again at the door, and leave for my own home. If at either of these times we spotted Beg Sahib coming along, we vanished quickly. Ayaz used to fear him, and, following Ayaz's lead, so did I. By the time I entered my youth, my fear of him had lessened considerably. Likewise my interaction with Ayaz had also become much less. He hardly ever visited me at my home even back then. Most of the time it was I who went to his place. But after I went to see him quite a few times and was told each time that he was out somewhere, I stopped going. At that time I didn't yet know that he had disappeared. Later Beg

Sahib came to my house several times to ask me about him. It was through him that I first learned that Ayaz had gone away somewhere without telling anybody. Beg Sahib also suggested that Ayaz had gone to live elsewhere of his own accord. I clearly remember that he never once mentioned the Garbage Dump during his inquiry. It was I who told him that back when we were boys Ayaz used to go there with me to watch the trash piling up. But Beg Sahib showed no interest in this information. Instead he began to ask me about some of Ayaz's other acquaintances. Beg Sahib didn't continue coming to our house for long. Perhaps he had guessed our financial condition in just a few days. After his last visit, he gave me a temporary job in his office. With the office staff his attitude was strictly professional, which they regretted somewhat. However with me he didn't just talk about work. The staff knew that I was a friend of Ayaz and had been frequenting Beg Sahib's house since childhood, so they understood his special treatment of me. Sometimes my coworkers also quizzed me about Ayaz. But, after hiring me, Beg Sahib never again brought up Ayaz with me; in fact, he never even mentioned his name once. Three days ago he had again mentioned his name. The first time, though, he had stopped right after he started. And now, today, it was the fourth day after his death, and I was standing on his verandah with his briefcase in my hand.

I was given a seat in the same outer room Beg Sahib had used as an office. I had been in this room several times before. Whenever a lot of work descended on the office suddenly, Beg Sahib would ask me to come over to his house to help him expedite it. He looked more like an officer at home than he did at the office. I used to feel reticent talking with him here, although I was treated with hospitality. At least twice while we worked Beg Sahib's wife sent tea and other things for us, and sometimes she brought the tea over herself. She was a simple homemaker. Now and then she engaged in formal conversation with me. The trace of affection in her tone, although perhaps natural and meant for everyone, somehow seemed to be exclusively for me, and I considered it a godsend compared to Beg's Sahib's dryness. She was acquainted with some women who were distant relatives of mine and she talked mostly about them. Until now, I didn't know that she was, in fact, the same Hajira Begam who worked for social causes in the city. I found this out only two days ago from the local newspapers where the news of Beg Sahib's death was printed under the headline: LOSS TO HAJIRA BEGAM: HUSBAND DIES SUDDENLY.

I used to see Hajira Begam mentioned often in the newspapers. She belonged to many women's organizations and reports of their activities appeared frequently. Occasionally a statement by her on some women's issue also found its way in, but without much fanfare.

At this moment I was sitting in Beg Sahib's office-like room, with his briefcase in front of me, waiting for Hajira Begam. I could have brought the briefcase over earlier, but the way the newspaper had headlined the news of Beg Sahib's death made me feel that the proper way would be to first send Rahmatullah to his house to ask for an appointment.

Hajira Begam entered the room quietly. She sat down in Beg Sahib's chair even before I could stand up. I wondered, feeling somewhat surprised, why I had thought she appeared to be just an ordinary housewife up until then. I pushed the briefcase toward her, trying to think of what I might say in sympathy at Beg Sahib's death. Just then she asked, "How did it all happen, Ghayas Mian?"

I gave her the same account I had told repeatedly to the office staff, and she listened with her head bowed. With her head still bowed she said, "He was late leaving for the office that day." Then she lifted her head and asked, "Was he able to get there on time?"

"Yes," I said. "He was never late."

"But that day he was unusually late leaving."

"He arrived exactly at the right time," I told her, then I clumsily offered my condolences on his death and assured her, still more clumsily, that he was a very good man. Hajira Begam listened inattentively to all of this and I thought that she must have heard similar things—but expressed more elegantly—for the past several days now. Feeling embarrassed by my superfluous expressions I thought I had better take my leave. I came up with a few parting sentences and said getting up, "The office was functioning very well because of him. But let's see …"

Hajira Begam beckoned me to sit down and said, "Yes. He always worried about the office. If he ran late he started to become angry. That day too …" She looked at me again, "Did he get there in time?"

I was feeling confused by this rather oblique conversation so I said, "Exactly on time. He took the lane to get there." Feeling that this too said nothing I told her, "Via the Garbage Dump."

She looked at me in silence for a while and then said, "That's the way he took every day."

"But not for some time now," I said. I was expecting her to say something equally indirect so I said, "He felt a slight chest pain whenever he stood in front of the Dump. Perhaps he told you that."

"No … yes. He did say something like that one day. I thought he was just joking."

"For some time now whenever he came near the Dump he shuddered and a pain started in his chest … so he began coming by way of the road instead."

Hajira Begam stared at me quietly. I remembered only one of the things I had thought up for taking my leave and I was about to forget that too, so I said without waiting for her response, "If there's anything I can do, I mean at the office."

I pushed the briefcase a bit more toward her and placed my hands on the desk. As I was getting up she said, "So the Garbage Dump killed him."

"Who can it kill, it looks dead itself."

"But then … why when he got there … when he got there …"

I turned around at the door. "He thought Ayaz lived there. Inside the Garbage Dump."

I heard a protracted gasp and I turned toward Hajira Begam. Right before my eyes such dreadful shock swept across her face that she couldn't hide it in spite of being a social figure. She began to look like an ordinary housewife as she had earlier. I sat down again.

"Did he tell you about that?"

"He said very little at home." She uttered this in a tone that sounded partly disappointed and partly displeased. "And about Ayaz—hardly ever anymore. Did he say something to you?"

"No. Only about the Garbage Dump.... He was thinking of starting a lawsuit to claim ownership of it, wasn't he? He had me work on preparing the documents."

"He never breathed a word to me about it."

I approached the desk and said, placing my hand on the briefcase, "All the papers are here."

Hajira Begam opened and closed the fasteners of the briefcase for a while and then said, "It all happened so suddenly. Now these papers ... you've read them, haven't you?"

"No, I've only seen them. He wanted me to make a list of these papers."

"Have you seen all the papers?"

"Almost all, but ... I don't understand legal matters. Have a lawyer look at them."

"I do recall that a lawyer visited him from time to time, but I don't know whether it had to do with the office or ..."

She opened and closed the fasteners once more, glancing at me and then at the briefcase. I remembered Beg Sahib's death and said, "That day he had asked me to make a list of the papers. He'd already arranged them in separate files himself."

I lifted up the flap of the briefcase. Hajira Begam casually looked over the papers in a couple of files at the top and said helplessly, "I won't understand a thing."

"I'll make the list. But first you must find a lawyer ..."

"You would be wasting your time for nothing."

"Why 'for nothing'?" I said. "It ... in a way, was his will ..."

Hajira Begam became sad and said in a hoarse voice, "He trusted you a lot."

"He was very kind to me," I said getting up and walking toward the door. Hajira Begam said once again, "You'll be wasting your time."

"Not at all," I said, saying goodbye to her and stepping out. "I have plenty of time after office hours."

I, of course, meant that I wouldn't have the time for it during office hours.

Then I proceeded straight to the office where the first news that greeted me was that my term of employment had ended. Beg Sahib had had me appointed temporarily especially to help him out, and perhaps he had renewed my appointment at the end of each term. My salary, too, was not paid monthly, but daily. My coworkers, referring to specific legal requirements, began telling me what I needed to do to obtain a renewal, but I knew all too well that whatever was needed was beyond my ability to accomplish. Even so, I expressed my intention to act on their advice and, after completing my last formal office duties, returned home.

My family was rather large. Several members had jobs, but there were also quite a few mouths to feed. Alone, I made about as much as the other wage-earning members did jointly and this had begun to have its effect on the external appearance of our household. That's why I was now feeling that both my family and my life had fallen into the path of some cataclysmic change. I spent a few days feeling pretty awful. Finally I reasoned with myself: actually the change was what had prevailed during the brief period of my temporary employment. The situation had now reverted to what it used to be. So it was like before. I accepted that; in fact, I accepted it so completely that before a month had passed I began to think of my office days as something that had occurred in dreams, so completely that I even forgot the faces of my coworkers. Even the face of Rahmatullah, whom I had seen the most, began to lose its clarity and fade, so, when he showed up at my house one day, I faltered as I said, "How are you ... Rahmatullah?"

He inquired after me in response, and, without my asking, began telling me about the office; namely, that it was functioning, but poorly, after Beg Sahib, and that he couldn't even get the new dust rag that Beg Sahib had already approved. Then he told me that he didn't like it there since I had left. At the very end he informed me that Hajira Begam wanted to see me.

"When?"

"She didn't say when. Shall I go find out?"

"Don't bother. Why make two trips?" I said. "Just tell her that I'll visit her tomorrow in the morning. But if she would rather see me at a different time, then come back and let me know when."

As soon as she saw me, Hajira Begam complained about my not having informed her of the termination of my job. Later she asked who had regular jobs in my family.

"And here I was thinking that it was because you had a heavier workload at the office after him that you didn't come here."

That's when I remembered about the list. "No," I said, "I just plain forgot. Otherwise the list would be ready by now."

"Ah yes, the list. Make it and be done with it."

She got up and went over to the cabinet by the wall, took out Beg Sahib's briefcase and placed it before me on the desk. I opened the flap, glanced at the files and asked, "Has a lawyer examined them yet?"

"No ... yes. He looked them over briefly. He also advised me to have a complete list drawn up first. He was saying that there are quite a few papers. The list will have to be fairly long."

"I'll make it ..." I stopped myself from saying "sir" just in time. "I'll come here and make it."

"Well then, whenever you have time."

"I have all the time."

Hajira Begam became somewhat dejected and hesitated a little before she said, "Let me have your diplomas, etc., sometime."

Then she said that she usually stayed home till about noon and that I could start that very day if I wanted to.

I started work that very day.

4

Beg Sahib had prepared the files very neatly. I had seen nearly all the papers in them and I had copied many of the documents myself. As a rule, he not only read each document himself, he also had someone else—usually me—read it out loud to him. But since besides these papers, and in fact more than them, my work was with office papers, my knowledge about the former didn't extend beyond the fact that they contained a variety of information about and references to some building dating from royal times. I never asked him about the matter, but one day he himself told me in a casual way that that building had been gifted to his family and he was now trying to reclaim it.

Working in Beg Sahib's office-like room, I initially began drawing up the list for Hajira Begam or her attorney with some degree of interest, but the papers were of many types. Most of them were things that had been filed in Beg Sahib's own office. Besides these, there were certified copies of all kinds of petitions, official notices, court rulings, etc., probably none of them less than a hundred years old. After it was put in a file, each paper assumed the appearance of a legal document, which was beyond my ability to understand, so, without probing deeply into it, I merely picked up and recorded each item on the list I was compiling. Beg Sahib had written a number on each file and on each paper in it and had also given each of them a title. This made my job considerably easier. I concentrated mainly on making sure that I didn't miss entering a single paper on the list. Now and then my attention did wander off though. That happened because there was a steady stream of women coming to see Hajira Begam and, except for her, none of them could keep their voices down when they spoke. Although, when one woman would stop and another start, I did sometimes feel that the woman before her had been speaking rather softly. On occasion all of the women broke out laughing at the same time and then I was obliged to backtrack to check some entries. That didn't bother me much because in my previous employment I had become accustomed to making errors and then correcting them. I must admit, though, that to correct some entries while working at Beg Sahib's home I was obliged to peruse certain legal papers and I found this tedious and boring.

But one day, after I had finished work on several legal files, a file with "The Big Garbage Dump" written on it caught my eye. I opened it with great interest, but all it contained was just one paper with the addresses of some properties from the distant past copied on it. Each address invariably contained either the line "Adjacent to Big Garbage Dump" or "In front of Big Garbage Dump." This file disappointed me. A similar disappointment awaited me when I looked into another file with no serial number but with "Ayaz" written on it in pencil. This one contained an incomplete genealogy of some family, with Ayaz's name appearing at the end. It didn't even tell me as much as I already knew about Ayaz. Beg Sahib had told me earlier that Ayaz was the last surviving member of his family, and I already knew that Beg Sahib had raised him from childhood. I wondered for quite a while whether something useful about Ayaz might only exist in his family tree.

When I looked at the list, I discovered that I had skipped Ayaz's file and was recording items from the one after it. God knows how many other errors I had already made. That day Hajira Begam's women visitors were speaking unusually loudly and also laughing more than at any other time. From the driblets of conversation that trickled into my ears, I surmised that Hajira Begam was out somewhere. Then I heard the clanking of teacups and such. I heard this noise at least twice during my hours working there. Each time it was followed shortly thereafter by a woman entering the room I was in through the door that was behind me. I would keep my eyes fixed on the file that was in front of me, while the woman, after placing a cup of tea near the other files, would quietly turn back on her heels. Sometimes, when Hajira Begam brought the tea over herself, she would tarry a little and talk about one or two things with me. I wasn't expecting any tea that day. I was also thinking that the house felt strangely still and quiet in her absence even though the women's noises were louder and sharper than before. In the midst of those loud noises I heard someone say, "Who will take the tea over?"

By then I was already busy counting the errors on my list, which seemed more numerous than usual. A short while later I heard the sound of a teacup being placed softly on the desk and I lost track of my count. I started all over again. Right after I began counting I heard an expressionless voice behind my back, "Why didn't you bring him along?"

"Him—who?" I blurted out, not thinking.

"Ayaz Bhai."

Then I turned around and looked at her, recognizing her after some uncertainty. "You're Shamima, aren't you?" I asked, and looked at her again. "Why, you've grown so big!"

My cordiality left her unaffected. She asked, again in an expressionless voice, "Please bring him from there, Ghayas Bhai."

"From where?"

"The Big Garbage Dump."

Is she still the way she used to be, I wondered to myself.

"Nobody can live in the Garbage Dump, Shamima."

"Why not? After all, you did, didn't you?"

Just then women's voices were heard outside on the

271

verandah. Hajira Begam's was among them. Then she herself entered the room. Shamima, pausing briefly as she started to leave the room, told her, "I had brought tea."

"That's good," Hajira Begam said absentmindedly as she came and stood near the desk. After waiting a while for her to say something, I said, "I saw Shamima today for the first time in a long time."

Hajira Begam looked a bit anxious and quite tired. She glanced at the files on the desk and said, "You've done quite a lot of work."

"It's not a lot really. It's just making a list after all."

"Were you able to understand the papers?"

"These are legal matters. Lawyers would understand them."

Suddenly I began to tire of my work. I made an estimate of the remaining files and the papers in them and said, "Only a little work remains. If I stay longer I may be able to wrap it all up today."

"Are you sure you don't have other work to do?" she asked, then said on her own, "Yes, it would be nice if you finished it today. You can eat here."

"A cup of tea would be fine halfway through. I'm used to eating only once a day."

"People your age should eat three or four times a day," she commented. "OK, you work," and she left the room.

The remaining work was less than what I had guessed. Then, too, I hurried to finish it. At some point a woman servant came in with tea. It was completely quiet in the house. I asked her, "Is Begam Sahiba in?"

"She's been gone for quite a while now," she said as she was leaving.

I had finished compiling the list by mid-afternoon. I checked that day's entries against the papers in the files and also made sure the files were arranged in serial order. As I was putting the list on top of the files, the woman servant walked in, again with tea. She put the cup down on the desk and said, "Let me know when you're leaving."

"I've finished the work and I'm just getting ready to go," I said. "You may close the door now."

"At least drink the tea first," she said, picking up the earlier teacup, and then she left the room.

I was repeatedly reminded of Shamima as I was putting the files and the list into the briefcase. She was just a little girl when I used to visit Ayaz during our childhood. Sometimes when he and I went out for a stroll, she would ask to accompany us without showing the least bit of eagerness. In answer, Ayaz always said the same thing, "No. Your clothes will get dirty." While she stood quietly watching us walk away he would tell her that the two of us were headed to the Garbage Dump. When we returned she would often be found standing at the door and she never failed to ask what all we had seen. But without paying much attention to our answer she just followed Ayaz into the house. The only things I knew about her were that she was Hajira Begam's sister, that she hung around Ayaz, and that she was a little weak in the head. She was absolutely a fanatic when it came to wearing spotlessly clean clothes. We considered this to be the result of her mental weakness—a weakness that showed on her face when she expressed her desire to go along with us, and also when she had brought tea for me. Perhaps that's the reason I had recognized her.

Had she not been weak in the head, I could have asked her quite a few things. But what things?—I hadn't the foggiest idea. I strained my mind for quite some time until I experienced the same weariness I'd had when I was making the list. The tea on the desk had turned cold. I gulped it down like water and left without letting the woman servant know.

5

Three or four days later Hajira Begam sent Rahmatullah to fetch me. That day her house was devoid of women's noises. Hajira Begam was seated in Beg Sahib's chair in the office-like room. She talked about this and that for quite a while. Then she hesitated just as she was about to say something, and said instead, "You've drawn up the list very neatly. The lawyer was full of praise."

"Has he examined the papers?"

"Yes. And so have I. But ..."

After that she spoke as if she was talking to herself. But everything she said was so convoluted that I really had to make my mind work very hard to understand it. All I could figure out was this: The legal proceedings would drag on for quite a while, and even then it would be difficult to prove to whom the Garbage Dump actually did belong. While the building belonging to Beg Sahib's family was definitely there, in the opinion of the lawyer the Garbage Dump had undoubtedly been there earlier. The lawyer also felt that either Beg Sahib had not carefully examined the files he had prepared or he had also been preparing another file that he wanted to pull out without warning. Assuming that he had won the case after so much trouble and headache, what would Beg Sahib have done with a dilapidated hall filled with garbage anyway? The lawyer was finding this hard to figure out, and so was Hajira Begam. Still worse, now the suit had to be brought to the court by Hajira Begam. Her remark, "Anything I say or do becomes the talk of the town," lingered in my memory. Obviously, if the suit prepared by Beg Sahib were to be pursued further, that would, no doubt, also attract a great deal of attention. And Hajira Begam would surely acquire a new nickname with "Garbage Dump" worked into it somehow. Exactly the same thing had happened with several well-known people in the city.

I was listening quietly. I remembered the absolutely bizarre nicknames tacked onto some of the city's prominent individuals and

I immediately understood Hajira Begam's worry. Not just that, I also understood why she was telling me all this. So I said, "I've taken every precaution to ensure that no one knows anything about this matter. I haven't even spoken to anyone at home about it."

"You did the right thing," she said. "Yes, the lawyer is of the same opinion: quash the matter where it now stands."

I concurred with what the lawyer said. Getting up, I was about to tell her that if, in the future, she needed my help in any matter, all she had to do was send Rahmatullah for me, but she beckoned for me to sit back down. She hesitated a bit, then, opening the desk drawer, she said in a tone as though she was addressing one of her own, "Ghayas Mian, refuse it only if you really want to hurt me." Then she pushed an envelope toward me.

Although the color in my face had perhaps changed a little, my hand moved forward as if by its own volition. Hajira Begam looked at me with downcast eyes and said, "Don't say another word." She looked even more downcast. "Think that you were working at the office for a while longer after him."

I sat tongue-tied, flipping the envelope back and forth. She too remained silent. Finally she said, "Do visit us now and then. Now that he's gone … you don't know …" and her voice gave way. When I lifted up my head after some time, she was already gone.

After going down the lane of stairs I came to a halt in front of the Garbage Dump. Eventually I continued on into the long lane and turned left. As usual, the lane was deserted and quiet, but not the kind of quiet that permeated the area around the Garbage Dump. Here it wasn't even broken by the loud shrill barking of dogs fighting among themselves. I remembered how, at the time I was getting Beg Sahib's papers ready, whenever I came to the Garbage Dump I stopped in front of it and I would sense some vague feeling in its silence, but I could never put it into words.

I turned around and once again went to stand in front of that dilapidated hall. I looked at the trash that was lying there. Something resembling steam was rising from the rubbish underneath, and that vague feeling now seemed to be somewhat like anticipation. My roving eyes stopped at the inner arches and I stepped, somewhat carefully, on the pile of garbage. While trying to avoid stepping on several useful objects, and trying to avoid tripping on them myself in the process, I managed to get as far as the first arch. Then I stuck out my head.

It was just as it had always been: extremely old trash, decayed and disintegrating, extending upwards about the distance of a couple of arm's lengths but unable to reach the highest serratures. The rubble that was used for the filler kind of soared upward behind it and, here and there, empty spaces were filled with the faint echo of vehicles as they moved along on the highway above.